The place: Midwich—a sleepy English village virtually undisturbed since the time of William the Conqueror.

The time: Precisely 10:17 on the night of September 26th, when Midwich is surprised by strange visitors.

The result: Every woman in Midwich pregnant—the first signs of a strange and terrifying threat to the whole human race.

"A flesh-creeper!"
—*Providence Sunday Journal*

The Midwich Cuckoos

John Wyndham

BALLANTINE BOOKS • NEW YORK

First Printing: March, 1959
Second Printing: December, 1960
Third Printing: November, 1966
Fourth Printing: October, 1972
Fifth Printing: June, 1973
Sixth Printing: August, 1973

Printed in the United States of America

BALLANTINE BOOKS, INC.
201 East 50th Street, New York, N.Y. 10022

THE MIDWICH CUCKOOS

PART ONE

1 · No Entry to Midwich

ONE OF THE LUCKIEST ACCIDENTS in my wife's life is that she happened to marry a man who was born on the 26th of September. But for that, we should both of us undoubtedly have been at home in Midwich on the night of the 26th-27th, with consequences which, I have never ceased to be thankful, she was spared.

Because it was my birthday, however, and also to some extent because I had the day before received and signed a contract with an American publisher, we set off on the morning of the 26th for London, and a mild celebration. Very pleasant, too. A few satisfactory calls, lobster and Chablis at Wheeler's, Ustinov's latest extravaganza, a little supper, and so back to the hotel where Janet enjoyed the bathroom with that fascination which other people's plumbing always arouses in her.

Next morning, a leisurely departure on the way back to Midwich. A pause in Trayne, which is our nearest shopping town, for a few groceries; then on along the main road, through the village of Stouch, then the right-hand turn on to the secondary road for— But, no. Half the road is blocked by a pole from which dangles a notice ROAD CLOSED, and in the gap beside it stands a policeman who holds up his hand.

So I stop. The policeman advances to the offside of the car. I recognize him as a man from Trayne.

"Sorry, sir, but the road is closed."

"You mean I'll have to go round by the Oppley road?"

"'Fraid that's closed, too, sir."

"But—"

There is the sound of a horn behind.

"'F you wouldn't mind backing off a bit to the left, sir."

Rather bewildered, I do as he asks, and past us and past

7

him goes an army three-ton lorry with khaki-clad youths lean-ing over the sides.

"Revolution in Midwich?" I inquire.

"Maneuvers," he tells me. "The road's impassable."

"Not *both* roads surely? We live in Midwich, you know, constable."

"I know, sir. But there's no way there just now. 'F I was you, sir, I'd go back to Trayne till we get it clear. Can't have parking here, 'cause of getting things through."

Janet opens the door on her side and picks up her shopping bag.

"I'll walk on, and you come along when the road's clear," she tells me.

The constable hesitates. Then he lowers his voice.

"Seein' as you live there, ma'am, I'll tell you—but it's confidential-like. 'T isn't no use tryin', ma'am. Nobody can't get into Midwich, an' that's a fact."

We stare at him.

"But why on earth not?" says Janet.

"That's just what they're tryin' to find out, ma'am. Now, 'f you was to go to the Eagle in Trayne, I'll see you're informed as soon as the road's clear."

Janet and I looked at one another.

"Well," she said to the constable, "it seems very queer, but if you're quite *sure* we can't get through . . ."

"I am that, ma'am. It's orders, too. We'll let you know, as soon as may be."

If one wanted to make a fuss it was no good making it with him; the man was only doing his duty, and as amiably as possible.

"Very well," I agreed. "Gayford's my name, Richard Gay-ford. I'll tell the Eagle to take a message for me in case I'm not there when it comes."

I backed the car further until we were on the main road and, taking his word for it that the other Midwich road was similarly closed, turned back the way we had come. Once we were the other side of Stouch village I pulled off the road into a field gateway.

"This," I said, "has a very odd smell about it. Shall we cut across the fields and see what's going on?"

"That policeman's manner was sort of queer, too. Let's," Janet agreed, opening her door.

What made it the more odd was that Midwich was, almost notoriously, a place where things did not happen.

Janet and I had lived there just over a year then, and found this to be almost its leading feature. Indeed, had there been posts at the entrances to the village bearing a red triangle and below them a notice:

MIDWICH
DO NOT
DISTURB

they would have seemed not inappropriate. And why Midwich should have been singled out in preference to any one of a thousand other villages for the curious event of the 26th of September seems likely to remain a mystery forever.

For consider the simple ordinariness of the place:

Midwich lies roughly eight miles west-northwest of Trayne. The main road westward out of Trayne runs through the neighboring villages of Stouch and Oppley, from each of which a secondary road leads to Midwich. The village itself is therefore at the apex of a road triangle which has Oppley and Stouch at its lower corners; its only other highway is a lane which rolls in a Chestertonian fashion some five miles to reach Hickham which is three miles north.

At the heart of Midwich is a triangular Green ornamented by five fine elms and a white-railed pond. The war memorial stands in the churchward corner of the Green, and spaced out round the sides are the church itself, the vicarage, the inn, the smithy, the post office, Mrs. Welt's shop and a number of cottages. Altogether, the village comprises some sixty cottages and small houses, a village hall, Kyle Manor, and the Grange.

The church is mostly Gothic, but with a Norman west doorway and font. The vicarage is Georgian; the Grange Victorian; Kyle Manor has Tudor roots with numerous later graftings. The cottages show most of the styles which have existed between the two Elizabeths, but even more recent than the two latest County Council cottages are the utilitarian wings that were added to the Grange when the Ministry took it over for research.

The existence of Midwich has never been convincingly accounted for. It was not in a strategic position to hold a market, not even across a packway of any importance. It appears, at some unknown time, simply to have occurred; the Domesday survey notes it as a hamlet and it has continued as little more, for the railway age ignored it as had the coach roads and even the navigation canals.

So far as is known it rests upon no desirable minerals; no

official eye ever saw it as a likely site for an aerodrome or
a bombing-range or a battle school; only the Ministry intruded,
and the reconditioning of the Grange had little effect upon village life. Midwich has—or rather, had—lived and drowsed
upon its good soil in Arcadian undistinction for a thousand
years; and had anyone, on the evening of the 26th of September, been second-sighted enough to tell of the unnatural
experience in store, with its alarming consequences to the inhabitants, the villagers would stoutly have laughed him to
scorn. "What! In Midwich?" they would have said. "Get along
with you! We don't have no queer goings-on in Midwich. If
you want to frighten folk with your nasty ideas, better go try
'em in Oppley or Stouch—there's a lot of shocking things
could happen there, I daresay. But not here. We're seemly folk
in Midwich; always have been, an' always will be." But
nobody had such second-sight. There was no faintest sense of
the sword that hung suspended over Midwich. Indeed, the
place gave every sign of being all set to drowse on for
the next millennium, too.

One must not, however, assume that Midwich is altogether
without history. It has had its moments. In 1931 it was the
center of an untraced outbreak of foot-and-mouth disease.
And in 1916 an off-course Zeppelin unloaded a bomb which
fell in a plowed field and fortunately failed to explode. And
before that Black Ned, a second-class highwayman, was shot
on the steps of the Scythe and Stone Inn by Sweet Polly
Parker. Although this gesture of reproof appears to have been
of a more personal than social nature, she was nevertheless
much lauded for it in the ballads of 1768.

Then, too, there was the sensational closure of the nearby
St. Accius' Abbey and the redistribution of the brethren for
reasons which have been a subject of intermittent local speculation ever since it took place, in 1493.

Other events include the stabling of Cromwell's horses in
the church and a visit by William Wordsworth who was inspired by the Abbey ruins to the production of one of his more
routine commendatory sonnets.

With these exceptions, however, recorded time seems to
have flowed over Midwich without a ripple.

Nor would the inhabitants—save, perhaps, some of the
youthful in their brief premarital restlessness—have it other-
wise. Indeed, but for the vicar and his wife, the Zellabys at
Kyle Manor, the doctor, the district nurse, ourselves and, of
course, the researchers, they had most of them lived there

for numerous generations in a placid continuity which had become a right.

During the day of the 26th of September there seems to have been no trace of a foreshadow. Possibly Mrs. Brant, the blacksmith's wife, did feel a slight uneasiness at the sight of nine magpies in one field, as she afterward claimed; and Miss Ogle, the postmistress, may have been perturbed on the previous night by a dream of singularly large vampire bats; but if so it is unfortunate that Mrs. Brant's omens and Miss Ogle's dreams should have been so frequent as to nullify their alarm value. No other evidence has been produced to suggest that on that Monday, until late in the evening, Midwich was anything but normal. Just, in fact, as it had appeared to be when Janet and I set off for London. And yet, on Tuesday the 27th . . .

We locked the car, climbed the gate and started over the field of stubble, keeping well in to the hedge. At the end of that we came to another field of stubble and bore leftward across it, slightly uphill. Halfway across the pasture beyond, we reached the top of the rise, and were able to look out across Midwich. Not much of it was visible for trees, but we could see a couple of wisps of grayish smoke lazily rising and the church spire sticking up by the elms. In the middle of the next field I could see four or five cows lying down, apparently asleep.

I am not a countryman, I only live there, but I remember thinking that there was something not quite right about that. Cows folded up, chewing cud, yes, commonly enough; but cows lying down fast asleep, well, no. But at the time I felt no more than a vague apprehension of something out of true. We went on.

We climbed the fence of the field where the cows were and started across that, too.

A voice hallooed at us, away on the left. I looked round and made out a khaki-clad figure in the middle of the next field. He was calling something unintelligible, but the way he was waving his stick was without doubt a sign for us to go back. I stopped.

"Oh, come on, Richard. He's miles away," said Janet impatiently, and began to run on ahead.

I hesitated, looking at the figure who was now waving his stick more energetically than ever, and shouting more loudly, though no more intelligibly. I decided to follow Janet. She had perhaps twenty yards' start of me by now, and then, just as I started off, she staggered, collapsed without a sound and lay quite still.

I stopped dead. Her fall was so sudden, so complete, that for a moment I thought, idiotically, that she had been shot. My pause was only momentary. Then I ran forward. Dimly I was aware of the man away on the left still shouting, but I did not bother about him. I hurried toward her . . .

But I did not reach her.

I went out so completely that I never even saw the ground come up to hit me.

2 · *All Quiet in Midwich*

AS I SAID, all was normal in Midwich on the 26th. I have looked into the matter extensively and can tell you where practically everyone was and what they were doing that evening.

At the Scythe and Stone, for instance, the regulars were gathered in their usual numbers. Some of the younger villagers had gone to the pictures in Trayne—mostly the same ones who had gone there the previous Monday. In the post office Miss Ogle was knitting beside her switchboard and finding, as usual, that real life conversation was more interesting than the wireless. Mr. Tapper, who used to be a jobbing gardener before he won something fabulous in a football pool, was in a bad temper with his prized color-television set, which had gone on the blink again in its red circuit, and was abusing it in language that had already driven his wife to bed. Lights still burned in one or two of the new laboratories shouldered onto the Grange, but there was nothing unusual in that; it was common for one or two researchers to conduct their mysterious pursuits late into the night.

Apparently all was normal, yet even the most ordinary day is special for someone. For instance, it was, as I have said, my birthday, so it happened that our cottage was closed and dark. And up at Kyle Manor it happened, also, to be the day when Miss Ferrelyn Zellaby put it to Mr. Alan (temporarily Second-Lieutenant) Hughes that, in practice, it takes more than two to make an engagement; that it would be a friendly gesture to tell her father about it.

Alan after some hesitation and demur allowed himself to be persuaded into Gordon Zellaby's study to make him acquainted with the situation.

He found the master of Kyle Manor spread comfortably about a large armchair, his eyes closed, and his elegantly white head leaning against the chair's right wing, so that at first sight he appeared to have been lulled to sleep by the excellently reproduced music that pervaded the room. Without speaking or opening his eyes, however, he dispelled this impression by waving his left hand at another easy chair and then putting his finger to his lips for silence.

Alan tiptoed to the indicated chair and sat down. There then followed an interlude during which all the phrases that he had summoned to the tip of his tongue drained back somewhere beyond its root, and for the next ten minutes or so he occupied himself by a survey of the room.

One wall was covered from floor to ceiling by books which broke off only to allow the door by which he had entered. More books, in lower bookcases, ran round most of the room, halting in places to accommodate the french windows, the chimney-piece, where flickered a pleasant though not quite necessary fire, and the record player. One of the several glass-fronted cases was devoted to the Zellaby Works in various editions and languages, with room on the bottom shelf for a few more.

Above this case hung a sketch in red chalk of a handsome young man who could, after some forty years, still be seen in Gordon Zellaby. On another case a vigorous bronze recorded the impression he had made on Epstein some twenty-five years later. A few signed portraits of notable persons hung here and there on the walls. The space above and about the fireplace was reserved for more domestic mementoes. Along with portraits of Gordon Zellaby's father, mother, brother and two sisters, hung likenesses of Ferrelyn and her mother (Mrs. Zellaby Number Two) and Ferrelyn's half-brother and half-sister and their mother (Mrs. Zellaby Number One).

A portrait of Anthea (the Number Three and current Mrs. Gordon Zellaby) stood upon the center piece and focus of the room, the large leather-topped desk where the Works were written.

Contemplating the Works, Alan wondered whether his timing was altogether propitious, for a new Work was in process of gestation. This was made manifest by a certain distraitness in Mr. Zellaby's recent behavior.

"It always happens when he's brewing," Ferrelyn had explained. "Part of him seems to get lost. He goes off on long walks and can't make out where he is and rings up to be brought home, and so on. It's a bit trying while it lasts, but it gets better once he starts to write. In the meantime, we just have to be firm with him, and see he has his meals and all that."

The room in general, with its comfortable chairs, convenient lights and thick carpet, struck Alan as a practical result of its owner's views on the balanced life. He recalled that in *While We Last*, the only one of the Works he had read as yet, Zellaby had treated asceticism and overindulgence as similar evidences of maladjustment. He remembered it as an interesting, but gloomy book; the author had not given proper weight to the fact that the new generation was more dynamic and rather more clear-sighted than those that had preceded it.

At last the music tied itself up with a neat bow, and ceased. Zellaby stopped the machine by a switch on the arm of his chair, opened his eyes and regarded Alan.

"I hope you don't mind," he apologized. "One feels that once Bach has started his pattern he should be allowed to finish it. Besides," he added, glancing at the playing-cabinet, "we still lack a code for dealing with these innovations. Is the art of the musician less worthy of respect simply because he is not present in person? What is the gracious thing? Should I defer to you, or you to me, or should both of us defer to genius—even genius at second-hand? Nobody can tell us. We shall never know. The world of the etiquette book fell to pieces at the end of the last century, and there has been no code of manners to tell us how to deal with anything invented since. Not even rules for an individualist to break, which is itself another blow at freedom. Rather a pity, don't you think?"

"Yes," said Alan. "I—"

"Though, mind you," Mr. Zellaby continued, "it is a trifle démodé even to perceive the existence of the problem. The true fruit of this century has little interest in coming to living-terms with innovations; it just wants to grab them all as they come along. Only when we encounter something really big do we become aware of a social problem at all, and then, rather than make concessions, we yammer for the impossibly easy way out, uninvention, suppression—as in the matter of the Bomb."

"I suppose so. What I—"

Mr. Zellaby perceived a lack of fervor in the response.

"When one is young," he said understandingly, "the unconventional, the unregulated, hand-to-mouth way of life has a romantic aspect. But such, you must agree, are not the lines on which to run a complex world. Luckily, we in the West still retain the skeleton of our ethics, but there are signs that the old bones are finding the weight of new knowledge difficult to carry with confidence, don't you think?"

Alan drew breath. Recollections of previous entanglements in the web of Zellaby discourse forced him to the direct solution.

"Actually, sir, it was on quite another matter I wanted to see you," he said.

When Zellaby noticed the interruptions of his audible reflections he was accustomed to take them in mild good part. He now postponed further contemplation of the ethical skeleton to inquire:

"But of course, my dear fellow. By all means. What is it?"

"It's that—well, it's about Ferrelyn, sir."

"Ferrelyn? Oh yes. I'm afraid she's gone up to London for a couple of days to see her mother. She'll be back tomorrow."

"Er—it was today she came back, Mr. Zellaby."

"Really?" exclaimed Zellaby. He thought it over. "Yes, you're quite right. She was here for dinner. You both were," he added triumphantly.

"Yes," said Alan, and holding his chance with determination, he plowed ahead with his news, unhappily conscious that not one of his prepared phrases remained in his mind. Zellaby listened patiently until Alan finally stumbled to a conclusion.

"So I do hope, sir, that you will have no objection to our becoming officially engaged." At that Zellaby's eyes widened slightly.

"My dear fellow, you overestimate my position. Ferrelyn is a sensible girl, and I have no doubt whatever that by this time she and her mother know *all* about you, and have, together, reached a well-considered decision."

"But I've never even met Mrs. Holder," Alan objected.

"If you had, you would have a better grasp of the situation. Jane is a great organizer," Mr. Zellaby told him, regarding one of the pictures on the mantel with benevolence. He got up.

"Well, now, you have performed your part very creditably; so I, too, must behave as Ferrelyn considers proper. Would you care to assemble the company while I fetch the bottle?"

In a few minutes, with his wife, his daughter and his prospective son-in-law grouped about him, he lifted his glass.

"Let us now drink," announced Zellaby, "to the adjunction of fond spirits. It is true that the institution of marriage as it is proclaimed by church and state displays a depressingly mechanistic attitude of mind toward partnership—one not unlike, in fact, that of Noah. The human spirit, however, is tough, and it quite often happens that love is able to survive this coarse, institutional thumbing. Let us hope, therefore—"

"Daddy," Ferrelyn broke in, "it's after ten, and Alan has to get back to camp in time, or he'll be cashiered, or something. All you really have to say is 'long life and happiness to you both.' "

"Oh," said Mr. Zellaby. "Are you sure that's enough? It seems very brief. However, if you think it suitable, then I say it, my dear. Most wholeheartedly I say it."

He did.

Alan set down his empty glass.

"I'm afraid what Ferrelyn said was right, sir. I shall have to leave now," he said.

Zellaby nodded sympathetically.

"It must be a trying time for you. How much longer will they keep you?"

Alan said he hoped to be free of the army in about three months. Zellaby nodded again.

"I expect the experience will turn out to have value. Sometimes I regret the lack of it myself. Too young for one war, tethered to a desk in the Ministry of Information in the next. Something more active would have been preferable. Well, good night, my dear fellow. It's—" He broke off, struck by a sudden thought. "Dear me, I know we all call you Alan, but I don't believe I know your other name. Perhaps we ought to have that in order."

Alan told him, and they shook hands again.

As he emerged into the hall with Ferrelyn he noticed the clock.

"I say, I'll have to step on it. See you tomorrow, darling. Six o'clock. Good night, my sweet."

They kissed fervently but briefly in the doorway, and he broke away down the steps, bounding toward the small red car parked on the drive. The engine started and roared. He gave a final wave and, with a spurt of gravel from the rear wheels, dashed away.

Ferrelyn watched the rear lights dwindle and vanish. She stood listening until the erstwhile roar became a distant hum, and then closed the front door. On her way back to the study she noticed that the hall clock now showed ten-fifteen.

Still, then, at ten-fifteen nothing in Midwich was abnormal.

With the departure of Alan's car peace settled down again over a community which was, by and large, engaged in winding up an uneventful day in expectation of a no less uneventful morrow.

Many cottage windows still threw yellow beams into the mild evening where they glistened in the dampness of an earlier shower. The occasional surges of voices and laughter which swept the place were not local; they originated with a well handled studio-audience miles away and several days ago, and formed merely a background against which most of the village was preparing for bed. Indeed, many of the very old and very young had already retired, and in upstairs bathrooms wives were now filling hot water bottles against the chill of night.

The last customers to be persuaded out of the Scythe and Stone had lingered for a few minutes in parting and gone their ways, and by ten-fifteen all but one Alfred Wait and a certain Harry Crankhart, who were still engaged in argument about fertilizers, had reached their homes.

Only one event of the day still impended, the passage of the bus that would bring the more dashing spirits back from their evening in Trayne. With that over, Midwich could finally settle down to sleep.

In the vicarage, at 10:15, Miss Polly Rushton was thinking that if only she had gone to bed half an hour ago she could be enjoying the book that now lay neglected on her knees, and how much pleasanter that would be than listening to the present contest between her uncle and aunt. For on one side of the room Uncle Hubert, the Reverend Hubert Leebody, was attempting to listen to a Third Program disquisition on The Pre-Sophoclean Conception of the Oedipus Complex, while, on the other, Aunt Dora was telephoning. Mr. Leebody, determined that scholarship should not be submerged by piffle, had already made two advances in volume and still had forty-five degrees of knob turning in reserve. He could not be blamed for failing to guess that what now struck him as a particularly nugatory exchange of feminine concerns would subsequently prove to be of importance.

The call was from South Kensington, London, where a Mrs. Cluey was seeking the support of her lifelong friend Mrs. Leebody. By 10:16 she had reached the kernel of the matter.

"Now, tell me, Dora—and, mind, I do want your *honest* opinion on this: do you think that in Kathy's case it should be white satin or white brocade?"

Mrs. Leebody stalled. Clearly this was a matter where the word "honest" was relative, and it was inconsiderate of Mrs. Cluey, to say the least, to phrase her question with no perceptible bias. Probably satin, thought Mrs. Leebody, but she hesitated to risk the friendship of years on a guess. She tried for a lead.

"Of course, for a very young bride . . . but then one wouldn't call Kathy such a *very* young bride, perhaps . . ."

"Not *very* young," agreed Mrs. Cluey, and waited.

Mrs. Leebody dratted her friend's importunity, and also her husband's radio program, which made thinking and finesse difficult.

"Well," she said at last, "both can look charming, of course, but for Kathy I really think—"

At which point her voice abruptly stopped.

Far away in South Kensington Mrs. Cluey joggled the receiver impatiently and looked at her watch. Presently she pressed the bar down for a moment and then dialed O.

"I wish to make a complaint," she said. "I have just been cut off in the middle of a most important conversation."

The exchange told her it would try to reconnect her. A few minutes later it confessed failure.

"Most inefficient," said Mrs. Cluey. "I shall put in a written complaint. I refuse to pay for a minute more than we had —indeed, I really don't see why I should pay at all in the circumstances. We were cut off at ten-seventeen exactly."

The man at the exchange responded with formal tact, and made a note of the time, for reference—22:17 hours, 26th September.

3 · Calling Midwich

FROM 10:17 P.M. that night information about Midwich becomes not only objective, but largely episodic. Undoubtedly the first person to be aware that there was something amiss was the operator at Trayne, who very properly reported it.

"Midwich! Oh, not Midwich again!" exclaimed the exchange supervisor. She looked helplessly at the operator. "Really, there are times when one wonders why places like Midwich are allowed to have telephones at all. I don't believe there's a single responsible person in the place. As for that Miss Ogle. . . . Try her on the other line."

"I've done that. She still doesn't answer," said the operator.

"Probably goes to bed leaving a call in. That's the third time in a month she's done something stupid. How do these Miss Ogles ever get their jobs? They're a menace. Keep on trying, and when you do get her let me have a word with her."

At Colewater Aerodrome the duty-officer heard his telephone ring at approximately 10:25. He picked it up.

"Midwich? No, old boy. Can't have been one of ours. No. We're all correct and accounted for. Sure it wasn't a meteorite, or something?"

He listened while the telephone chattered.

"Well, it didn't come in this way. *Our* radar hasn't picked up anything. And it certainly wasn't one of our aircraft. None of 'em been in that sector, or near it. . . . Well, you might try Basinghill. They've got some kind of a show on there tonight, I believe. . . . Not at all, old man. Sorry I can't help."

"Midwich?" said the traffic manager of the South Hundreds Omnibus Company. "Well, man, *ring up* Midwich, for heaven's sake! Find out if it's stuck there, or what's happened. You're in charge. No need to bother me at this time of night. . . . Oh, you have. Why couldn't you say so before? Might've expected that, with a one-eyed place like Midwich.

But if it left Oppley on time and it's not reached Stouch, it obviously *must* be in Midwich, or thereabouts. There's nowhere else *for* it to be. . . . Yes, I know that's what you said. The point is, what have you *done*? You're in charge there. It's your job to do things. . . . Never mind what I said last time; this is *this* time. Of *course* the truck'll have to go out and find it. Get it away at once. Ought to have been on the job twenty minutes ago. . . ."

And in Trayne:

The engine roared, the building thrummed and the scarlet appliance swept magnificently out of the station.

"Midwich," explained the firewoman at the switchboard to those who remained standing by. "Report came from Oppley. The man's seen something alight over in Midwich. Thinks it's a house—or could be a rick. Midwich phone's apparently out of service."

"Would be," said the man beside her. "What else would you expect from bloody Midwich?"

And, also in Trayne:

"Oh, Midwich," said the desk sergeant. "Yes, we've had a report in about that. The patrol car's on its way there now. I'll ring you back when we hear from it."

He wrote the number and the time of the call on his sheet, and regarded it.

"H'm," he said, after thought, "would you suppose, Constable Jones, that the name Midwich could have anything to do with witchcraft?"

Constable Jones fancied it more likely to be a corruption of the Anglo-Saxon "wick," denoting a living-place.

"Oh," said the sergeant. He regarded his subordinate pensively for a moment. You never knew what you were going to find in the force nowadays. "Well, anyway," he went on, "the place seems to be bewitched tonight. The South Hundreds mislay a bus there; the R.A.F. says it has a radar report on an aircraft coming down there, which may or may not be the reason that Oppley reports a fire there. The South Hundreds send a truck to find their bus and proceed to lose that, too. The Fire Service sends a dispatch rider to find out why the devil their appliance has made no report, and not a word comes from him, either. Oppley reports a second fire and that it can't see anything being done about it, or about the first one either, for that matter. *Still* nobody in bloody

Midwich answers the bloody telephone. And *now* what the hell has happened to our patrol car?"

He turned round in his chair and pulled aside a small panel in the charge-room wall.

"Anything from that car yet?" he called.

The constable looked up and lifted away one earphone.

"No, sarge. Nothing since they were leaving Stouch, on the Midwich road."

"That was about half an hour ago, man."

"Twenty-one minutes, sarge," said the constable, looking at his watch.

The sergeant slapped the panel shut, irritably. He stared at the opposite wall for a few seconds and then picked up the telephone again.

"Get me Constable Gobby, in Stouch," he directed. He drummed with the fingers of his right hand while he waited, then: "Ah, Gobby? Sergeant Floyd here. Sorry to dig you out at this hour, but I want you to get over to Midwich as quick as may be and find out what the hell's going on there." He outlined a few of the reasons. "Yes, it is. A very rum do, altogether. Let us have some word on it as soon as you can. I'll tell the exchange to expect you through from Midwich post office—push the door in there, if you have to. I'll deal with Miss Ogle. . . . Good man. My apologies to Mrs. Gobby." He put the phone back.

"Sound fellow, Gobby," he said. "Now perhaps we'll begin to make some sense of it."

Away in Stouch, Constable Gobby switched on the light, dragged himself out of his warm bed and dressed sleepily to the accompaniment of a dissertation on the unhappy lot of a policeman's wife. Descending to the outhouse, he presently succeeded in disentangling his bicycle from the perambulator, and pedaled away.

Thereafter, he vanished into a silence just as uncommunicative as that which already covered the bus, the truck, the fire engine, the dispatch-rider, the police car and, indeed, all that had to do with Midwich.

4 · Requiescat Midwich

THE DAWN of the 27th was an affair of slatternly rags soaking in a dishwater sky, with a gray light weakly filtering through. Nevertheless, in Oppley and in Stouch cocks crowed and other birds welcomed it more melodiously. In Midwich, however, no birds sang.

In Oppley and Stouch, too, as in other places, hands were soon reaching out to silence alarm clocks, but in Midwich the clocks rattled on till they ran down.

In other villages sleepy-eyed men left their cottages and encountered their work-mates with sleepy good mornings; in Midwich no one encountered anyone.

For Midwich lay entranced.

While the rest of the world began to fill the day with clamor, Midwich slept on. Its men and women, its horses, cows and sheep; its pigs, its poultry, its larks, moles and mice all lay still. There was a pocket of silence in Midwich, broken only by the whispering of the leaves, the chiming of the church clock, and the gurgle of the Opple as it slid over the weir beside the mill.

And while the dawn was still a poor, weak thing an olive-green van, with the words "Post Office Telephones" just discernible upon it, set out from Trayne with the object of putting the rest of the world into touch with Midwich again.

In Stouch it paused at the village call box to inquire whether Midwich had yet shown any signs of life. Midwich had not; it was still as deeply incommunicado as it had been since 22:17 hours. The van re-started and rattled on through the uncertainly gathering daylight.

"Cor!" said the lineman to his driver companion. "That there Miss Ogle ain't 'alf goin' to cop 'erself a basinful of 'Er Majesty's displeasure over this little lot."

"I don't get it," complained the driver. " 'F you'd asked me I'd of said the old girl was *always* listenin' when there was anyone on the blower, day or night. Just goes to show," he added, vaguely.

22

A little out of Stouch, the van swung sharply to the right
and bounced along the byroad to Midwich for half a mile or
so. Then it rounded a corner to encounter a situation which
called for all the driver's presence of mind.

He had a sudden view of a fire-engine, half heeled over,
with its near-side wheels in the ditch, and a black car which
had climbed halfway up the bank on the other side a few
yards further on, with a man and a bicycle lying half in the
ditch behind it. He pulled hard over, attempting an "S" turn
which would avoid both vehicles, but before he could complete it his own van ran on to the narrow verge, bumped
along for a few more yards, then plowed to a stop, with its
side in the hedge.

Half-an-hour later the first bus of the day rattled round
the same corner to jam itself neatly into the gap between the
fire-engine and the van, and block the road completely.

At roughly the same time Major Dramley, retired, a resi-
dent of Oppley, was taking his morning constitutional and
approaching Midwich's other road, the one connecting it
with Oppley. He had noticed nothing amiss as he came
across the field-path, with his terrier sniffing at his heels, but
now, as he climbed the stile he stood immobilized astride of
it and surveyed the prospect with consternation.

By precedent, he should have debouched upon an empty
second-class road distinguished only by a lone white stone
announcing "MIDWICH ¾." Instead he found himself gazing
upon a mélange of vehicles giving an impression that the
highway had been converted overnight into a dump.

At the far end of the medley was a private car, skewed
across the road and looking as if it had been shoved along
by a bus which now rested at an oblique angle, with its front
halfway through a hedge. The bus had apparently in its turn
been charged on the starboard quarter by a light truck. A
tractor which had evidently attempted the narrow gap that
remained had slewed in an attempt to climb the bank, and
overturned. A man who might well have been its driver now
lay clear of it, asprawl and unmoving in the forefront of the
tangle.

Major Dramley was surprised into the use of an expression
more common in his youth.

"By jove!" he said, with concern. "By *jove!*"

He stepped clear of the stile, onto the road, and began to
hurry toward the entangled vehicles. Then, as he drew closer,
something prompted him to stop short.

"Had a feeling there was something deuced odd," he explained later to me. "Old campaigner, you know. Get a sense when things are a bit off color. Learn not to ignore it."

The warning was, however, something more than psychic. For one thing, he was able to see the heads of several passengers who were sitting in the bus, and not one of them moved. Moreover, he noticed that the bus's interior lights were still dimly on. Also, he caught sight of the truck's driver still sitting at the wheel.

"Didn't care for the look of that, you know," he explained. "Right off the wicket, what? Fellow sitting there like a dummy, with his radiator pushing the back of the bus in. Fellow wouldn't, you know. 'Dashed odd, that,' I said to myself. *'Dashed* odd!' "

The oddness—or, at any rate, the implication in the oddness—was less apparent to the Major's terrier bitch. She did pause for a moment to survey the unusual scene, but then curiosity sent her trotting forward to investigate.

"Here, ———! Heel!" commanded the Major.

The terrier hesitated, but the lure ahead was too strong. She trotted on. Then, when she was within a foot or so of the back of the truck, her legs crumpled. Without a sound she fell on her side and lay motionless.

Major Dramley stared from widened eyes. For some seconds he stood quite still, incredulity frozen on his face. Then he blanched a little, and withdrew a step.

"GAS!" he announced, at battalion strength. "GAS!"

After glancing left and right he retreated in an orderly manner, withdrawing his invisible troops from the danger area and round the bend on the road. There he halted to consolidate, and to mop his brow with a large white handkerchief. He became aware of the silence all about him, and of an uneasy feeling that was hostile. A minute later he was relieved to hear the sound of a motor. The noise hummed steadily closer, slowed for the next turn, and then revealed itself in a blaze of scarlet glory as the Royal Mail.

Major Dramley strode out, and stood squarely in its way, waving like a human windmill.

"GAS!" he roared, as the van shuddered to a stop.

A head pushed out of the offside window.

"Good morning, Major Dramley, sir. This isn't the Oppley delivery, it's the Midwich—"

The Major recognized the face under the peaked cap.

"Ah! Sergeant Bray!" he exclaimed with satisfaction. "This road is unserviceable, sergeant. Contaminated area ahead."

The driver was less quick to drop back into half-forgotten jargon.

"A what, sir?" he inquired.

"Contaminated area. Gas, man, gas," explained the Major. The driver's memory caught up.

"Oh, I see, sir. 'Fraid all that's nothing to do with me these days. Maneuvers or no maneuvers, the mail has to go——"

"But I tell you there's *gas* ahead, sergeant. *Gas!*" repeated the Major.

The driver drew his head in and looked at his companion with raised eyebrows.

"It's got the old boy at last," he said. "Knew it would, one of these days."

"Oh, flip 'im. Let's get on," said the other.

The Major came round to the window.

"In any case you can't get through. The road's obstructed," he told them.

The driver shook his head.

"We'll have to try, sir," he said, and let in his clutch, with decision.

Major Dramley made a gesture as if he would hold the van back, but dropped his arm as it drew away. It whisked round the corner and out of sight.

Presently there came a sound of brakes hard on. The Major walked to a point which gave him a view round the corner. The van had pulled up in the middle of the road, the men were out of it and curiously approaching the congestion of vehicles ahead. He waved his stick and called to them.

"Hey, there, sergeant!" he shouted.

The driver paused and looked round. His companion held on his way, showing a contemptuous back.

"Keep clear, man. GAS, I tell you. GAS!" repeated the Major.

The driver hesitated, and then decided to ignore the old duffer. He turned round again, just in time to see his companion fold up and go down beside the body of the dog.

He stared, then he ran to his van. He backed up to the bend and stopped. The Major poked his head in the window.

"Smell anything?"

The driver had little drops of sweat on his brow. He shook his head.

"What do you reckon it is, sir?" he said, in a shaken voice.

"Some kind of gas. That's what I've been trying to tell you."

The driver surveyed the scene, with his fallen mate in the forefront.

"Gas," he repeated vaguely. "But who? Why . . . ? I don't get it."

Major Dramley had already passed through that stage. He shrugged.

"Never can tell these days, sergeant. Foreign agents, you know. Subversive elements. Damned scientists always up to something, too. It's probably escaped from somewhere," he added, rather as if gas were part of a traveling circus. A thought struck him. "There's that government research place at the Grange," he said. "Very likely something to do with that. Always said they'd no right to put it there."

The driver looked at his mate again.

"Reckon I'd better get on the blower, and have 'em fetch Bill and the rest out of there, pretty sharp," he decided.

"Just what I was going to suggest, sergeant," agreed the Major. "My house is as near as any. Use my phone. Several ambulances, I'd say. Ten or eleven people at least in there. I'll stay here. Can't leave a thing like this unguarded, you know."

"No-o . . ." admitted the driver, "but suppose it starts shifting this way?"

It was the rolling phrase "contaminated area" that had been uppermost in the Major's mind, connoting something established and stationary, but he met this uneasy possibility stoutly.

"Have to chance that, sergeant. Can't win wars without taking risks, you know."

"Wars?" repeated the driver, wonderingly. "Do you mean—?"

"Manner of speaking," the Major explained, with some reluctance. "Now you cut along to my place and stir up those ambulance people."

The van backed further until it reached a spot where it could turn. Major Dramley waved his stick in a reassuring farewell as it drove off; then squared his shoulders and settled down to duty.

From time to time he approached the corner and cocked a wary eye at the tangle of vehicles further along. All appeared to be quite static, with no sign of anything "shifting" his way. But then, what sort of a sign would there be if it was?

Meanwhile a similar state of affairs on the Stouch road had been discovered by the prudent driver of a baker's van, who had stopped short of it. Twenty minutes later almost identical action was taking place on both roads. Ambulances swept up to the trouble centers. Rear doors opened. Uniformed men emerged, fastening their tunic buttons, and providently pinching the embers from half-smoked cigarettes. They surveyed the pile-ups in a knowledgeable, confidence-inspiring way, unrolled stretchers and prepared to advance.

On the Oppley road Major Dramley attempted to offer the benefit of his advice. The ambulance men regarded him simply as one of those who are magnetized out of nowhere by the presence of disaster. They brushed him and his warnings aside with deaf, official firmness.

The two leading bearers approached the prone postman briskly and competently, but then, as the one ahead drew level with the sprawled body, he wilted, sagged and subsided across the last casualty's legs. The hind bearer goggled and his jaw dropped. Out of the babble behind him his ears picked up the Major's voice saying "Gas." He dropped the stretcher-handles as if they had turned hot and stepped back hastily.

There was a pause for consultation. Presently the ambulance driver shook his head.

"Not our kind of job," he said, with the satisfaction of one recalling a useful decision. "More in the fire-chaps' line, if you ask me. Better give 'em a buzz—and warn 'em to bring masks."

Major Dramley snorted.

"Smoke-masks! Absurd. No good taking half-measures with a thing like this. Colonel Latcher over at Cufton Camp, friend of mine, knows the Chief Constable, too. I'll get him to send some volunteers over with the proper gear. Good experience for 'em."

"The fire chaps—" began the ambulance-driver again.

"All right. If you like. Nothing against them personally. Fine men in their way, no doubt. But poison gas. Job for the army. Stands to reason," said the Major, and marched off purposefully toward his home.

5 · Operation Midwich

ABOUT THE TIME that Janet and I were approaching Trayne on the road from London, Lieutenant Alan Hughes was standing beside Leading-Fireman Norris on the Oppley road into Midwich, surveying the blockage. After frowning at it awhile he inquired:

"Do they teach firemen to spin a rope—a lasso?" The Leading-Fireman stared at him, and then caught on.

"Not in our mob, anyway," he admitted, "but now we've got an idea where the edge is. I reckon a ceiling hook might reach one or two of 'em."

He gave instructions, and they watched while the hook grappled at the ambulance man. Presently . lodged in his clothes, and two men hauled it in. The body w is dragged a couple of yards along the tarmac, then it sat up abruptly and swore.

It seemed to Alan that he had never heard more beautiful language. Already, the acute anxiety of the rescue party had been allayed by the discovery that the victims were quietly, but quite definitely, breathing. Now it was established that one, at least, of them showed no visible ill effects of quite ninety minutes' experience of whatever-it-was.

"Good," Alan said. "If he's all right, it looks as if the rest may be—though it doesn't get us much nearer to knowing *what* it is."

The next to be pulled out was the postman. He had been there somewhat longer than the ambulance man, but his recovery was every bit as spontaneous and satisfactory.

"Funny," said the Leading-Fireman. "Kind of hits 'em like a hammer. But the line seems to be quite sharp, and stationary. Whoever heard of a stationary gas?"

Alan shook his head. "Besides," he agreed, "anything really volatile would have cleared by now."

"I wonder how far it stretches?" mused the Leading-Fireman. "Must be fairly wide, or we'd see things what were trying to come this way."

They continued to gaze in perplexity toward Midwich. Beyond the vehicles the road continued, clear and innocent-looking to the next turn. Now that the morning mist had lifted it was possible to see the tower of Midwich church jutting above the hedges. When one disregarded the immediate foreground, the prospect was completely normal; the very negation of mystery.

The firemen continued to drag out the forms within easy reach, including one of their own number who had ventured too close. The victims who had not been there long sat up alertly, maintaining with obvious truth that they needed no help from the ambulance men. The experience left no impression on them; indeed, the Major's terrier bounded exuberantly into the zone again, and had to be retrieved once more.

With the sprawled figures pulled clear, the next problems was to drag out the vehicles and their occupants. The Leading-Fireman left Alan and went forward to direct his squad.

Alan watched for some moments, still with a puzzled frown. Then he turned away and climbed over the stile by which Major Dramley had approached earlier. He did not, however, follow the path to the left, but kept straight ahead, climbing a small rise, from which he was able to see several roofs, including those of Kyle Manor and the Grange. A scene of uninformative placidity. But a few more yards further brought him to a point where he could see four sheep lying motionless in a field. Although they would no doubt recover, the sight troubled him. It indicated that the barrier zone was wider than he had hoped. In Kyle Manor Ferrelyn, too, must be lying helpless and inert, the thought distressed him. It did not occur to him that there might be unseen activities going on in the area which would produce results far more alarming in their implications. If the present gave him cause for concern, the future, luckily, was still hidden. After he had watched a little longer, he turned and walked thoughtfully back to the road.

A group from the working party were heaving on a rope which they had somehow attached to the tractor.

"Sergeant Decker," he called.

The sergeant broke off, came across and saluted.

"Sergeant," Alan said thoughtfully, "do you think you could get hold of a canary—in a cage, of course?"

The sergeant blinked.

"Er—a canary, sir?" he asked, uneasily.

"Yes. There ought to be some in Oppley. You'd better take the jeep."

The sergeant still hesitated.

"Yes, sir. Er—you did say a canary, sir?"

"Well, a budgerigar would do just as well, if it's easier, but some kind of a bird."

The sergeant's eyes strayed uncertainly to a point somewhere over Alan's shoulder.

"I—ah—" he began.

"Cut along now, sergeant," Alan told him. "I just want that bird here as soon as you can manage it. Tell them it's urgent and there'll be compensation if necessary."

"Very good, sir. A canary," said the sergeant. He saluted, and walked over to the jeep, his opinion of the assignment showing clearly through his back.

I became aware that I was slithering along the ground, face down. Very odd. One moment I was hurrying towards Janet, then, with no interval at all, this. . . .

The motion stopped. I sat up to find myself surrounded by an odd collection of people. There was a fireman, engaged in disentangling a murderous-looking hook from my clothing, a St. John's ambulance man regarding me with a professionally hopeful eye, a very young private carrying a pail of white-wash, another holding a map, and an equally young corporal armed with a bird cage on the end of a long pole. Also an unencumbered officer. In addition to this somewhat surrealistic collection there was Janet, still lying where she had fallen. I got to my feet just as the fireman, having freed h¨ hook, reached it toward her and caught the belt of her mackintosh. He began to pull, and of course the belt broke, so he reached it over her and began to roll her toward us. At the second time over, she sat up, looking disarranged and indignant.

"Feeling all right, Mr. Gayford?" asked a voice beside me.

I looked round and recognized the officer as Alan Hughes, whom we had met at the Zellabys' a couple of times.

"Yes," I said. "But what's going on here?"

He disregarded that for the moment and helped Janet to her feet. Then he turned to the corporal.

"I'd better get back to the road. Just carry on with this, corporal."

"Yes, sir," said the corporal. He lowered his pole from the vertical and, with the cage still dangling at its end, thrust it forward tentatively. The bird fell off its perch and lay on the sanded floor of the cage. The corporal withdrew the cage slightly. The bird gave a slightly indignant tweet and hopped back on its perch. One watching private stepped forward with his bucket and daubed a little whitewash on the grass, the other made a mark on his map. The party then moved along a dozen yards or so and repeated the performance.

This time it was Janet who inquired what on earth was happening. Alan explained as much as he knew and added:

"There's obviously no chance of getting into the place while this lasts. Your best course would be to make for Trayne and wait there for the all-clear."

We looked after the corporal's party, just in time to see the bird fall off its perch once more, and then across the innocent fields to Midwich. After our experience there did not appear to be any useful alternative. Janet nodded. So we thanked young Hughes and presently parted from him to make our way back to the car.

At the Eagle Janet insisted that we should book a room for the night, just in case, and then went up to it. I gravitated to the bar.

The room was unusually full for noon, and almost all of them were strangers. The majority of them were talking somewhat histrionically in small groups or pairs; though a few individuals were drinking privately and thoughtfully. I wormed my way to the counter with some difficulty, and as I was working back out again, drink in hand, a voice at my shoulder said:

"Now, what on earth would you be doing in this lot, Richard?"

The voice was familiar and so, when I looked round, was the face, though it took me a second or two to place it—there was not only the veil of years to be drawn aside, but a military cap had to be juggled into the place of the present tweed. But when this had been done, I was delighted.

"My dear Bernard!" I exclaimed. "This is wonderful! Come along out of this mob." And I seized his arm and towed him into the lounge.

The sight of him made me feel young again: took me back to the beaches, the Ardennes, the Reichswald and the Rhine. It was a good meeting. I sent the waiter for more drinks. Half an hour later, when the first ebullition had leveled out, he brought me back to the point.

"You never answered my first question," he reminded me, looking at me carefully. "I'd no idea you'd gone in for that sort of thing."

"What sort of thing?" I inquired.

He lifted his head slightly, toward the bar.

"The Press."

"Oh, is that it! I was wondering why the invasion."

One eyebrow descended a little.

"Well, if you're not part of it, what are you?"

"I just live in these parts."

At that moment Janet came into the lounge, and I introduced him.

"Janet, dear, this is Bernard Westcott. He used to be Captain Westcott when we were together, but I know he became a major, and now——?"

"Colonel," admitted Bernard, and greeted her charmingly.

"I am so glad," Janet told him. "I've heard a lot about you. I know one says that, but this time it happens to be true."

She invited him to lunch with us, but he said that he had business to attend to, and was already overdue. His tone of regret was genuine enough for her to say:

"Dinner, then? At home, if we can get there, but here if we are still exiled?"

"At home?" queried Bernard.

"In Midwich," she explained. "It's about eight miles away."

Bernard's manner changed slightly.

"You *live* in Midwich?" he inquired, looking from her to me. "Have you been there long?"

"About a year now," I told him. "We'd normally be there now, but——" I explained how we came to be stranded at the Eagle.

He thought for some moments after I finished, and then seemed to come to a decision. He turned to Janet.

"Mrs. Gayford, I wonder if you would excuse me if I were to take your husband along with me? It's this Midwich business that has brought me here. I think he might be able to help us, if he's willing."

"To find out what's happened, you mean?" Janet asked.

"Well, let's say in connection with it. What do you think?" he added to me.

"If I can, of course. But who is *us?*" I inquired.

"I'll explain as we go," he told me. "I really ought to have been there an hour ago. I'd not drag him off like this if it weren't important, Mrs. Gayford. You'll be all right on your own here?"

Janet assured him that the Eagle was a safe place, and we rose.

"Just one thing," he added before we left, "don't let any of those fellows in the bar pester you. Get them slung out if they try. They're all a bit peevish since they've learned that their editors won't be touching this Midwich business. Not a word to any of 'em. Tell you more about it later."

"Very well. Agog, but silent. That's me," Janet agreed as we left.

H.Q. had been established a little back from the affected area on the Oppley road. At the police block Bernard produced a pass which earned him a salute from the constable on duty, and we passed through without further trouble. A very young three-pipper sitting forlornly in a tent brightened up at our arrival and decided that as Colonel Latcher was out inspecting the lines it was his duty to put us in the picture.

The caged birds had now, it seemed, finished their job and been returned to their doting and reluctantly public-spirited owners.

"We'll probably have protests from the R.S.P.C.A., as well as claims for damages when they contract croup or something," said the Captain, "but here's the result." And he produced a large-scale map showing a perfect circle almost two miles in diameter, with Midwich Church lying somewhat south and a little east of its center.

"That's *it*," he explained, "and as far as we can tell it *is* a circle, not just a belt. We've got an o.p. on Oppley church tower, and no movement in the area has been observed—and there are a couple of chaps lying in the road outside the pub who haven't moved, either. As to *what* it is, we're not much further.

"We've established that it is static, invisible, odorless, non-registering on radar, non-echoing on sound, immediate in effect on at least mammals, birds, reptiles and insects; and apparently has no aftereffects—at least, no direct effects, though naturally the people in the bus and the others who were in it for some time are feeling roughish from exposure. But that's about as far as we go. Frankly, as to what it really is, we haven't a clue yet."

Bernard asked him a few questions which elicited little more, and then we made our way in search of Colonel Latcher. We found him after a while, in company with an older man who turned out to be the Chief Constable of Wintonshire. Both of them, with some lesser lights in attendance, were standing on a slight rise regarding the terrain. Their grouping suggested an eighteenth-century engraving of generals watching a battle that was not going too well, only there was no visible battle. Bernard introduced himself and me. The Colonel regarded him intently.

"Ah!" he said. "Ah yes. You're the chap on the phone who told me this had to be kept quiet."

Before Bernard could reply, the Chief Constable came in:

"*Kept quiet!* Kept quiet, indeed. A two-mile circle of country completely blanketed by this thing, and you'd like it kept quiet."

"That was the instruction," said Bernard. "The Security—"

"But how the devil do they think—?"

Colonel Latcher cut in, heading him off.

"We've done our best to put it around as a surprise tactical exercise. Bit thin, but it makes something to say. Had to say something. Trouble is, for all we know it may be some little trick of our own gone wrong. So much damned secrecy nowadays that nobody knows anything. All these scientists in back rooms ruining the profession. Soldiering'll soon be nothing but wizards and wires."

"The news agencies are on to it already," grumbled the Chief Constable. "We've headed some of 'em off. But you know what they are. They'll be sneaking round some way, pushing their noses into it. And how are we going to keep *them* quiet?"

"That, at least, needn't worry you much," Bernard told him. "There's been a Home Office advice on this already. Very sore they are. But I think it will hold. It really depends on whether it turns out to have enough sensation in it to make trouble worth while."

"H'm," said the Colonel, looking out across the somnolent scene again. "And I suppose *that* depends on whether, from a newspaper view, the sleeping beauty would be a sensation, or a bore."

Quite an assortment of people kept on turning up in the course of the next hour or two, all apparently representing the interests of various departments, civil and military. A larger tent was erected beside the Oppley road, and in it a conference was called for 16:30. Colonel Latcher led off with a review of the situation. It did not take long. Just as he was concluding it a Group Captain arrived. He marched in with a malevolent air, and slapped a large photograph down on the table in front of the Colonel.

"There you are, gentlemen," he said grimly. "That cost two good men in one good aircraft, and we were lucky not to lose another. I hope it was worth it."

We crowded round to study the photograph, and compare it with the map.

"What's *that?*" asked a Major of Intelligence, pointing.

The object he indicated showed as a pale oval outline, with a shape, judging by the shadows, not unlike the inverted bowl of a spoon. The Chief Constable bent down, peering more closely.

"I can't imagine," he admitted. "Looks as if it *might* be some unusual kind of building—only it can't be. I was round by the Abbey ruins myself less than a week ago, and there was no sign of anything there then; besides, that's British Heritage Association property. They don't build, they just prop things up."

One of the others looked from the photograph to the map, and back again.

"Whatever it is, it's in just about the mathematical center of the trouble," he pointed out. "If it wasn't there a few days ago, it must be something that's landed there."

"Unless it could be a rick, with a very bleached cover," someone suggested.

The Chief Constable snorted. "Look at the scale, man—and the shape. It'd have to be the size of a dozen ricks, at least."

"Then what the devil is it?" inquired the Major.

One after another we studied it through the magnifier.

"You couldn't get a lower altitude picture?" suggested the Major.

"Trying that was how we lost the aircraft," the Group Captain told him curtly.

"How far up does the whatsit—this affected area—extend?" someone asked.

The Group Captain shrugged. "You could find that out by flying into it," he said. "This," he added, tapping the photograph, "was taken at ten thousand. The crew noticed no effect there."

Colonel Latcher cleared his throat.

"Two of my officers suggest that the area may be hemispherical in form," he remarked.

"So it may," agreed the Group Captain, "or it may be rhomboidal, or dodecahedral."

"I gather," said the Colonel mildly, "that they observed birds flying into it; getting a fix on them at the moment they became affected. They claim to have established that the edge of the zone does not extend vertically like a wall—that it definitely is not a cylinder, in fact. The sides contract slightly. From that they argue that it must be either domed, or conical. They say their evidence favor a hemisphere, but they have had to work on too small a segment of too large an arc to be certain."

"Well, that's the first contribution we've had for some time," acknowledged the Group Captain. He pondered. "If they're right about a hemisphere, that should give it a ceiling of about five thousand over the center. I suppose they didn't have any helpful ideas on how we establish that without losing another aircraft?"

"As a matter of fact," Colonel Latcher said, diffidently, "one of them did. He suggested that perhaps a helicopter dangling a canary in a cage on a few hundred feet of line and slowly reducing height . . . Well, I know it sounds a bit—"

"No," said the Group Captain. "It's an idea. Sounds like the same fellow who got the perimeter taped."

"It is." Colonel Latcher nodded.

"Quite a line of his own in ornithological warfare," commented the Group Captain. "I think perhaps we can improve on the canary, but we're grateful for the idea. A bit too late for it today. I'll schedule it for early tomorrow, with pictures from the lowest safe altitude while there's a good cross-light."

The Intelligence Major emerged from silence.

"Bombs, I think," he said reflectively. "Fragmentation, perhaps."

"Bombs?" asked the Group Captain, with raised brows.

"Wouldn't do any harm to have some handy. Never know what these Ivans are up to. Might be a good idea to have a wham at it, anyway. Stop it getting away. Knock it out so that we can have a proper look at it."

"Bit drastic at this stage," suggested the chief constable. "I mean, wouldn't it be better to take it intact, if possible?"

"Probably," agreed the Major, "but meanwhile we are just allowing it to go on doing whatever it came to do, while it holds us off with this whatever-it-is."

"I don't see what it *could* have come to do in Midwich," another officer put in, "therefore I imagine that it force-landed and is using this screen to prevent interference while it makes repairs."

"There's the Grange . . ." someone said tentatively.

"In either case the sooner we get authority to disable it further, the better," said the Major. "It had no business over our territory, anyway. Real point is, of course, that it mustn't get away. Much too interesting. Apart from the thing itself, that screen effect could be very useful indeed. I shall recommend taking any action necessary to secure it; intact if possible; but damaged if necessary."

There was considerable discussion, but the only decisions I can recall were that parachute flares would be dropped every hour for observation purposes, and that the helicopter would attempt to get more informative photographs in the morning. Beyond that nothing definite had been achieved when the conference broke up.

I did not see why I had been taken along at all—or, for that matter, why Bernard had been there, for he had made not a single contribution to the conference. As we drove back I asked:

"Is it out of order for me to inquire where you come into this?"

"Not altogether. I have a professional interest." .

"The Grange?" I suggested.

"Yes. The Grange comes within my parish, and naturally anything untoward in its neighborhood interests us. One might call this very untoward, don't you think?"

"Us" I had already gathered from his self-introduction before the conference, could be either Military Intelligence in general, or his particular department.

"I thought," I said, "that the special branch looked after that kind of thing."

"There are various angles," he said, vaguely, and changed the subject.

We managed to get him a room at the Eagle, and the three of us dined together. I had hoped that after dinner he might make good his promise to "explain later," but though we talked of a number of things, including Midwich, he was clearly avoiding any more mention of his professional interest in it. But for all that it was a good evening that left me wondering how one can be so careless as to let some people drift out of one's life.

Twice in the course of the evening I rang up the Trayne police to inquire whether there had been any change in the Midwich situation, and both times they reported that it was quite unaltered. After the second call, we decided it was no good waiting up, and after a final round we retired.

"A nice man," said Janet, as our door closed. "I was afraid it might be old-warriors-together which is so boring for wives, but he didn't let it be a bit like that. Why did he take you along this afternoon?"

"That's what's puzzling me," I confessed. "He seemed to have second thoughts and become most reserved, once we actually got close to it."

"It really is very queer," Janet said, as if the whole thing had just struck her afresh. "Didn't he have anything at all to say about what it is?"

"Neither he, nor any of the rest of them," I assured her. "About the one thing they've learned is what we could tell them—that you don't know when it hits you, and there's no sign afterward that it did."

"And that at least is encouraging. Let's hope that no one in the village comes to any more harm than we did," she said.

While we were still sleeping, on the morning of the 28th, a meteorology officer gave it as his opinion that ground mist in Midwich would clear early, and a crew of two boarded a helicopter. A wire cage containing a pair of lively but perplexed ferrets was handed in after them. Presently the machine took off, and whimmered noisily upwards.

"They predict," remarked the pilot, "that six thousand will be dead-safe, so we'll try at seven thou for luck. If that's okay, we'll bring her down slowly."

The observer settled his gear, and occupied himself with teasing the ferrets until the pilot told him:

"Right. You can lower away now, and we'll make the trial crossing at seven."

The cage went through the door. The observer let three hundred feet of line unreel. The machine came round, and the pilot informed ground that he was about to make a preliminary run over Midwich. The observer lay on the floor, observing the ferrets through glasses.

They were doing fine at present, clambering with non-stop sinuousness all round and over one another. He took the glasses off them for a moment, and turned toward the village ahead, then:

"Oy, skipper," he said.

"Uh?"

"That thing we're supposed to photograph, by the Abbey?"

"What about it?"

"Well, either it was a mirage, or it's flipped off," said the observer.

6 · Midwich Reviviscit

AT ALMOST the same moment that the observer made his discovery, the picket at the Stouch-Midwich road was carrying out its routine test. The sergeant in charge threw a lump of sugar across the white line that had been drawn across the road, and watched while the dog, on its long lead, dashed after it. The dog snapped up the sugar and crunched it.

The sergeant regarded the dog carefully for a moment, and walked close to the line himself. He hesitated there a moment, and then stepped across it. Nothing happened. With increasing confidence he took a few more paces. Half a dozen rooks cawed as they passed over his head. He watched them flap steadily away over Midwich.

"Hey, you there, Signals," he called. "Inform H.Q. Oppley. Affected area reduced and believed clear. Will confirm after further tests."

A few minutes earlier, in Kyle Manor, Gordon Zellaby had stirred with difficulty and given out a sound like a half-groan. Presently he realized that he was lying on the floor; also that the room which had been brightly lit and warm, perhaps a trifle over-warm, a moment ago, was now dark, and clammily cold.

He shivered. He did not think he had ever felt quite so cold. It went right through so that every fiber ached with it. There was a sound in the darkness of someone else stirring. Ferrelyn's voice said, shakily:

"What's happened? Daddy . . . ? Anthea . . . ? Where are you?"

Zellaby moved an aching and reluctant jaw to say:

"I'm here, nearly frozen. Anthea, my dear?"

"Just here, Gordon," said her voice unsteadily, close beside him.

There was a sound of movement across the room.

"Gosh, I'm stiff! Oh, dear!" complained Ferrelyn's voice. "Oo-ow-oo! I don't believe these are my legs at all."

39

Zellaby's eyes went to the grate. He stared at it in disbelief. A moment ago he had put a new log on the fire, now there was nothing there but a few ashes. Anthea, sitting up on the carpet a yard away from him and Ferrelyn, by the window, were both staring at the grate, too.

"What on earth—?" began Ferrelyn.

"The champagne?" suggested Zellaby.

"Oh, really, Daddy." Ferrelyn crossed unsteadily to the fireplace. She reached a hand toward it, and stood there, shivering.

"I think it's dead," she said.

She tried to pick up *The Times* from the chair, but her fingers were too numb to hold it. She looked at it miserably, and then managed to scrumble it between her stiff hands and stuff it into the grate. Still using both hands she succeeded in lifting some of the smaller bits of wood from the basket and dropping them on the paper.

Frustration with matches almost made her weep.

"My fingers *won't*," she wailed miserably.

In her efforts she spilled the matches on the hearth. Somehow she managed to light one by rubbing the box on them. It caught another. She pushed them all closer to the paper bulging out of the grate. Presently it caught, too, and the flame blossomed up like a wonderful flower.

Anthea got up and staggered stiffly closer. Zellaby made his approach on all fours. The wood began to crackle. They crouched toward it, greedy for warmth. The numbness in their outstretched fingers began to give way to a tingling. After a while the Zellaby spirit began to show signs of revival.

"Odd," he remarked through teeth that still showed a tendency to chatter, "odd that I should have to live to my present age before appreciating the underlying soundness of fire-worship."

On both the Oppley and Stouch roads there was a great starting up and warming of engines. Presently two streams of ambulances, fire appliances, police cars, jeeps and military trucks started to converge on Midwich. They met at the Green. The civilian transport pulled up, and its occupants piled out. The military trucks for the most part headed for Hickham Lane, bound for the Abbey. An exception to both categories was a small red car that turned off by itself and went bouncing up the drive of Kyle Manor to stop in grooves of gravel by the front door.

Alan Hughes burst into the Zellaby study, pulled Ferrelyn out of the huddle by the fire and clutched her firmly.

"Darling!" he exclaimed, still breathing hard. "Darling! Are you all right?"

"Darling!" responded Ferrelyn, rather as if it were an answer.

After a considerate interval Gordon Zellaby remarked: "We, also, are all right, we believe, though bewildered. We are also somewhat chilled. Do you think—?"

Alan seemed to become aware of them for the first time.

"The—" he began, and then broke off as the lights came on. "Good-oh," he said. "Hot drinks in a jiffy." And he departed, towing Ferrelyn after him.

" 'Hot drinks in a jiffy,' " murmured Zellaby. "Such music in a simple phrase. All the same, Anthea my dear, if your hands are now warm enough to turn a knob and withdraw a stopper, the brandy decanter is in the usual cupboard."

And so, when we came down to breakfast eight miles away, we were greeted by the news that Colonel Westcott had gone out a couple of hours before, that Midwich was no longer forbidden territory; and that we could now go home.

7 · *Midwich Settles Down*

THERE WAS still a police picket on the Stouch road, but as residents of Midwich we passed through promptly, drove on through a scene which looked much as usual and reached our cottage without further hindrance.

We had wondered more than once what state of affairs we might find, but there was no need for alarm. The cottage was intact, and exactly as we had left it. We went in and re-settled ourselves just as we had intended to on the previous day, with no inconvenience except that the milk in the refrigerator had gone sour on account of the cut in the electricity supply. Indeed, within half an hour of returning, the happenings of the previous day were beginning to seem unreal; and when we went out to visit the Zellabys we found that for those who had actually been involved the feeling of unreality was even more pronounced.

Nor was that surprising, for, as Mr. Zellaby pointed out, their knowledge of the affair was limited to an awareness that they had failed to go to bed one night and had awakened, feeling extremely cold, one morning: the rest was a matter of hearsay, and highly improbable hearsay, at that. He appeared to believe that some kind of swindling machination was afoot, and advanced a number of arguments to support this contention. Not until he had checked with several distant sources of information by telephone and been confronted with copies of what appeared to him to be tomorrow's newspapers would he concede that the day had been the 28th, and that the rest of the world must inexplicably be right. Even so, he wore the air of one worsted by a trick; as though he had been cheated of one of the days to which he was entitled.

Most of the village, however, simply shrugged and wrote the day off; a dismissal that turned out at the time to be surprisingly easy, for it is doubtful whether the affair—even had it not lain beneath the intimidating muzzles of the Official Secrets Act—could at this stage have made a really useful newspaper sensation. As a dish, it had a number of promising aromas, but it proved short on substance. There were, in all, eleven casualties, and something might have been made of them, but even they lacked the details to excite a blasé readership, and the stories of the survivors were woefully undramatic, for they had nothing to tell but their recollections of a cold awakening.

Frankly, the suspense element had been brief, and the end an anti-climax. The nature, source and motivation of the event were all obscure. Radar did seem to have detected an unidentified flying object on the night of the 26th, but it was by no means the first of such detections, and unlikely to be the last. Some kind of flying-saucer story might have been put across, but unfortunately the one rather unsatisfactory photograph which could have supported it was government property.

Moreover, there was the utter undistinction of Midwich; even if it had somehow managed to lose a month, or more, instead of just a day, no effect would have been perceptible outside its immediate neighborhood.

Such shortcomings did much to modify the professional indignation of the press and radio. Among themselves, correspondents conceded that, with so little to build up, the attempt would very likely have been a flop, anyway, and as things fell out it would have been pushed aside by a railway accident on the evening of the 27th which provided a richesse of sensational, personal stories.

In Midwich, therefore, we were able to assess our losses, dress our wounds and generally readjust ourselves from the experience which afterward became known as the Dayout, with a quite unexpected degree of privacy.

Of our eleven fatalities: Mr. William Trunk, a farmhand, his wife and their small son, had perished when their cottage burned down. An elderly couple called Stagfield had been lost in the other house that caught fire. Another farmhand, Herbert Flagg, caused some comment by being discovered dead of a broken neck at the foot of the stairs in the Harrimans' cottage, Mrs. Harriman being upstairs, while Harriman himself was at work in his bakery at the time of the accident. Harry Crankhart, one of the two men whom the Oppley church-tower observers had seen lying in front of the Scythe and Stone, succumbed shortly afterward to double pneumonia. Mrs. Droxson was found floating face-down in her bath, having apparently been overcome in the act of leaving it. The other three were all elderly persons, for whom the shock of falls, followed by prolonged unconsciousness while dressed only in thin clothes, had proved too great a strain.

Mr. Leebody preached a thanksgiving sermon on behalf of the rest of us at an unusually well-attended service the following Sunday, and with that, and his conduct of the last of the funerals, the dreamlike quality of the whole affair became established.

It is true that for a week or so there were a few soldiers about, and there was quite a deal of coming and going in official cars, but the center of this interest did not lie within the village itself, and so disturbed it little. The visible focus of attention was close to the Abbey ruins where a guard was posted to protect a large dent in the ground which certainly looked as if something massive had rested there for a while. Engineers had measured this phenomenon, made sketches and taken photographs of it. Technicians of various kinds had then tramped back and forth across it, carrying mine-detectors, geiger-counters and other subtle gear. Then, abruptly, the military lost all interest and withdrew.

Investigations at the Grange went on a little longer, and among those occupied with them was Bernard Westcott. He dropped in to see us several times, but he told us nothing of what was going on and we asked no details. Not until the evening of his departure for London did he speak of the Day-out and its consequences. Then, following a lull in conversation, he said:

"I've got a suggestion I'd like to put to you two. But I'm afraid it is a thing I'll have to ask you to forget altogether if you don't want to take it on."

"Sounds mysterious," I said. "But I think we can undertake to be good forgetters, if required. What is it?"

"Well, first, I'll have to confess that I've had you both looked up and checked. I remembered that you did some useful work for the Military Government. As for Petty-Officer Janet Drummond, late of the W.R.N.S., I find that she also received praise from her superiors for work of a very confidential nature. Now, I have no doubt that on the strength of these reports, and subject to certain formalities under the Official Secrets Act, I could, if you were willing, arrange your temporary attachment to my department."

We looked at him, and then at one another, with some astonishment.

"Well," I said, cautiously. "Perhaps we had better hear what you're after before we try to comment on that."

"Essentially it is this: we feel that it is rather important for us to keep an eye on this village for a time, and know what goes on here. We could introduce one of our own men to help keep us posted, but there are points against that. For one thing, he would have to start from scratch, and it takes time for any stranger to work into the life of any village. For another, it is doubtful whether we could justify the detachment of a good man to full-time work here at present—and if he were not full-time it is equally doubtful whether he could be of much use. If, on the other hand, we could get someone who already knows the place and the people to keep us posted on possible developments it would be more satisfactory all round. What do you think?"

I considered for a moment.

"Not very much," I told him. "It rather depends, I suppose, on what is involved." I glanced across at Janet. She spoke somewhat coldly.

"It rather sounds as if we were being invited to spy on our friends, and neighbors. I think perhaps a professional spy might suit you better."

"This," I backed her up, "is our home."

He nodded, rather as if that were what he had expected. "You consider yourselves a part of this community?" he said.

"We are trying to be and, I think, beginning to be," I told him.

He nodded again. "Good. At least, good if you feel that you have begun to have an obligation toward it. Midwich needs, and is getting, outside protection. And we can best give it that protection if we have adequate information on what goes on inside it."

"What sort of protection—and from what?"

"Chiefly, at present, from busybodies," he said, "My dear fellow, surely you don't think it was an accident that the Midwich Dayout wasn't splashed across the papers *on* the Dayout? Or that there wasn't a rush of journalists of all kinds pestering the life out of everyone here the moment it lifted?"

"Of course not," I said. "Naturally I knew there was the security angle—you told me as much yourself. I don't know what goes on at the Grange, but I do know it is very hush."

"It wasn't simply the Grange that was put to sleep," he pointed out. "It was everything for a mile around."

"But the Grange must have been the focal point. Quite possibly the influence, whatever it is, doesn't have less than that range—or perhaps the people, whoever they were, thought it safer to have that much elbow room for safety."

"That's what the village thinks?" he asked.

"Most of it—with a few variations."

"That's the sort of thing I want to know. They all pin it on the Grange, do they?"

"Naturally. What other reason could there be in Midwich?"

"Well then, suppose I tell you I have reason to believe that the Grange had nothing whatever to do with it. And that our very careful investigations all confirm that?"

"But that would make nonsense of the whole thing," I protested.

"Surely not—not, that is, any more than any accident can be regarded as a form of nonsense."

"Accident? You mean a forced landing?"

Bernard shrugged. "That I can't tell you. It's possible that the accident lay more in the fact that the Grange happened to be located where the landing was made. But my point is this: almost everyone in this village has been exposed to a curious and quite unfamiliar phenomenon. And now you, and all the rest of the place, are assuming it is over and finished with. Why?"

Both Janet and I stared at him.

"Well," she said, "it's come, and it's gone, so why not?"

"And it simply came, and did nothing, and went away again, and had no effect on anything?"

"I don't know. No visible effect—beyond the casualties, of course, and they mercifully can't have known anything about it," Janet replied.

"No visible effect," he repeated. "That means rather little nowadays, doesn't it? You can, for instance, have quite a serious dose of X-rays, gamma-rays and others, without immediate visible effect. You needn't be alarmed, it *is* just an instance. If any of them had been present we should have detected them. They were not. But something that we were unable to detect was present. Something quite unknown to us that is capable of inducing—let's call it artificial sleep. Now, that is a very remarkable phenomenon—quite inexplicable to us, and not a little alarming. Do you really think one is justified in airily assuming that such a peculiar incident can just happen and then cease to happen and have no effect?"

Janet weakened a little.

"You mean, you want us, or someone, to watch for and note any effects?"

"In a way, that's it. Midwich has been exposed to an influence of unknown potentialities; somebody must watch the place and see if it shows any unusual symptoms as a result. If it does they may require action. Probably the person best placed to perceive them would be your Dr. Willers, but it would put him in a difficult position. What passes between a doctor and his patients is confidential, and he would be subject to conflicting loyalties. Therefore it would seem better to depend on someone who, though he does not have the same specialized opportunities as a doctor, is accustomed to using his powers of observation. I know Richard's reports used to be highly regarded, and I am sure I could depend on them. But my own experience of villages is that much that is general knowledge among the women doesn't reach the men—either because they simply aren't interested themselves, or because it may be the kind of small talk they don't think others would be interested in. It struck me, though, that you two working together ought to be able to keep tabs on the state of the place pretty thoroughly."

Janet looked at him steadily for a moment.

"Just what are you expecting to happen here, Bernard?" she asked.

"Would I have to make this suggestion to you if I knew?" he countered. "I'm taking precautions. We don't know what this thing is or does. We can't slap on a quarantine order without evidence. But we can watch for evidence. At least, you can. So what do you say?"

"I'm not sure," I told him. "Give us a day or two to think it over, and I'll let you know."

"Good," he said. And we went on to talk of other things.

Janet and I discussed the matter several times in the next few days. Her attitude had modified considerably.

"He's got something up his sleeve, I'm sure," she said. "But what?"

I did not know. And:

"It isn't as if we were being asked to watch a particular person, is it?"

I agreed that it was not. And:

"It wouldn't be really different in principle from what a Medical Officer of Health does, would it?"

Not very different, I thought. And:

"If we don't do it for him, he'd have to find someone else to do it. I don't really see who he'd get, in the village. It wouldn't be very nice, or efficient, if he did have to introduce a stranger, would it?"

I supposed not.

So, mindful of Miss Ogle's strategic situation in the post office, I wrote, instead of telephoning, to Bernard telling him that we thought we saw our way clear to co-operation provided we could be satisfied over one or two details, and received a reply suggesting that we should arrange a meeting when we next came to London. The letter showed no feeling of urgency, and merely suggested that we should keep our eyes open in the meantime.

We did. But there was little for them to perceive. A fortnight after the Dayout, only very small rumples remained in Midwich's placidity.

The small minority who felt that Security had cheated them of national fame and pictures in the newspapers had become resigned: the rest were glad that the interruption of their ways had been no greater. Miss Polly Rushton, almost the only visitor to the district to be involved, concluded her holiday with her uncle and aunt and returned home to London. Alan Hughes found himself, to his disgust, not only inexplicably posted to the north of Scotland, but also listed for release several weeks later than he had expected, and was spending much of his time up there in documentary argument with his regimental record office, and most of the rest of it, seemingly, in correspondence with Miss Zellaby. Mrs. Harriman, the baker's wife, after thinking up a series of not very convincing circumstances which could have led to the discovering of Herbert Flagg's body in her cottage, had taken refuge in attack and was belaboring her husband with the whole of his known and suspected past. Almost everyone else went on as usual.

Midwich had, in fact, simply twitched—curiously, perhaps, but only very slightly—for the third or fourth time in its thousand-year doze.

And now I come to a technical difficulty, for this, as I have explained, is not my story; it is Midwich's story. If I were to set down my information in the order it came to me I should be flitting back and forth in the account, producing an almost incomprehensible hodge-podge of incidents out of order, and effects preceding the causes. Therefore it is necessary that I rearrange my information, disregarding entirely the dates and times when I acquired it, and, by putting it into chronological order of happening, give proper weight to various indications on incidents which appeared to me, and to all of us, insignificant, or perhaps unrelated, at the time. If this method of approach should result in the suggestion of disquieting omniscience in the writer, the reader must bear with it the assurance that it is entirely the product of hindsight. In the presence of the events he played a part that was not only undistinguished, but extensively uncomprehending until he began to find that some of his pieces would fit together, and was thereby inspired to search for others that were missing.

It was, for instance, not current observation, but later inquiry which revealed that a little while after the village had seemingly returned to normal there began to be small swirls of localized uneasiness in its corporate peace; certain disquiets that were, as yet, isolated and unacknowledged. This would be somewhere about late November, even early December—though perhaps in some quarters slightly earlier. Approximately, that is, when Miss Ferrelyn Zellaby mentioned, in the course of her almost daily correspondence with Mr. Hughes, that a tenuous suspicion had perturbingly solidified.

In what appears to have been a not very coherent letter, she explained—or, perhaps one should say, intimated—that she did not see how it could be and, in fact, according to all she had learned, it couldn't be, so she did not understand it at all, but the fact was that in some mysterious way she seemed to have started a baby—well, actually "seemed" wasn't a very good word because she was pretty sure about it, really. So did he think he could manage a week-end leave, because one did rather feel that it was the sort of thing that needed some talking over. . . ?

8 · Coming Events

IN POINT of fact, investigations have shown that Alan was not the first to hear Ferrelyn's news. She had been worried and puzzled for some little time, and two or three days before she wrote to him had made up her mind that the time had come for the matter to be known in the family circle: for one thing, she badly needed advice and explanation that none of the books she consulted seemed able to give her; and, for another, it struck her as more dignified than just going on until somebody should guess. Anthea, she decided, would be the best person to tell first—Mother, too, of course, but a little later on, when the organizing was already done; it looked like one of those occasions when Mother might get terribly executive about everything.

Decision, however, had been rather easier to take than action. On the Wednesday morning Ferrelyn's mind was fully made up. At some time in that day, some relaxed hour, she would draw Anthea quietly aside and explain how things were.

Unfortunately, there had been no hour of Wednesday when people were really relaxed. Thursday morning did not feel suitable somehow, either, and in the afternoon Anthea had had a Women's Institute meeting which made her look tired in the evening. There was a moment on Friday afternoon that might have done—and yet it did not seem quite the kind of thing one could raise while Daddy showed his lunch visitor the garden, preparatory to bringing him back for tea. So, what with one thing and another, Ferrelyn arose on Saturday morning with her secret still unshared.

"I'll really *have* to tell her today—even if everything doesn't seem absolutely right for it. A person could go on this way for weeks," she told herself firmly, as she finished dressing.

Gordon Zellaby was at the last stage of his breakfast when she reached the table. He accepted her good morning kiss absentmindedly, and presently took himself off to his routine—once briskly round the garden, then to the study and the Work in progress.

Ferrelyn ate some cornflakes, drank some coffee and accepted a fried egg and bacon. After two nibbles she pushed the plate away decisively enough to arouse Anthea from her reflections.

"What's the matter?" Anthea inquired from her end of the table. "It ought to be fresh."

"Oh, there's nothing *wrong* with it," Ferrelyn told her. "I just don't happen to feel eggy this morning, that's all." An inside voice seemed to prompt her: *Why not now?* So she took a breath. By way of introducing the matter gently she said:

"As a matter of fact, Anthea, I was sick this morning."

"Oh, indeed?" said her stepmother, and paused while she helped herself to butter. In the act of raising her marmaladed toast, she added: "So was I. Horrid, isn't it?"

Now she had taxied on to the runway, Ferrelyn was going through with it. She squashed the opportunity of diverting to nice cozy hypochondriacal chit-chat.

"I think," she said, steadily, "that mine was rather special kind of being sick. The sort," she added, in order that it should be perfectly clear, "that happens when a person might be going to have a baby, if you see what I mean."

Anthea regarded her for a moment with thoughtful interest, and nodded slowly.

"I do," she agreed. With careful attention she buttered a further area of toast, and added marmalade. Then she looked up again.

"So was mine," she said.

Ferrelyn's mouth fell a little open as she stared. To her confusion, she found herself feeling slightly shocked. Anthea was only sixteen years older than herself, so it was all very natural really, only . . . Her thoughts whirled on in a bewildered way. The Zellaby family was no tidy, formal unit at best, but a baby who was going to be a half-brother, or half-sister, to herself, some sort of half-aunt or half-uncle to the grandchildren who were already four or five years old—and also to her own baby which would be the same age—was going to reduce the proper relationship of the generations to chaos. Besides, it was all so unexpected.

She went on staring at Anthea, unable to find the right-sounding thing to say, because everything had somehow turned the wrong way round.

Anthea was not seeing Ferrelyn. She was looking straight down the table, out of the window at something much further away than the bare, swaying branches of the chestnut. Her dark eyes were bright and shiny.

The shininess increased and sparkled into two drops sparkling on her lower lashes. They welled, overflowed and ran down Anthea's cheeks.

A kind of paralysis still held Ferrelyn. She had never seen Anthea cry. Anthea wasn't that kind of person. . . .

Anthea bent forward suddenly, and put her face in her hands. Ferrelyn jumped up as if she had been suddenly released. She ran to Anthea, put her arms round her and felt her trembling. She held her close, and stroked her hair, and made small, comforting sounds.

In the pause that followed Ferrelyn could not help feeling that a curious element of miscasting had intruded. It was not an exact reversal of roles, for she had had no intention of weeping on Anthea's shoulder; but it was near enough to it to make one wonder if one were fully awake.

Quite soon, however, Anthea ceased to shake. She drew longer, calmer breaths, and presently sought for a handkerchief.

"Phew!" she said. "Sorry to be such a fool, but I'm so happy."

Anthea blew, blinked, and dabbed.

"You see," she explained, "I've not really dared to believe it myself. Telling it to somebody else suddenly made it real. And I've always wanted to, so much, you see. But then nothing happened, and—well, I'd just about decided I'd have to try to forget about it and make the best of things. And now it's really happening after all, I—I—" She began to weep again, quietly and comfortably.

A few minutes later she pulled herself together, gave a final pat with the bunched handkerchief and decisively put it away.

"There," she said, "that's over. I never thought I was one to enjoy a good cry, but it does seem to help." She looked at Ferrelyn. "Makes one thoroughly selfish, too—I'm sorry, my dear."

"Oh, that's all right. I'm glad for you," Ferrelyn said, generously she thought because, after all, one had been a bit anti-climaxed. After a pause, she went on:

"Actually, I don't feel weepy about it myself. But I do feel a bit frightened."

The word caught Anthea's attention. It was not a response she expected from Ferrelyn. She looked at her step-daughter for a thoughtful moment, as if the full import of the situation were only just reaching her.

"Frightened, my dear? I don't think you need feel that. It isn't very proper, of course, but—well, we shan't get anywhere by being puritanical about it. The first thing to do is to make sure you're right."

"I *am* right," Ferrelyn said, gloomily. "But I don't understand it. It's different for you, being married, and so on."

Anthea disregarded that.

"Well, then, the next thing must be to let Alan know."

"Yes, I suppose so."

"Of course it is. And you don't need to be frightened of that. Alan won't let you down. He adores you."

"Are you sure of that?"

"Why, yes, you silly. One only has to look at him. Of course it's all quite reprehensible, but I shouldn't be surprised if you find he's delighted. Why, Ferrelyn, what's the matter?" She broke off, startled by Ferrelyn's expression.

"But—but you don't understand. It wasn't Alan."

The look of sympathy died from Anthea's face. Her expression was cold. She started to get up.

"No," exclaimed Ferrelyn, desperately, "you *don't* understand, Anthea. It wasn't Alan. *It wasn't anybody! That's* why I'm frightened."

A week or so later, Mrs. Willers, the doctor's wife, laden with a stringbag of shopping and on her way home from the bus, perceived a small group of people clustered on the right hand side of the road ahead of her. Most of the party were women, she noticed. Their expressions varied a little, but their concentration was general, and rapt.

Mrs. Willers' first thought was that the Harrimans, whose cottage it was, must in some way have achieved color television, and so installed it that others could envy them. Coming nearer, however, she caught sounds of conflict which, though muffled, had a quality of realism seldom achieved in a studio. A woman's voice was raised in protesting cries and squawks, and the language used by a male voice would not have suited either the B.B.C., or the purposes of commerce. Mrs. Willers' intention was to keep to the far side of the road, but the sounds caused her to change her mind and join the peepshow on the Harrimans' domestic affairs. She arrived just in time to witness a maneuver which brought a yelp of increased poignancy from Mrs. Harriman.

"Well, really!" said Mrs. Willers. "Aren't any of you men going to do anything?"

The group contained only two men. They did not look her way, and appeared not to hear her.

"A fine lot you are," she told them, scathingly.

She opened the gate, stumped sturdily up the two yards of brick path, lifted the front latch and pushed hard. The door swung back and hit the wall with a crash.

Mrs. Willers stepped inside and planted herself squarely on the mat.

"Stop that at once!" she ordered decisively.

Fred Harriman looked round, red-faced and furious.

"What the bloody 'ell—" he began.

Mrs. Willers glared back at him.

"Stop that, I tell you," she said again.

Fred straightened up, allowing his left hand to loosen its grip on his wife's hair. The buckle-ended strap still swung in his right hand as he regarded Mrs. Willers through narrowed eyes.

For a moment she thought he was going to attack her. She tightened her hold on her only weapon, the stringbag with its load of knobbly objects, and stood her ground. Their eyes held for some seconds, then he pushed past her, buckling the strap back round his waist as he went. She looked down at Mrs. Harriman crouching, sobbing and disheveled, on the floor. Out of her experience she decided that the next move would be better left to a neighbor, and turned to survey the group that still lingered outside.

"One of you look after her," she directed. "And you can tell Harriman when he comes back that if I hear of any more of this kind of thing Constable Gobby will be along to see about it."

Then, feeling a little breathless and a trifle shaky at the knees, but seeming to walk as sturdily as ever, she resumed her homeward journey.

Mrs. Willers was pensive at dinner, but it was not until the latter part of the meal that she inquired:

"Would I be right, Charles, in thinking that Mrs. Harriman could be pregnant again?"

Dr. Willers regarded her across the table. He raised his eyebrows.

"The hare of instinct versus the tortoise of diagnosis," he remarked. "It was only this afternoon she came here. And between ourselves, she's even less happy about it this time than last."

"She's even more unhappy about it now, poor woman," Mrs. Willers told him, and described the interruption of her walk from the bus. "More sound and fury than real harm, I imagine, or somebody would have been along for you to repair the damage," she added. "But quite enough sound to start one thinking."

The doctor looked troubled.

"The Midwich bush-telegraph," he said. "Someone must have noticed her coming in here, and her husband heard of it and put two and two together."

"From what was going on, it might well be more than two and two, I think. After all, there was that awkward business of Flagg's body being found in their house after the Dayout, remember."

"I'd forgotten that," the doctor admitted.

Both of them pursued their reflections for a while. Presently Mrs. Willers said: "Of course, I may be just imagining it, but aren't there rather a lot of pregnancies just now? Above average, I mean?"

The doctor looked displeased. His professional discretion was sensitive.

"These things fluctuate," he said, with automatic evasion. But the vertical line between his brows deepened, and after a minute's silence he continued: "Naturally, one does not want to gossip. But just at present—well, yes, there are several on the books that worry and surprise me. Ones that I wouldn't expect, and don't at all understand."

After thirty years Mrs. Willers had a fair working knowledge of her husband's mental processes.

"Unmarried, you mean?" she suggested.

He nodded, slowly.

"But it's not just that. The improprieties are their own business. It's the improbabilities that worry me. There are going to be sticky patches ahead—some very sticky patches, I'm afraid."

Mrs. Willers pondered that. She knew better than pry into details, but she could not help running over a number of possibilities in her mind. Suddenly her expression livened into astonishment.

"Good gracious!" she exclaimed.

"Good gracious, what?" said her husband, with a touch of disapproval.

"No. I must be wrong." She shook her head. "All the same . . . No, it couldn't be . . ."

"Less cryptically," suggested the doctor.

"Well, when I got off the bus, I remembered we were out of stamps, so I thought I'd better get some. Miss Ogle had closed the post office really, but she obligingly allowed me in and let me have some. She was just about to start her tea. It seemed odd to me then, but now I come to think of it . . . Oh, I don't know, there's probably nothing in it . . . I mean it's so unlikely . . ."

"My dear, are you telling me, or are you just arguing with yourself? Why should it be so unlikely for Miss Ogle to have her tea?"

"It's nothing. Perhaps I shouldn't have mentioned it. After all, Miss Ogle . . ."

"One either mentions things or one doesn't mention them. Now you've started you might as well finish," the doctor said, a little shortly.

"Well," admitted Mrs. Willers, "it wasn't just the tea, it was the *kind* of tea. Such an odd choice. Slices of bread and butter spread with herring-paste nearly half an inch thick, and a saucer with a whole heap of gherkins and pickled onions on it . . ." She let the sentence trail off.

Her husband stared at her.

"Milly, really! You must be mistaken. Good God, not Miss Ogle! It's fantastic! I won't believe it!"

"Well, I must say it doesn't seem very *likely*," Mrs. Willers conceded. "All the same, it was rather a funny sort of meal to choose, wasn't it?"

9 · Heads Together

THE HUGHES-ZELLABY WEDDING, a ceremony which I had understood to be scheduled for late March or early April, took place quietly, as they say, at the beginning of January.

"Quietly," in this case, meant a reception to some seventy

guests at Kyle Manor. The bride looked charming, self-possessed, and cut her cake with decisive competence. The best man, now less harassed than in the earlier stages of the occasion, made a pleasant response for the bridesmaids with an air of having got into the straight at last. The bride's father's speech began in an atmosphere of some nervousness, but, being delivered under the regimental eye of his second wife, the bride's mother, turned out to be brief for him, and mostly suitable in content. All in all, the affair was felt to have passed off very well.

While I was waiting for Janet to fetch her coat the only other occupant of the hall for the moment was Dr. Willers. His air was contemplative, and he got himself into his coat with a progressive deceleration until by the time it was on he had reached a stage of pensive immobility, with his scarf dangling idly in one hand. In this arrested condition he had remained for fully a minute before he was recalled by the approach of Mr. Leebody. He looked up, as if a little surprised to find himself where he was, and then came out of his abstraction.

"Oh, hullo, Vicar. A very nice little service indeed. Bride looked charming, don't you think? He seems a nice young fellow, too. Ought not to be any regrets there."

Mr. Leebody nodded.

"Thank you, Doctor. A fine young couple. Yes, very well suited, one would think."

His gaze wandered. If similar reflections occurred in both their minds, they remained unexpressed.

"Can I give you a lift, Vicar?" the doctor offered.

"That's very kind of you, Doctor."

Mr. Leebody took his coat from a peg. The doctor reached out to hold it for him. But the vicar did not turn round at once; instead he paused, his eyes looking at the other's.

"I've been meaning to ask you for some days, Doctor. Do you think we could have a word together—some time when it's convenient?"

Dr. Willers nodded.

"I've been intending to ask you the same thing, Vicar. Would it suit you now? I've managed to fix myself a clear afternoon for this affair."

"Good. Excellent," agreed Mr. Leebody, with a note of relief in his voice. As he allowed himself to be helped on with his coat, he added: "We shall be undisturbed at the vicarage, I think."

I watched them go off together, each without doubt gravely

concerned about something. At the time I had scarcely an inkling what that something might be, and it was not until much later that I was given an account of the conversation which followed their departure.

Arrived at the vicarage, the vicar led the way to his study and roused the fire to a blaze.

Dr. Willers shed his coat and sat down in one of the armchairs, holding his hands out to the warmth. The Reverend Hubert took the chair on the other side of the fireplace and watched the flames for some little time before he spoke. At length, he said:

"In these days, one is not, perhaps, a confidant to the extent one's predecessors were—the faith of many seems to have shifted, temporarily at least, from theology to the newer sciences. It may well be, therefore, that your knowledge of my parishioners is in some respects greater than my own.

"Both of us are, in our fields—fields which nowadays overlap considerably—confessors: the recipients of confidences. And though I must admit that the ethics of the situation between two persons who have been the recipients of identical confidences are not entirely clear to me, I cannot help feeling that when a grave problem of wide, one might even say general, concern is involved, consultation between such parties would not be unethical—provided, of course, that one avoids particulars."

He removed his gaze from the flames and looked across at the other, questioningly. Doctor Willers nodded.

"Yes," he agreed. "Yes, with that provision, I think it might be considered permissible, in unusual circumstances."

"I am glad to hear that; very glad," said the vicar. "For, quite frankly, Doctor, I cannot recall being more worried, or feeling less capable of comforting certain of my parishioners than I do at present. I don't imagine you can be uncertain what matters I have in mind."

"No," said the doctor decisively. "I have been worried myself, for some time now—and am likely to be more so, I think. My concern, however, is on a somewhat different plane from yours and probably less harassing—that is to say my job is to take some practical action about the effects; I do not have to concern myself with the causes."

"Yes," said the vicar. He gazed unhappily into the fire. "When you lose a patient you have done your best, but medical knowledge has proved inadequate: when I lose a member of my church, when one of them strays, it is I personally who have fallen short because I have not the degree of faith to inspire others. Preventive medicine grows stronger, but I am afraid that preventive morality seems to grow weaker. The immunity they develop is the measure of one's failure." He sighed.

"Appearances can be deceptive, you know, Vicar," the doctor said. "If one makes proper allowance for the greater prevalence of more ingenious devils these days, I doubt whether the weakness is really as serious as it may appear. You seem to me to work under two handicaps—the temptations are now more subtle, and the penalties for yielding to them are less obvious because they are less severe. But it is far too early to talk of failure." He paused, and then, as if brushing out of the way the preamble of generalities introduced by the vicar, he came to the point. "The trouble is, of course, all these pregnancies?"

The vicar nodded.

"I would qualify that by saying that they are, in a large part, the practical manifestation of it—though I am by no means sure that they are the most important part."

The doctor frowned a little.

"I think we must try to be practical, Vicar. The moral issues have their importance, no doubt, but the practical side is more urgent, I think."

"Oh, that was not the aspect I had in mind at the moment, important though it is."

"I don't think I quite see what you're getting at, Vicar."

The Reverend Hubert hesitated on the brink, and then made up his mind.

"It is this," he said. "I can instance three young women in the parish—we agreed not to use names, so I will not—but two of them from excellent homes, the third from one scarcely less so, and all have come to see me within the last three weeks. They came to me for encouragement, because they wanted help; they did not come in shame, or contrition; they felt no guilt; they came simply because they are frightened." He paused, frowning. "Nothing very unusual in that these days, you may perhaps say. Social values have changed, so the quality of response to them has changed too. But with these it was different. They came to me, as I said, because they are frightened; I tried to help them, but by the time the third had gone I, too, was frightened." He paused again at some length, and then went on:

"I have learned a little of human nature. I baptized all these three. I have watched them grow up. I am as sure of them as I am of any human being. So what am I to say, what am I to think when each of the three denies completely, and with a sincerity that I cannot doubt, that she has ever been in a situation which could have 'got her into trouble,' as the phrase goes?" He shook his head slowly.

"One knows only too well the stupid obstinacy which protests innocence in the face of every proof—but they these women are not stupid, nor are they ignorant, or uniformed; indeed, it is for that very reason that they are frightened.

"One of them said to me: 'If I could account for it, Vicar, I'd be worried, of course, and I expect I'd be ashamed too—but I'd know what it was about. I wouldn't be scared stiff, the way I am now!' Another of them took almost the same line. She told me: 'It's not knowing, not understanding, that frightens me. I don't suppose a man *could* really understand how it feels. To have such a thing happen to you, without any idea why or how, is terrifying.'

"I am sure there had been no collusion. Each of these young women was telling what she believed to be the truth. They honestly *do not know* of any cause. It *is* terrifying—most particularly for them, of course; but scarcely less so for the rest of us. . . .

"Ever since the first one came to me, I have been asking myself, what am I to think? The temptation was to disbelieve them, but I don't. I know they are sincere. So—well, I just don't know what to do. And I cannot help them as I would wish. I am right out of my depth. Perhaps there are cases I haven't heard of. I wondered if you, as a medical man . . ? One would like to know if there are any records, any known or suspected conditions which might cause such a thing to happen? After all, it is not just one isolated case."

He finished, bending forward with his hands clasped between his knees, watching Willer's face anxiously.

The doctor methodically pressed down the tobacco as he lit his pipe. When it was going he said:

"I think we had better get one thing clear right away, Vicar. What you are hoping and, I suspect, against your better judgment, is that I may be able to produce a documented—or at least a circumstantial—account of a similar occurrence in some other community. Well, I'm afraid your better judgment is right. I can't. I have never heard of anything like this."

"You would entirely discredit the statements of these young women?" asked the vicar unhappily.

The doctor shook his head.

"Simply as a member of the scientific profession, I suppose

I ought to. But from what I have heard as a human being practicing that profession, I, too, am inclined to believe that they are speaking the truth—as far as they are aware of it."

"I am glad to hear you say that, Doctor. Very glad. But 'as far as they are aware of it'—what does that imply? An obliteration of memory? Of course, there are things that our minds hide away in the subconscious, one knows. But it's difficult to believe that in such a matter . . . Besides, all three of them! I've wondered, could hypnotism be involved, do you think? Someone who hypnotically induces amnesia in his victims and wipes the whole matter out of their memories? Would such a thing, perhaps, be possible?"

Dr. Willers, puffing at his pipe, stared into the fire for nearly a minute before he replied. Then he turned his head and looked earnestly at the Reverend Hubert's distressed face.

"We'd better face it now, Vicar. We shall have to, sooner or later. You are, I know, in close touch with many of your flock; I probably know most of my patients less well, but I do get a pretty fair cross-section of the whole village, and extra-professionally, too, one hears things that might not come your way, so I'll tell you this. It is not simply a matter of three young women—it is a situation in which, if something is not done soon, we shall see a large part of the village going neurotic, or worse."

The vicar looked startled.

"A large part?" he asked weakly. "How large?"

The doctor did not answer that. He went on:

"You have been speaking of three young women who are frightened although they are intelligent. But I can tell you that there are a number of others equally frightened, but less intelligent. Some of them in a worse situation than those three. You heard about young Mrs. Dorry?"

"I know she's been unwell. My wife has called. Is she . . ?"

The doctor said seriously.

"I am going to break a professional confidence—I think it's justified, to give you an idea of what we are facing. About a week ago young Tom Dorry came home on leave from the navy. It's eighteen months since he was last home, and what does he find? He finds his wife distracted with worry, and at last gets it out of her that she's going to have a baby. Well, he's no Harriman; he doesn't beat her up. Instead, he goes sort of numb, collects his things and moves out. He goes over to his mother's cottage and tells her why he's come. To his surprise she sticks up for the girl and tells him to go back. He says he's damned if he will. They argue a bit, until she brings out the last shot in her locker. Guess what that is—yes, she's pregnant too. And not an idea how it can have happened, she says. A respectable widow for years, and there it is—and if it can happen to her, it can happen to others.

"Well, young Tom doesn't know whether he's on his head or his heels. He pushes off from his mother's place and wanders about for an hour or two, in a daze. Then what his mother has said sinks in a bit. He's still bewildered but, anyway, he decides to go home. What he finds when he gets there is his wife on the floor, with a large, empty aspirin bottle beside her. Luckily he has the sense to fetch me right away."

The Reverend Hubert shook his head in distress.

"Poor girl," he said. "Oh, poor girl . . . I had no idea . . ."

"In point of fact," the doctor went on, practically, "she'd quite likely have come round on her own—but that doesn't alter the tragic intention. If there are others feeling nearly as desperate, and I'm pretty sure they are, we may have a real tragedy at any moment . . .

"Besides," he added, "there is another aspect that is scarcely less worrying. In the last fortnight I have been called to two women who have fallen downstairs, and one who had stewed herself into a state of collapse in a hot bath. I can't be sure, of course, but in the circumstances I feel obliged to regard such things as pointers. One notices things—such as, for instance, a certain young woman who has suddenly bought herself a bicycle and is now likely to be encountered pedaling madly up any hill in the district.

"So you'll see, Vicar, why I said I was on the point of approaching you. This sort of thing can't be allowed to go on. Up till now we have been lucky—so far as I know—but we cannot go on counting on luck. It's got to be taken in hand."

The Reverend Hubert's face had become bleak.

"This is shocking," he said. "I don't mean just conventionally shocking. It's—it's so alarming . . . one doesn't understand . . . How many do you think are involved?"

Doctor Willers hesitated. "I am only certain of comparatively few, but from indications, and what the district nurse tells me, and my wife's observations, I should certainly say quite a number."

The Reverend Hubert showed irritation. He said brusquely:

" 'Quite a number' means practically nothing to me. Would

you put it at ten, or perhaps a dozen? We must have some idea of the size of the problem before we can tackle it."

The doctor re-lit his pipe, then removed it from his mouth and regarded it carefully. From there he transferred his gaze to the vicar for some seconds.

"One can't *know*, you understand," he said. "But I should put it at—well, perhaps a few over sixty."

The Reverend Hubert stared back at him speechlessly. His mouth opened silently for a moment, then he tried again:

"Over *sixty*—did you say?"

Dr. Willers nodded.

"But why sixty? Couldn't it just as well be fifty, or thirty, or twenty?"

"I suppose it could," admitted the doctor, "but sixty, or one or two over that, happens to be my estimate of the number of women of child-bearing age in the village."

There was a long silence. The vicar looked bleaker than before. He clenched his interlocked fingers, and worked his palms hard together.

"But Willers, you *can't* mean that . . . You *can't* . . . Not every one of them?"

"Speaking as a man of science, Vicar, the number itself doesn't impress me. I find one just as unbelievable as sixty. In fact, if like conditions give like results, the latter is *less* surprising. But there will, undoubtedly, be a certain percentage of error."

"But how on earth could such a thing happen?"

"I don't pretend to have the least idea," the doctor told him. "Anyhow that can wait. The urgent question now is, what is to be done about it? Particularly about the single women, they'll be the ones who'll be suffering most. As I see it, the first and most important thing is to get it into the open. Break up the secrecy, and stop them being afraid to share their trouble. It will get rid of a lot of muddle, guilt and bewilderment. I want that done quickly, before any more of my patients start throwing themselves downstairs, and so on."

"Yes, yes, of course. I see that," agreed the vicar. "But you'll have to let me think a little. This is a great shock."

Dr. Willers continued to press his point, however.

"There's little time to think. This is *urgent*. Every day's delay is dangerous. As it is I've delayed a couple of days more than I wanted, to get this wedding over, because I think we need Zellaby in with us."

"Zellaby?" the vicar repeated, with a touch of doubt.

"Well, in point of fact, in order to get hold of Mrs. Zellaby. My wife's suggestion, and a sound one, I think. Mrs. Zellaby's a capable, intelligent woman, still quite young, but old enough to carry weight. She's sensible. She *looks* right, and they'll listen to her—the more so because she—er—shares the situation with them."

The vicar considered for a moment. Even though he was fairly sure Mrs. Leebody also shared the situation, and that she, as his wife, ought to have some standing in the matter, he had to admit that he could not see her in the part. Moreover, it was undeniable that Mrs. Zellaby had ability, influence and greater campaign value. He nodded agreement.

"Good," approved the doctor. "In the circumstances one can scarcely tackle Zellaby this evening, but I'll see if we can't fix a meeting for some time tomorrow. Then if Mrs. Zellaby—" He broke off at the sound of the front door knocker. The vicar excused himself to answer it. He came back quickly.

"Young Platch wanting you, Doctor. He says his sister's suddenly 'taken very queer' and can you come at once?"

An hour and a half later Doctor Willers again drove his car up to Kyle Manor. In the time which had intervened since his talk with the vicar his feeling of urgency had considerably increased. Moreover, it had occurred to him that they had overlooked a somewhat ticklish point, for it was to be assumed that Mrs. Zellaby would be taking it for granted that her pregnancy was entirely normal—which, for all one knew, it might be. But acquainting her with the situation and asking her help was going to sow doubts.

Nevertheless, it was essential that Mrs. Zellaby should have a full understanding of the problem before she was asked to join a council of action, and important that some such council should meet as soon as possible.

It was unfortunate that it must be so hurriedly called, but hurry was necessary. For all he could tell, there might at this very moment be several women trying to collect enough courage for a desperate course, one that might have worse effects than that of the poor, terrified Platch child who had drunk half a bottle of disinfectant . . .

Nobody came to Kyle Manor door to answer his knock, so he walked in. The confetti had been brushed up and the hall restored to its normal appearance. From the back regions came a clatter of crockery and the sound of several women chattering. The doctor crossed to the study door and knocked.

A muffled voice told him to come in. Zellaby was lying in a fatigued position in an easy chair.

"What is it?" he inquired without looking round. "I have done my stint. Meticulously I have performed all the tasks allotted to me. The hall is—oh, it's you, Doctor. Come along in. I thought they were after me again. Sit down. You can be a witness. Did you in your passage through the hall perceive so much as one single residual fertility symbol? I thought not. It still astonishes me that the simple decision of male and female to mate should require all this semi-public upset. I recall that at my first wedding—"

Experience had taught the doctor that if the initiative were not wrested away from Gordon Zellaby with firmness, it would remain with him. He therefore interrupted, forthrightly:

"It is a serious and u.. at matter I've come about, Mr. Zellaby. I wouldn't be here intruding now if it weren't. Can you spare a quarter of an hour or so?"

"Of course, my dear fellow. Do take off your coat and sit down. You'll like a drink? There's still an assortment about. It seems a pity just to let it—"

The doctor declined the offer.

"Mr. Zellaby," he continued steadily. "I have just come from seeing the vicar. A situation has arisen in which we are agreed that we used your help—and, even more, your wife's help—very urgently."

The tone of his voice told. Zellaby abandoned his hunt for the sherry and sat down.

"Don't tell me something got left out. Surely they're properly married after all that."

"Of course they are," said the doctor impatiently. "This is another matter entirely. It concerns the whole village. It's of vital importance to all of us."

Zellaby looked at him more carefully. He noted what he saw there, and nodded. He leaned back, composing himself to listen.

"Go ahead, my dear fellow," he said.

The doctor did. He put forward his evidence, its implications, and his fears. He concluded:

"The last thing I did before I came here was to send a girl off in the ambulance to Trayne hospital. She tried to kill herself, poor child—at seventeen."

When he had finished they both gazed into the fire in silence for some minutes. Presently Zellaby said:

"We will dispense with the protests of incredulity. You are

a man of science—which means that outside your own field you may be as credulous as the rest of us, but within it you demand proof. Since your professional reputation is involved you will obviously have done your damnedest to ignore the evidence of your own senses and observations, and you must have failed. I am getting too old to waste my time fighting facts out of loyalty to prejudice. So let us take it from there.

"You tell me that you believe almost every woman in Midwich, capable of pregnancy, to be pregnant—and that, furthermore, they are, with a few exceptions, in the same stage of pregnancy. This you find, not to put too fine a point on it, abnormal. Now, we have recently had another occurrence here which was also abnormal. So it is possible that the present situation is somewhat intimately connected with what the village calls its Dayout. Is that the conclusion you and the vicar have reached?"

"I myself think it probable," admitted Dr. Willers, "but I can't speak for the vicar. I fancy that at the moment he is too bowled over to have any clear conclusions or ideas at all."

Zellaby nodded.

"Understandably. The matter is so very much in his province as well as in yours—and, unlike yourself, the poor man lacks the consolations of science."

"Science," observed the doctor, "is giving me very small consolation at the moment."

Zellaby shook his head.

"You are mistaken there, Doctor. *You* know that effects have causes and can sooner or later be traced back to them. The vicar's situation is far more uncomfortable. He has to include a whole extra range of metaphysical hypotheses— not exclusive of diabolical visitation—which must be a highly disquieting contemplation for a man in his position. A herd, or coven, of incubi—"

"Perhaps we could let the causes wait," the doctor suggested, with a touch of impatience. "It is the existing situation, and the urgent need to deal with it, that has brought me here. I wondered if Mrs. Zellaby—" He broke off, wondering how best to put it. Zellaby forbore to interrupt. The doctor changed his approach and explained the necessity of, first of all, decreasing the tension. "Then," he said, "once we've brought the neuroses out of the dark we shall be able to get on with some planning."

"And my wife? Where does she come in?"

The doctor repeated the commendations of Mrs. Zellaby

that he had given to the vicar. "You see, it is the right approach that I feel is so important at this moment. I *could*, of course, call a meeting and talk to them myself, but it seems to me what's needed is a sense of solidarity, of mutual support, something that would be better achieved from leadership within the group, rather than from outside."

Zellaby frowned a little and looked hard at the doctor. "Leadership within the group . . ." he murmured. And then remained thoughtfully silent for some minutes. At last:

"I see," he said. "Or do I see? And I suppose the answer is that you simply don't know?"

"It is," confessed the doctor. "And that raises another difficulty. While most of the married women are presumably easy in their minds now, this is going to come as a shock to them, too. It is inevitable that they should have doubts once they hear about the rest. I don't know—perhaps you would prefer me to explain the whole situation to Mrs. Zellaby?"

Zellaby nodded.

"That would probably be best," he agreed. "But not for a few minutes. I rather think I want a drink. You too, I imagine?"

This time the doctor accepted. Zellaby poured out two stiff brandies and sodas. He was just raising his to his lips when he abruptly set it down again.

"My God!" he said. "Ferrelyn, too . . .?"

He stared at her picture above the fireplace for a minute, and then shook his head slowly, in a bemused way. He pushed back his white hair, picked up the glass and drank half its contents right off. Then he lapsed into his chair and remained gazing at the carpet for some minutes. Presently he roused himself to drink half the remaining brandy. Then with studied detachment of manner he observed:

"There are three—no, perhaps four—possibilities that suggest themselves. However, since you have not mentioned it I take it that whatever may have happened during the Dayout it was not that which is likely to be the first thought of the normal, as well as of the lewd. We can rule that out?"

"Quite definitely," agreed the doctor.

Zellaby nodded. "Then it is possible, is it not, in some of the lower forms at any rate, to induce parthenogenesis?"

"But not, as far as is known, among mammals, or any of the higher forms."

"I see. We bear in mind 'as far as is known,' there. Well then, there is artificial insemination."

"There is," admitted the doctor.

"But you don't think so?"

"I can't say. It seems improbable."

"Then also," Zellaby went on, a little grimly, "there is implantation, which *could* result in what someone—Huxley, I fancy—has called 'xenogenesis.' That is, the production of a form unlike that of the parent, or should one perhaps say host?"

Dr. Willers frowned.

"Do you think that will occur to them? I have been hoping that it will not. Of course, I realized you yourself would think of it, and very likely some of those people up at the Grange, but do you think the rest of the village will?"

"Yes," said Zellaby. "Not, perhaps, as a practical proposition, but in the circumstances I imagine a certain amount of morbid fantasy will be inevitable."

"I suppose you're right. I was trying to dodge it." Dr. Willers pressed his lips tightly together and shook his head. "We must do our best to check that. It's panicky stuff. Will you undertake to convincingly pooh-pooh any suggestion of the kind that may come your way?—and I'll get on to Crimm and his people about that, too."

"I will—a very good case for benign censorship," agreed Zellaby. "It is difficult to appreciate how a woman sees these matters. All I can say is that if I were to be called upon, even in the most propitious circumstances, to bring forth life, the prospect would awe me considerably. If I had reason to suspect that it might be some unexpected form of life I should probably go quite mad. Most women wouldn't, of course, they are mentally tougher, but some might, so a convincing dismissal of the possibility will be best."

He paused, considering. Gradually his look of concern grew into a frown.

"Oh God," he said suddenly.

"What now?" asked the doctor.

"I've just realized. The thing doesn't rest with us—not for long. Once the newspapers get hold of it that is only one of the suggestions they'll be making, with very little delay. It has just the right ghoulish note to delight the readers of, say *The Reflector*. And nearly six months of gloriously mounting speculation ahead. Just their stuff, Doctor. Symposia of articles on every aspect, day-by-day commentary— they'll wring the last drop of sensation out of it—and there'll be nothing we can do to stop them."

Dr. Willers thought for some minutes. Then he said heavily:

"You're right, of course. It's an aspect I had overlooked. There's only one possible answer—*they must not know.*"

"H'm," said Zellaby, skeptically. "H'm."

"It *should* be possible," insisted the doctor. "To begin with, it's by no means easy to believe. They'll suspect a hoax—who wouldn't?—so they'll be wary. After all, they've been hoaxed before. They'd need a lot of evidence before they'd even touch it. Remember, *if* they were to run it, it would have to be full-scale stuff. It couldn't be done as a tucked-away second feature, obviously. Therefore, they'd want to be mighty sure that they weren't going to come out of it as an equally full-scale laughing-stock. Then, the libel aspect should worry them quite a bit—it'd take them on to some very tricky ground indeed. I'm only just beginning to see *how* tricky."

"I see your point—it's a good one too," Zellaby admitted. "But that isn't necessarily going to make them throw away a chance like this."

"I think there's a way. Crimm, of course, will have to be brought in. He should be able to tip off Security if there's any sign of press interest. They're still sitting on the Dayout affair, remember. But the first line, I'm sure, is to keep it quiet. Not to let out that there is anything, or any evidence of it, to go after. That's the *safe* way."

"Undoubtedly—*if* it can be done," agreed Zellaby.

"Damn it, Zellaby, it's *got* to be done. We've a duty to all these women to see that it *is* done. They're my patients. I'm not going to have them driven crazy by a lot of sensation-mongers."

"We'll do our best," agreed Zellaby, and went on looking at the doctor thoughtfully. "I hope you will forgive me, Doctor, for bringing up a point which I imagine you have considered already. It has, of course, occurred to you that you will be discarding the opportunity of world-wide fame?"

"There are different classes of fame," Willers replied. "Some that one would not wish for. I am keeping records which may be publishable one day."

Zellaby nodded, and reverted to the previous question. "Six months," he said. "It *may* be just possible. We can only do our best. After the dénouement it will matter comparatively little."

"And should be easier—providing the children are normal," Willers agreed.

"And if the children are *not* normal?"

The doctor looked bleakly at him, and shook his head.

"I don't know."

It was Zellaby who broke the long pause which followed. "I had better fetch my wife," he said.

The door clicked behind him. Doctor Willers sat unmoving while he waited. His forearms rested on his thighs, his hands hung slackly between his knees, and he leaned forward in a slump, gazing without sight somewhere beyond the red caverns of the fire.

10 · Keep It Dark

THE CANVASSING for attendance at what was not very informatively described as a 'Special Emergency Meeting of great importance to every woman in Midwich' was intensive and conscientious. We ourselves were visited by Gordon Zellaby who managed to convey quite a dramatic sense of urgency through a considerable wordage which gave practically nothing away. He had no difficulty in extracting Janet's promise to attend at the village hall on the following afternoon.

Our attempts to pump him were firmly fended off.

"You must forgive me," he said, "but it is a matter of putting the whole thing on the right footing. We're forming a small unofficial committee," he explained. "One on which we should be glad to have your help if, after your wife has heard what is to be said, and you have discussed it together, you should feel disposed to assist us."

The meeting itself was remarkably well attended. It was reckoned that something like ninety per cent of the Midwich women were present, and that the planned repeat meeting for those who could not attend would be small.

Once people had been convinced that it was not simply a matter of another civil defense drive, or any other of the hardy perennials, they became inquisitive as to what it could possibly be that could put the doctor, the vicar, their wives, the district-nurse, and both the Zellabys, too, to the trouble of seeing that everyone was called on and given a personal invitation.

The two chief convenors sat on the platform with Anthea Zellaby, looking a little pale, between them. The doctor smoked, with a nervous intensity. The vicar seemed lost in an abstraction from which he would rouse himself now and then to make a remark to Mrs. Zellaby, who responded to it with an absentminded air. They allowed ten minutes for laggards, then the doctor asked for the doors to be closed, and opened the proceedings with a brief, but still uninformative, insistence on their importance. The vicar then added his support. He concluded:

"I earnestly ask every one of you here to listen very carefully indeed to what Mrs. Zellaby has to say. We are greatly indebted to her for her willingness to put the matter before you. And I want you to know in advance that she has the endorsement of Dr. Willers and myself for everything she is going to tell you. It is, I assure you, only because we feel that this matter may come more acceptably and, I am sure, more ably, from a woman to women that we have burdened her with the task.

"Dr. Willers and I will now leave the hall, but we shall remain on the premises. When Mrs. Zellaby has finished we shall, if you wish, return to the platform, and do our best to answer questions. And now I ask you to give Mrs. Zellaby your closest attention."

He waved the doctor ahead of him and they both went out by a door at the side of the platform. It swung to behind them, but did not close entirely.

Anthea Zellaby drank from a glass of water on the table before her. She looked down for a moment at her hands resting on her notes. Then she raised her head, waiting for the murmurs to die down. When they had, she looked her audience over carefully as if noticing every face there.

"First," she said, "I must warn you. What I have to tell you is going to be difficult for me to say, difficult for you to believe, too difficult for any of us to understand at present." She paused, dropped her eyes, and then looked up once more.

"I," she said, "am going to have a baby. I am very, very glad, and happy about it. It is natural for women to want babies and to be happy when they know they are coming. It is *not* natural and it is *not* good to be afraid of them. Babies should be joy and fun. Unhappily, there are a number of women in Midwich who are not able to feel like that. Some of them are miserable, ashamed and afraid. It is for their benefit we have called this meeting. To help the unhappy ones and assure them that they need be none of these things."

She looked steadily round her audience again. There was a sound of caught breath here and there.

"Something very, very strange has happened here. And it has not happened just to one or two of us, but to almost all of us—to almost all the women in Midwich who are capable of bearing children."

The audience sat motionless and silent, every eye fixed upon her as she put the situation before them. Before she had finished, however, she became aware of some disturbance and shushing going on on the right-hand side of the hall. Glancing over there, she saw Miss Latterly and her inseparable companion, Miss Lamb, in the middle of it.

Anthea stopped speaking, in mid-sentence, and waited. She could hear the indignant tone of Miss Latterly's voice, but not its words.

"Miss Latterly," she said clearly. "Am I right in thinking that you do not find yourself personally concerned with the subject of this meeting?"

Miss Latterly stood up, she spoke in a voice trembling with indignation.

"You most certainly are, Mrs. Zellaby. I have never in all my life—"

"Then, since this is a matter of the gravest importance to many people here, I hope you will refrain from further interruptions. Or perhaps you would prefer to leave us?"

Miss Latterly stood firm, looking back at Mrs. Zellaby.

"This is—" she began, and then changed her mind. "Very well, Mrs. Zellaby," she said. "I shall make my protest against the extraordinary aspersions you have made on our community at another time."

She turned with dignity, and paused, clearly to allow Miss Lamb to accompany her exit.

But Miss Lamb did not move. Miss Latterly looked down at her with an impatient frown. Miss Lamb continued to sit fast.

Miss Latterly opened her lips to speak, but something in Miss Lamb's expression checked her. Miss Lamb ceased to meet her eyes. She looked straight before her, while a tide of color rose until her whole face was a burning flush.

An odd, small sound escaped from Miss Latterly. She put out a hand, and grasped a chair to steady herself. She stared down at her friend without speaking. Then with a great effort she pulled herself together. She lifted her head decisively and, straight-backed, but a little uncertain in her steps, she made her way up the aisle to the back of the hall, alone.

Anthea stood waiting. She expected a buzz of comment, but there was none. The audience looked shocked and bewildered. Every face turned back to her, in expectation. In the silence she picked up where she had stopped, trying to reduce by matter-of-factness the emotional tension which Miss Latterly had increased. With an effort she continued factually to the end of her preliminary statement, and then broke off.

The expected buzz of comment rose quickly enough this time. Anthea took a drink from her glass of water, and rolled her bunched handkerchief between her damp palms while she watched the audience carefully. When she decided that the first impact had had long enough to register she rapped the table. The murmurs died away, there were a few sniffs, and then rows of expectant faces turned toward her once more. Anthea took a deep breath and started again.

"Nobody," she said, "nobody but a child, or a child-minded person, expects life to be fair. It is not, and this is going to be harder on some of us than on others. Nevertheless, fair or unfair, whether we like it or not, we are all of us, married and single alike, in the same boat. If any married woman here is tempted to consider herself more virtuous than her unmarried neighbor, she might do well to consider how, if she were challenged, she could *prove* that the child she now carries is her husband's child. This is a thing that has happened to all of us. We must make it bind us together for the good of all." She paused, and then turned to another aspect.

"You must all know how the cheap papers seize upon anything to do with birth, particularly anything unusual. We have all read of one instance of a multiple birth where the papers took it up, then the medical profession, backed by the government, with the result that the parents were virtually deprived of their own children quite soon after they were born.

"Well I, for one, do not intend to lose my child that way, and I expect and hope that all of you will feel the same. Therefore, I warn you that if this should become generally known we may be exposed to the very real probability that our babies will be taken away from us on one excuse or another by doctors and scientists. We must, every one of us, resolve not to mention, or even hint outside the village, at the present state of affairs.

"If people in Trayne, or elsewhere, are inquisitive, or strangers come here asking questions, we must, for our babies' sakes and our own, tell them nothing. It is not their business, it is *ours*. There is no one, no one at all who has a better right, or a higher duty, to protect our children from exploitation than we who are to be their mothers."

She surveyed them steadily, almost individually once more, as she had at the start. Then she concluded:

"I shall now ask the vicar and Dr. Willers to come back. I know there must be a great many questions you are wanting to ask."

She slipped off into the little room at the side.

"Excellent, Mrs. Zellaby. Really excellent," said Mr. Leebody.

Dr. Willers took her hand and pressed it.

"I think you've done it, my dear," he told her, as he followed the vicar onto the platform.

Zellaby guided her to a chair. She sat down, and leaned back with her eyes closed. Her face was pale and she looked exhausted.

"I think you'd better come home," he told her.

She shook her head.

"No, I'll be all right in a few minutes. I must go back."

"They can manage. You've done your part, and very well, too."

She shook her head again.

"I know what those women must be feeling. You know, it isn't true, Gordon, what I said just now."

"Which part, my dear? You said a lot, you know."

"About my being glad and happy. Two days ago it was quite, quite true. I wanted the baby, yours and mine, so very much. Now I'm frightened about it—I'm frightened, Gordon."

He tightened his arm round her shoulders. She rested her head against his, with a sigh.

"My dear, my dear," he said, stroking her hair gently. "It's going to be all right. We'll look after you."

"Not to *know*," she exclaimed. "To know there's something growing there—and not to be sure how, or what. . . . It's so— so abasing, Gordon. It makes me feel like an animal."

He kissed her cheek softly and went on stroking her hair.

"You're not to worry," he told her. "I'm prepared to bet that when he or she comes you'll take one look and say: 'Oh dear, there's that Zellaby nose.' But if not, we face it together. You're not alone, my dear, you must never feel that you are alone. I'm here, and Willers is here. We're here to help you, always, all the time."

She turned her head and kissed him.

"Gordon, darling," she said. Then she pulled away, and sat up. "I must get back. There are girls of seventeen and eighteen out there, Gordon, with no kind husbands—and middle-aged spinsters like that Miss Ogle, who are even more alone. I must go back to them."

She bent down to give him a peck of a kiss, then squared her shoulders and went through the door, back onto the platform.

Zellaby gazed after her a moment. Then he moved a chair closer to the unclosed door, lit a cigarette and settled himself to listen critically to the mood of the village as it showed in its questions.

•

11 · Midwich Comes to Terms

THE TASK for January was to cushion the shock and steer the reactions, and thus to establish an attitude. The initiation meeting could be considered a success. It let the air in and a lot of anxiety out; and the audience, tackled while it was still in a semi-stunned condition, had for the most part accepted the suggestion of communal solidarity and responsibility.

Once the bewilderment of the first impact had subsided, the feeling grew that there were capable hands at the helm. The self-appointed committee could feel that at least it had succeeded in getting things on to the right lines.

By this time the original committee had been augmented, first by Janet and myself who offered our services in any useful capacities, and then by the co-opting of Mr. Arthur Crimm to represent the interests of those researchers at the Grange who now found themselves linked, willy-nilly, with the domestic life of Midwich.

My own duties to begin with were not very closely defined, and consisted chiefly of trying to make the more awkward among the men take it quietly and, if possible, see reason; in addition I was secretary of the meetings, and, less officially, the archivist.

Dr. Willers, naturally in charge of the medical side, with the assistance of Nurse Daniels and Mrs. Willers, took the chair by consensus, rather than by election. Social welfare was nominally the concern of Mr. and Mrs. Leebody, but something rather overlapping it which might be called practical morale had been adopted by Anthea Zellaby as her field; while Janet engaged herself on an allied task in the nature of visiting nurse. Gordon Zellaby's activities were useful, but hard to classify; he himself described them as roving, with an ear to the ground.

But though the feeling at the committee meeting held some five days after the village hall meeting could be fairly summarized as "so far, so good," members were well aware that the achievement could not be left to take care of itself. The attitude that had been successfully induced might, it was felt, slip back all too easily into normal conventional prejudices if it was not carefully tended.

"What we need to produce," Anthea summed up, "is something like the companionship of adversity, but without suggesting that it is an adversity—which, indeed, so far as we know, it is not. If we can, we must make it appear as—well, as a sort of specialness, a kind of emergency which we are going to deal with in the way that is most beneficial for everyone."

The sentiment gained the approval of everyone but Mrs. Leebody, who looked doubtful.

"But," she said hesitantly, "I think we ought to be honest, you know."

The rest of us looked at her inquiringly. She went on:

"Well, I mean, it *is* an adversity, isn't it? After all, a thing like this wouldn't happen to us for no reason, would it? There must *be* a reason; so isn't it our duty to search for it?"

Anthea regarded her with a small, puzzled frown.

"I don't think I quite understand . . ." she said.

"Well," explained Mrs. Leebody, "when things—unusual things like this—suddenly happen to a community there *is* a reason. I mean, look at the plagues of Egypt, and Sodom and Gomorrah, and that kind of thing."

There was a pause. Zellaby felt impelled to relieve the awkwardness.

"For my part," he observed, "I regard the plagues of Egypt as an unedifying example of celestial bullying; a technique now known as power-politics. As for Sodom—" He broke off and subsided as he caught the vicar's eye.

Anthea came to the rescue.

"I really don't think you need worry about that, Mrs. Leebody. Barrenness is, of course, a classical form of curse; but I really can't remember any instance where retribution took the form of fruitfulness. After all, it scarcely seems reasonable, does it?"

"That would depend on the fruit," Mrs. Leebody said, darkly.

Another uneasy silence followed. Everybody, except Mr. Leebody, regarded Mrs. Leebody. Dr. Willers' eyes swiveled to catch those of Nurse Daniels, and then went back to Dora Leebody who showed no discomfort at being the center of attention. She glanced round at all of us in a faintly apologetic manner.

"You are kind," she said. "I know you want to spare me. But there is a time for confession. I am a sinner, you see. If I had had my child twelve years ago, none of this would have happened. Now I must pay for my sin by bearing a child that is not my husband's. It is all quite clear. I am very sorry to have brought this down on the rest of you. But it is a judgment, you see. Just like the plagues . . ."

The vicar, flushed and troubled, broke in before she could continue: "I think—er—perhaps if you will excuse us—"

There was a general pushing back of chairs. Nurse Daniels crossed quietly to Mrs. Leebody's side and began a conversation with her. Dr. Willers watched them for a moment until he became aware of Mr. Leebody beside him, mutely inquiring. He laid a hand reassuringly on the vicar's shoulder.

"It has been a shock to her. Not surprising at all. I fully expected a number of   before this. Quite a temporary effect. No need to worry. I'll get Nurse Daniels to see her home and give her a sedative. Very likely a good sleep will make all the difference. I'll look in tomorrow morning."

A few minutes later we dispersed, in a subdued and thoughtful mood.

The policy advocated by Anthea Zellaby was carried out with considerable success. In late February I was able to report to Bernard that things were going, on the whole, smoothly—more smoothly, at any rate than we had dared to hope at first. I gave him details of the happenings in the village since my last report, but information regarding the attitude and views prevailing at the Grange which he had asked for I could not supply. Perhaps the researchers were of the opinion that the affair somehow came within the compass of their oaths of secrecy, or perhaps the habit of non-fraternizing had become too well rooted for them to loosen it. Mr. Crimm held a kind of position as nuncio to the village, and they left relations to him. It seemed to me that to learn anything from him Bernard had better see Mr. Crimm and talk to him officially. As a result, the next time Mr. Crimm visited his Ministry, he carried with him an invitation to luncheon with Colonel Westcott at the In and Out.

Mr. Crimm remembered Colonel Westcott as one of the less sticky investigators that the Dayout had brought to the Grange, but he did not allow the realization of an ulterior motive to interfere with a good meal, and appreciated his host's deferment of the raison d'être to the stage of coffee and brandy in the lounge. Only then, after he had settled himself comfortably and made sure that his cigar was burning evenly, did Bernard observe, in a conversational tone:

"They tell me that your place has its little problems."

"We're never without them," Mr. Crimm assured him. "If it's not the Ministry itself, there's always the Treasury."

"I was thinking at the moment more of the staff side—the social questions that must be involved."

"They can be troublesome in all these tucked-away research departments," Mr. Crimm admitted. "There are times when I feel that I am in charge of a boarding-school, but unfortunately without the forthright powers of a headmaster."

"H'm," said Bernard, bearing over from the general toward the particular. "I wonder what a headmaster would do if he were to be faced with a sudden high incidence of fecundity?"

Mr. Crimm watched the roof of a bus pass by on its way up Piccadilly. He said:

"At least he would not have an establishment section to badger him. Establishments do so worship tidiness. There are matters of allowances, you see, and absences, and the deplorable effect upon their nice, neat leave-roster. *I* am perturbed at the effect on our schedule."

Bernard nodded.

"Perplexing all round," he said. "But I am told you yourself have been helping to align the various interests by consenting to serve on a local committee."

Mr. Crimm nodded.

"It is wonderful how much you people at the heart of things manage to know about the darker corners of the Empire," he observed.

"It is, rather," Bernard agreed. "Do you think this committee is making a good job of it?" he added.

Again Mr. Crimm nodded.

"I doubt that anyone could have done better, so far."

"Will they, do you think, be able to see it through successfully?"

Mr. Crimm considered for a moment.

"I would say that if they are left to themselves there's a reasonably good chance that they may, barring accidents. But the question is: Will they be left to themselves? People chattering carelessly, a journalist with a good nose—any one of a number of things might set off awkward curiosity. The main safeguard isn't really anything we can do—it is the average man's and woman's elemental views on the subject; the loud guffaw which would dismiss the facts."

"I appreciate that," agreed Bernard. "Judging by the resistance to belief shown in my own department, it should be a valuable protection. I hope it remains so. If your committee succeeds in keeping the whole thing strictly local knowledge it will save a lot of trouble. If you can't, and there has to be overt official action, it will mean isolating the place; and heaven knows what that would involve—questions in the House, special Act of Parliament, most likely. Very undesirable from every point of view."

"Yes," agreed Mr. Crimm. He pondered a moment. "The precise significance of your use of the word 'overt'—?" he suggested.

"We shall do what we can to help, unobtrusively—I stress 'unobtrusively.' If the village were to know we are interested it would be likely to confuse matters. So long as they can handle it for themselves, so much the better all round. But if the affair does show any signs of breaking into the open I'd be glad if you'd let me know at the first hairline of a crack— any time: we'd rather have a dozen false alarms than miss one that might be critical."

"You seem to be kept pretty well informed already," Mr. Crimm remarked.

"About the village, but not about the Grange. You have a different type of people there, with different responses. I am told that six of your young women are directly affected. For that reason we are hoping you will be able to contrive a standstill order among your staff until—well, next July, at least. A thing we particularly don't want is for young women to disperse to other establishments and then get themselves involved in trying to account for the state of their affairs."

Mr. Crimm considered that a little.

"I'll do my best over that, but it would help if other projects could be discouraged from applying to have personnel transferred from us."

"I'll see if something can be done about that. And do you think it would be possible to draw your people into closer relationship with the village? I know that is the reverse of usual policy—but in this case an increased sense of mutual responsibility might help. Would, indeed, be quite valuable, I should think, to your particular six."

"Yes, I see, better solidarity. I'll put it to them as policy."

"Good. But not, of course, a breath about us if it can be helped."

"Very well," agreed Mr. Crimm. "In point of fact, except for our meeting after the Dayout, I don't *know* much more than a breath about you. I suppose you aren't at liberty to—er—?"

Bernard shook his head.

"Sorry. Not at present, anyway."

Mr. Crimm looked disappointed.

"I was afraid so. Pity. I've seldom come up against anything as intriguing as the idea of an Obstetrics Division of Military Intelligence."

A few minutes later Bernard showed his guest to the door. As they shook hands Mr. Crimm regarded him thoughtfully.

"It might, might it not," he suggested, "be more efficient if, instead of working alone, I were to co-operate with, shall we say, Mr. and Mrs. Gayford?"

"Oh," said Bernard, "so you've rumbled that, have you? Has anyone else?"

"I don't imagine so. It sort of came to me about ten minutes ago who it must be."

"Well, I hope you'll do your best to stop it coming to anyone else. But now it has occurred to you, yes, go and see Gayford by all means. The fuller the picture gets, the better."

Mr. Crimm lost no time in doing so. He called in that same evening on his way back, and together with Janet we considered means by which the Grange, and particularly his six problems there, could be better integrated with the life of the village.

Life appeared to be going on smoothly enough in Midwich for the present, but it was only a little later that one of the undercurrents broke surface and gave us a flutter of anxiety.

After the committee meeting which she had brought to a premature close, Mrs. Leebody ceased, not altogether surprisingly, to play any further active part in the promotion of village harmony. When she did reappear after a few days' rest, she seemed to have recovered her balance by a decision to regard the whole unfortunate situation as a distasteful subject.

On one of the early days in March, however, the vicar of St.

Mary's in Trayne, accompanied by his wife, brought Mrs. Lee-body home in their car.

"A most unhappy affair, I am so sorry," he said, after the two women had gone upstairs and Mr. Leebody had tele-phoned for the doctor. "Most distressing for us all."

"I am not quite clear yet as to exactly what occurred," Mr. Leebody confessed.

"My wife found her. She just happened to be passing through Trayne market, shopping, you know. And she saw Mrs. Leebody. She had quite a little difficulty, I believe, in persuading her to come away, but in the end she got her to the vicarage, and gave her some tea while she telephoned for me. We thought the best course was to bring her home at once."

"I am most grateful to you for that," Hubert Leebody assured him. "But I still don't quite understand. I mean, I know she went to stop in Trayne. It was quite natural for her to go to the market, surely?"

"Yes, yes, of course. It was not that, it was her behavior there. When my wife noticed her, Mrs. Leebody was stand-ing on an upturned box, and talking—preaching, I suppose one might say. She had quite a crowd round her, my wife says. Not at all a sympathetic crowd, one is afraid—a certain ribald element, you understand. Not at all pleasant. In spite of that, Mrs. Leebody was reluctant to leave. Fortunately, however, my wife has a somewhat decisive way with her when she chooses to use it."

"It was indeed most kind of your wife, Vicar. She must have found it an embarrassing and distasteful situation, which puts us the more in her debt."

"I think all her concern was on Mrs. Leebody's behalf," the Vicar of St. Mary's assured him.

After a pause Mr. Leebody inquired, with a tinge of hesi-tation:

"Preaching, you said. You can't tell me what was the—er—theme?"

"Oh, well—quite fantastical, I gather," said the vicar of St. Mary's, evasively.

"But I think I ought to know. The doctor will be sure to ask about it."

The other hesitated, but conceded the point.

"I understand that it was in the nature of a call to re-pentence; I expect you will have come across the kind of thing—revivalist doom. The people of Trayne must repent and pray forgiveness for fear of wrath, retribution and hell-fire. Rather nonconformist, I'm afraid. Lurid, you know. And, it seems, they must particularly avoid having anything to do with the people of Midwich, who are already suffering under divine disapproval. If the Trayne people do not take heed and mend their ways, punishment will inevitably descend on them, too."

"Oh," said Mr. Leebody, keeping his tone level. "She did not say what form our suffering here is taking?"

"A visitation," the vicar of St. Mary's told him. "Specifically, the infliction of a plague of—er—babies. That, of course, prompted most of the ribaldry. A lamentable business altogether. Of course, once my wife had drawn my attention to Mrs. Leebody's—er—condition the matter became more intelligible, though still more distressing. I—oh, here is Dr. Willers, now." He broke off with relief.

A week later, in the middle of the afternoon, Mrs. Leebody took up a position on the lowest step of the war memorial and began to speak. She was dressed for the occasion in a garment of hessian, her feet were bare and there was a smudge of ash on her forehead. Fortunately there were not many people about at the time, and she was persuaded home again by Mrs. Brant before she had well begun. Word was all round the village in an hour, but her message, whatever it may have been, remained undelivered.

Midwich was not alarmed, and heard the quickly following news of Dr. Willers' recommendation to rest in a nursing-home with sympathy rather than surprise.

About mid-March Alan and Ferrelyn made their first visit since their marriage. With Ferrelyn putting in the time until Alan's release in a small Scottish town entirely among strangers, Anthea had been against causing her worry by attempting to explain the Midwich state of affairs in a letter; so now it had to be laid before them.

Alan's expression of concern deepened as the predicament was explained. Ferrelyn listened without interruption, but with a swift glance now and then at Alan's face. It was she who broke the silence that followed.

"You know," she said, "I had a sort of feeling all along that there was something funny. I mean, it oughtn't—" She broke off, struck apparently by an ancillary thought. "Oh, how dreadful! I kind of shot-gunned poor Alan. This probably makes it coercion, or undue influence, or something heinous. Could it be grounds for divorce? Oh, dear. Do you want a divorce, darling?"

Zellaby's eyes crinkled a little at the corners as he watched his daughter.

Alan put his hand over hers.

"I think we ought to wait a bit, don't you?" he told her.

"Darling," said Ferrelyn, twining her fingers in his. Turning her head after a long look at him she caught her father's expression. Treating him to a determinedly unresponsive look, she turned to Anthea and asked for more details of the village's attitude. Half an hour later they went out, leaving the two men alone together. Alan barely waited for the door to latch before he broke out.

"I say, sir, this *is* a bit of a facer, isn't it?"

"I'm afraid it is," Zellaby agreed. "The best consolation I can offer is that we find the shock wears off. The most painful part is the opening assault on one's prejudices—I speak for our sex, of course. For the women that is, unfortunately, only the first hurdle. I admire their fortitude with awe, though it doesn't do, of course, to go about looking awed."

Alan shook his head.

"This is going to be a terrible blow for Ferrelyn, I'm afraid—as it must have been to Anthea," he added, a little hurriedly. "Of course, one can't expect her, Ferrelyn, I mean, to take in all the implications at once. A thing like this needs a bit of absorbing . . ."

"My dear fellow," said Zellaby, "as Ferrelyn's husband you have the right to think all sorts of things about her, but one of the things you must not do, for your own peace of mind, is to underestimate her. Ferrelyn, I assure you, was away ahead of you. I doubt that she's missed a trick. She was certainly far enough ahead to put in a lightweight remark because she knew that if she seemed worried you would worry about her."

"Oh, do you think so?" said Alan, a little flatly.

"I do," said Zellaby. "Furthermore, it was sensible of her. A fruitlessly worrying male is a nuisance. The best thing he can do is to disguise his worry and stand staunchly by, impersonating a pillar of strength while performing certain practical and organizational services. I offer you the fruit of somewhat intensive experience.

"Another thing he can do is represent Modern Knowledge and Commonsense—but tactfully. You can have no idea of the number of venerable saws, significant signs, old wives' sooths, gypsies' warnings, and general fiddle-faddle that has been thrown up by this in the village lately. We have become a folklorist's treasure-chest. Did you know that in our circumstances it is dangerous to pass under a lych-gate on a Friday? Practically suicide to wear green? Very unwise indeed to eat seed-cake? Are you aware that if a dropped knife, or needle, sticks point down in the floor it will be a boy? No? I thought you might not be. But never mind. I am assembling a bouquet of these cauliflowers of human wisdom in the hope that they may keep my publishers quiet."

Alan inquired with belated politeness after the progress of the Current Work. Zellaby sighed sadly.

"I am supposed to deliver the final draft of *The British Twilight* by the end of next month. So far I have written three chapters of this supposedly contemporary study. If I could remember what they deal with I've no doubt I should find them obsolete by now. It ruins a man's concentration to have a crêche hanging over his head."

"What is amazing me as much as anything is that you've managed to keep it quiet. I'd have said you hadn't a chance," Alan told him.

"I *did* say it," Zellaby admitted. "And I'm still astonished. I think it must be a kind of inversion of the Hitler Big Lie— a truth too big to be believed. Mind you, both Oppley and Stouch are saying unneighborly things about some of us that they've noticed. I'm told that there is a theory current that we have all been indulging in one of those fine old uninhibited rustic frenzies on Hallowe'en. I must say that our people have restrained themselves commendably under some provocation."

"But do you mean that only a mile or two away they've no idea what's really happened?" Alan asked incredulously.

"I'd not say that, so much as that they don't want to believe it. They must have heard fairly fully I imagine, but they choose to believe that this is all a tale to cover up something more normal, but disgraceful. The scoffing attitude in the other villages really helps. It means that a newspaper is unlikely to get anything to go on unless it is directly informed by someone inside the village."

Zellaby rambled on for half an hour or more with reassuring anecdotes illustrative of Midwich solidarity until Alan asked thoughtfully:

"You did say that some of the women who might be expected to be involved, actually are not, didn't you?"

"About half a dozen," Zellaby agreed.

"Did you look into the question of where they were during the Dayout?"

"I don't think so—though I expect Willers has. Now let me see, who were they?" He thought for a moment, and then produced several names, including Janet's.

"Mrs. Gayford scarcely counts," Alan pointed out. "She only had a half-hour experience of it, anyway. But Betsy Shuttler—I remember that name. Wasn't she one of the ones in the bus on the Oppley road? There were four women in that bus. Do you remember who the others were?"

Zellaby did. They were four of the names he had just given. "That's odd," he added. "I wonder how I missed that?"

"Well, it means that it didn't happen to any of those we had under observation that day. So that would pretty well establish that it can't have been an effect of the radiation, or whatever it was, that put everyone to sleep. Though that doesn't really get us a lot further."

"Oh, I don't know," said Zellaby. "At least it helps toward dissipating *one* of one's uneasy speculations as to what science, as the *enfant terrible* of our time, may have achieved."

12 · Well Played, Midwich

"I AM REALLY SORRY," Bernard Westcott wrote to me early in May, "that circumstances preclude well-deserved official congratulations to your village on the success of the operation to date. It has been conducted with a discretion and communal loyalty which, frankly, has astonished us; most of us here were of the opinion that it would prove necessary to take official action well before this. Now, with only some seven weeks to go before D-day, we are hopeful that we may get through without it. What is your own opinion? Do you think Midwich will last it out?"

That was far from easy to answer. If there was no major upset, I thought it might stand a good chance: on the other hand, one could not fail to be anxiously aware of the unexpected, lurking round any corner—the small detonator that might set things off.

We had had our moments of panic, though, and managed to get through them. Sometimes they seemed to come from nowhere and spread like an infection. The worst, which looked at one time like becoming a panic, was allayed by Dr. Willers who hurriedly arranged X-ray facilities and was able to show that all appeared to be quite normal.

Mid-May, however, brought something of a change to the village. Hitherto, its spirit had been well attuned with that of the burgeoning season all about it; but now there seeped in an air of abstraction. Its mien was more thoughtful, its strings somewhat muted. Zellaby mentioned it to Willers, and the doctor nodded agreement:

"Scarcely surprising," he said. "It's getting near enough now to be seen as a reality, for good or bad. The next few weeks are the part I've been dreading most ever since it began. This is where we stiffen up the sinews."

"The old women's nattering isn't helping," Zellaby said. "Anthea's fresh-air-and-all-above-board line isn't holding them off as well as it did. Can't something be done to shut them up?"

"Nobody's ever found a way." The doctor shook his head.

"We've already accomplished more than one thought possible—and nearly all of it due to Mrs. Zellaby."

Zellaby hesitated, and then made up his mind.

"I'm rather concerned about her, Willers. I wonder if you could—well, have a talk with her."

"A talk?"

"She's more worried than she has let us see. It came out a bit a couple of nights ago. Nothing particular to start it. I happened to look up and found her staring at me as if she were hating me. She doesn't you know . . . Then, as if I had said something, she broke out: "It's all very well for a man. How can *he* know what it feels like to lie awake at night with the humiliating knowledge that one is simply being used?—As if one were not a person at all, but just a kind of mechanism, a sort of incubator. . . ."

Zellaby paused, and shook his head.

"There's so damned little one can do. I didn't try to stop her. I thought it would be better for her to let it out. I think it did help her a bit. But I'd be glad if you would talk to her, convince her. She knows that all the tests and X-rays show normal development—but she's got it into her head that it would be professionally necessary for you to say that, in any case. And I suppose it would."

"But it's true, thank heaven," the doctor told him. "I don't know what the devil I'd have done if it weren't. I assure you the patients can't be more relieved that it is so than I am. So don't you worry, I'll set her mind at rest on that point, at any rate. She's not the first to think it, and she'll certainly not be the last. But, you know, when we do get that fixed I'm afraid they'll find other aspects to worry themselves with.

"This is going to be a very, very dodgy time all round. . . ."

In a week it began to look as if Willers' prophecy would prove a pale understatement. The feeling of tension was contagious, and almost palpably increasing day by day. At the end of another week Midwich's united front had weakened sadly. Mr. Leebody arranged special daily services and for the rest of the day drove himself on from one parishioner to another, giving what encouragement he could.

Zellaby found himself quite superfluous. Rationalism was in disfavor. He maintained an unusual silence and would have accepted invisibility, too, had it been offered.

"Have you noticed," he inquired, dropping in one evening at Mr. Crimm's cottage, "have you noticed the way they glare at one? Rather as if one had been currying favor with the Creator in order to be given the other sex. Quite unnerving at times. Is it the same at the Grange?"

"It began to be," Mr. Crimm admitted, "but we got them away on leave a day or two ago. Those who wanted to go home have gone there. The rest are in billets arranged by the doctor. We are getting more work done, as a result. It was becoming a little difficult."

"Understatement," said Zellaby. "As it happens, I have never worked in a fireworks factory, but I know just what it feels like. I feel that at any moment something ungoverned and rather horrible may break out. And there's nothing one can do but wait and hope it doesn't happen. Frankly, how we are going to get through another month or so of it, I don't know." He shrugged and shook his head.

At the very moment of that despondent shake, however, the situation unexpectedly improved.

For Miss Lamb, who had adopted the custom of a quiet evening stroll, carefully supervised by Miss Latterly, that evening underwent a misadventure. One of the milk bottles neatly arranged outside the back door of their cottage had somehow been overturned and, as they left, Miss Lamb stepped on it. It rolled beneath her foot, and she fell.

Miss Latterly carried her back indoors and rushed to the telephone. . . .

Mrs. Willers was still waiting up for her husband when he came back, five hours later. She heard the car drive up, and when she opened the door he was standing on the threshold, disheveled, and blinking at the light. She had seen him like that only once or twice in their married life, and caught his arm anxiously.

"Charley. Charley, my dear, what is it?"

"Rather drunk, Milly. Sorry. Take no notice," he said.

"Oh, Charley! Was the baby—?"

"Reaction, m'dear. Jus' reaction. Baby's perfect, you see. Nothing wrong with the baby. Nothing 'tall. Perfect."

"Oh, thank God for that," exclaimed Mrs. Willers, meaning it as fervently as she had ever meant any prayer.

"Got golden eyes," said her husband. "Funny—but nothing against having golden eyes, is there?"

"No, dear, of course not."

"Perfect, 'cept for golden eyes. Not wrong at all."

Mrs. Willers helped him out of his coat and steered him into the sitting-room. He dropped into a chair and sat there slackly, staring before him.

"So s-silly, isn't it?" he said. "All that worrying. And now it's perfect. I—I—I—" He burst suddenly into tears and covered his face with his hands.

Mrs. Willers sat down on the arm of his chair, and laid her arm round his shoulders.

"There, there, my darling. It's all right, dear. It's over now." She turned his face toward her own, and kissed him.

"Might've been orange, or green, or like a monkey. X-rays no good to tell that," he said.

"I know, my dear, I know. But now you don't need to worry about that any more. You said it's perfect."

Dr. Willers nodded emphatically several times and recovered himself somewhat.

"That's right. Perfect," he repeated with another nod. " 'Cept for golden eyes. Perfect . . . Lambs may safely graze . . . safely graze . . . Give me another drink, Milly, dear. Oh, God . . . !"

A month later Gordon Zellaby found himself pacing the floor of the waiting room in Trayne's best nursing-home, and forced himself to stop it and sit down. It was a ridiculous way to behave at his age, he told himself. Very proper in a

young man, no doubt, but the last few weeks had brought
the fact that he was no longer a young man rather forcibly to
his notice. He felt about twice the age he had a year ago.
Nevertheless when, ten minutes later, a nurse rustled starchily
in she found him pacing the room again.

"It is a boy, Mr. Zellaby," she said. "And I have Mrs. Zellaby's special instructions to tell you he has the Zellaby nose."

13 · Harvest Home

ON A FINE AFTERNOON in the last week of July Gordon Zellaby, emerging from the post office, encountered a small family
party coming from the church. It centered about a girl who
carried a baby wrapped in a white woolen shawl. She looked
very young to be the baby's mother; scarcely more than a
schoolgirl. Zellaby beamed benevolently upon the group and
received their smiles in return, but when they had passed his
eyes followed the girl a little sadly.

As he approached the lych-gate the Reverend Hubert Leebody came down the path.

"Hullo, Vicar. Still signing up the recruits, I see," he said.

Mr. Leebody nodded and fell into step beside him.

"It's easing off now, though," he said. "Only two or three
more to come."

"Making it one hundred per cent?"

"Very nearly. I must confess I had scarcely expected that,
but I fancy they feel that though it can't exactly regularize
matters, it does go some way toward it. I'm glad they do." He
paused reflectively. "This one," he went on, "young Mary
Histon, she's chosen the name Theodore. Chose it all on her
own, I gathered. And I must say I rather like that."

Zellaby considered for a moment, and nodded.

"So do I, Vicar. I like it very much. And, you know, that
embodies no mean tribute to you."

Mr. Leebody looked pleased, but shook his head.

"Not to me," he said. "That a child like Mary should want
to call her baby 'the gift of God' instead of being ashamed of
it is a tribute to the whole village."

"But the village had to be shown how, in the name of humanity, it ought to behave."

"Teamwork," said the vicar. "Teamwork, with a fine captain in Mrs. Zellaby."

Zellaby contemplated.

"I wonder," he observed, "what sort of conclusion is to be drawn from the fact that when something wildly *extra mores* occurs your Christian response to it and our agnostic one should turn out to be virtually identical? Does that seem to you reasonably to be expected?"

"Perhaps one could take it as a sign of a creed's strength that though its forms may be abandoned its ethics persist?" suggested Leebody.

"A palpable point," Zellaby admitted.

They continued for a few paces in silence, then he said:

"Nevertheless, the fact remains that, however the girl takes it, she has been robbed. She has been swept suddenly from childhood into womanhood. I find that saddening. No chance to stretch her wings. She has to miss the age of true poetry."

"One would like to agree—but, in point of fact, I doubt it," said Mr. Leebody. "Not only are poets, active or passive, rather rare, but it suits more temperaments than our times like to pretend to go straight from dolls to babies."

Zellaby shook his head regretfully.

"I expect you're right. All my life I have deplored the Teutonic view of women, and all my life ninety per cent of them have been showing me that they don't mind it a bit. Is it an illusion, I wonder, that when I was a young man I used to meet many intelligent young women, whereas now I seem rarely to meet one who is not a lazy-minded conformist?"

"Probably. Times are never what they were. But, to revert, there are some who certainly have not been robbed of anything."

"You're right. I've just been looking in on Miss Ogle. She hasn't. Still a bit bewildered, perhaps, but delighted too. You'd think it was all some kind of conjuring trick she had invented for herself, without knowing how."

He paused, and then went on: "My wife tells me that Mrs. Leebody will be home in a few days. We were most happy to hear that."

"Yes. The doctors are very pleased. She's made a wonderful recovery."

"And the baby is doing well?"

"Yes," said Mr. Leebody, a shade unhappily. "She adores the baby."

"There are signs of that even in those who were most indignant—a sound provision of nature," Zellaby said. "But, as a male, I must admit to finding things a bit flat now. There's an empty, after-the-battle feeling."

"It *was* a battle," agreed Mr. Leebody, "but, after all, battles are just the highlights of a campaign—and this was only the opening battle. We now have the responsibility for fifty-eight new souls in our community in all. Five of them, including your son, are—well, one hesitates to reflect on the rest by saying 'normal,' but they are the usual, not the golden-eyed kind. Of the fifty-three of the latter kind, thirty-two belong to married women and are technically legitimate—that is to say that, lacking evidence to the contrary, there would be a legal assumption that the women's husbands are their fathers. Which leaves twenty-one who are frankly illegitimate, twelve of them mothered by girls between seventeen and twenty-four years old. Looking after their interests is going to be part of the campaign, too, I think."

"True. There'll be problems," Zellaby agreed. "And, of course, not all the golden-eyed children are actually in this community. Five young women from the Grange went away in the end, to their homes, or elsewhere. There is also my daughter, Ferrelyn."

"And my niece, Polly, poor girl," said Mr. Leebody.

"Making sixty in all—sixty whats? What are they? Why are they? We're not a fraction nearer knowing that than we were in January. You've heard, of course, that Willers considers all of them quite unusually well developed at birth—in everything but size, luckily?"

Mr. Leebody nodded.

"One can perceive that for oneself. And there's something about the way they look at one with those curious eyes. They are—strangers, you know." He hesitated before adding: "I realize it is not a way of thinking that will commend itself to you, but somehow I find myself continually returning to the idea that this must be some kind of test."

"A test," Zellaby repeated. "But by whom, of whom?"

Mr. Leebody shook his head.

"Possibly we shall never know that. Though it has already shown itself something of a test to us."

"I wonder," said Zellaby. "There seems to be no reason why it should be us rather than Oppley, or Stouch, or any of one of a thousand villages. On the other hand, the actual happening itself is clearly no accident. Possibly, therefore, it *is* a kind of test—of something. Could we be a randon sample under test? After all, there was the question: would we accept the situation thrust upon us or would we take steps to reject it? Well, we've answered that one. But that is, surely, quite a secondary question. Behind it are the bigger questions of who made the test? And why was it made?—Not to mention the still perplexing 'how'? You know, in the practical anxieties we seem rather to have lost sight of the incredible and quite monstrous aspect. As you said, these are strangers . . . we mustn't forget. . . . We might do well to stand back now and then and remind ourselves consciously of it— they are strangers, sent among us for an unknown purpose . . . or does that sound too fanciful . . . ?"

"Who can say?" asked Mr. Leebody. "But what can we do but watch and hope to learn? Whether we do learn or not we have felt a sense of obligation and accepted a duty toward them. Now, if you will excuse me . . ." He lifted the latch of the Foreshams' gate.

Zellaby watched him disappear up the path, and then, still with an abstracted air, turned to stroll back by the way they had come.

Not until he was approaching the Green was his attention turned outward, and then it was by the sight of Mrs. Brinkman, still at some distance, but coming toward him in a hurry, behind a new and shiny perambulator. Possibly it was because Mrs. Brinkman, the widow of a naval commander, the mother of a boy at Eton and a girl at Wycombe, did not customarily hurry that he noticed her; indeed, a second or two after he had noticed her she stopped.

She stood for a moment looking down into the perambulator with a helpless, troubled air. Then she picked the baby up and carried it the few steps to the War Memorial. There she sat down on the second step, unbuttoned her blouse and held the baby to her.

Zellaby continued his stroll. As he drew near he raised his somewhat ramshackle hat. An expression of annoyance came over Mrs. Brinkman's face, and a suffusion of pink, but she did not move. Then, as if he had spoken, she said defensively:

"Well, it's natural enough, isn't it?"

"My dear lady, it's classical. One of the great symbols," Zellaby assured her.

"Then go away," she told him, and abruptly began to weep. Zellaby hesitated. "Is there anything I can—?"

"Yes. Go *away*," she repeated. "You don't think I *want* to make an exhibition of myself, do you?" she added, tearfully.

Zellaby was still irresolute.

"She's hungry," Mrs. Brinkman said. "You'd understand if yours was one of the Dayout babies. Now, will you please go *away!*"

It did not seem the moment to pursue the matter further. Zellaby lifted his hat once more, and strolled on. The puzzled frown on his brow gradually deepened into displeasure as he realized that somewhere he had missed a trick; something had been kept from him.

Halfway up the drive to Kyle Manor the sound of a car behind made him draw in to the side for it to pass. It did not pass, however. It drew up beside him. Turning, he saw not the tradesman's van he had assumed it to be, but a small black car with Ferrelyn at the wheel.

"My dear," he said, "how nice to see you. I had no idea you were coming. I wish they wouldn't forget to tell me things."

But Ferrelyn did not give him smile for smile. Her face, a little pale, remained tired-looking.

"Nobody had any idea I was coming—not even me. I didn't intend to come." She looked down at the baby in the carrycot on the passenger seat beside her. "He *made* me come," she said.

14 · *Midwich Centrocline*

ON THE FOLLOWING DAY there returned to Midwich, first, Dr. Margaret Haxby from Norwich, with baby. Miss Haxby was no longer on the staff of the Grange, having resigned two months before, nevertheless it was to the Grange she went, demanding accommodation. Two hours later came Miss Diana Dawson, from the neighborhood of Gloucester, also with baby, also demanding accommodation. She presented slightly less of a problem than Miss Haxby since she was still a member of the staff, though not due to return from leave for some weeks yet. Third came Miss Polly Rushton from London, with baby, in a state of distress and confused emotions, asking help and shelter of her uncle, the Reverend Hubert Leebody.

The day after that two more ex-staff from the Grange arrived, with their babies, admitting their resignations from the Service, but at the same time making it perfectly clear that it was the Grange's duty to find them a room of some kind in Midwich. In the afternoon young Mrs. Dorry, who had been staying in Devonport to be near her husband in his latest posting, arrived unexpectedly, with her baby, and opened up her cottage.

And on the next day there showed up from Durham, with baby, the remaining member of the Grange staff involved. She, too, was technically on leave, but insisted that a place must be found for her. Finally appeared Miss Latterly, with Miss Lamb's baby, urgently returning from Eastbourne whither she had taken Miss Lamb for recuperation.

This influx was observed with varying emotions. Mr. Leebody welcomed his niece warmly, as though she were putting it within his power to make some amends. Dr. Willers was perplexed and disconcerted—as was Mrs. Willers, who feared it might cause him to postpone the much-needed holiday she had arranged for him. Gordon Zellaby had the air of one regarding an interesting phenomenon with judicial reserve. The person upon whom the development pressed most hardly was, without doubt, Mr. Crimm: he began to wear a distraught look. ·

Janet and I decided that the time had come for a conference. I rang up Bernard (on the Grange line) putting it to him that though the worst hurdle had been crossed and the babies had arrived without nationwide obstetrical interest, this new development would now require dealing with if he still hoped to avoid publicity. Plans for the care of the children would have to be drawn up. The whole affair must be placed on a new footing, and in the process it was likely that the government's interest would have to be acknowledged— at least within the village. He agreed to come down for a discussion the following week.

The next Thursday he arrived in time for luncheon, and afterward we were joined by Mr. Crimm and Dr. Willers. It was Bernard's first personal meeting with the doctor, and he again said his piece, lamenting that congratulations could not be official and public at present, but hoping that one day the doctor would receive his due. Dr. Willers was pleased, but shook his head. ·

"Official ceremonies aren't much in my line anyway, Colonel," he replied. "And, in any case, might it not be better to wait a little and see whether it is, in fact, going to turn out to be a matter for congratulations?"

"At this stage it is," Bernard insisted. "On the babies themselves, however, my information so far is rather sketchy."

"And so," Dr. Willers told him, "is mine. Indeed, from the purely scientific point of view a hundred per cent survival rate is not without disadvantages. But of course I don't know how much information you do have—or whether it is accurate."

"Well, let's take the most obvious characteristic first, their eyes. How do they differ from ordinary eyes?"

"In structure they appear not to differ at all. It is simply that the color of the iris strikes one at once. It is a bright, almost fluorescent-looking gold, and the shade of gold is exactly the same in all of them."

"Are there other unusual characteristics?"

"Several. Their hair, which is unusually soft and fine, does not accord with any ordinary type. Under the microscope, in section, it is almost flat on one side while the other is an arc —somewhat the shape of a narrow capital D. It is the same with half a dozen specimens I have examined from different subjects and, as far as I can discover, there is no record of such a hair type. The finger and toe nails are slightly unusual, too. They are narrower, covering less of the upper surface of the digit—but as flat as normal nails; no suggestion of claw formation. The shape of the occiput strikes me as a little unusual, too, but it is early to be sure about that."

"Blood group?" inquired Bernard.

The doctor shook his head.

"The blood group distribution is about what you would expect. Not exactly, but in a small group there could well be some differences. We haven't yet checked all the minor groups."

"But apart from these minor points, would you call them normal?"

Dr. Willers scratched his cheek.

"Such a difficult word, 'normal.' They certainly appear to have all we expect to find in a human being, but if you ask me to place them ethnically, I can't. They are a species of homo sapiens undoubtedly—but so, too, are the Nordics, the Chinese, the Bushmen and the Andamanese. The most I can say is that not only are they all clearly members of the same ethnic stock, whatever it may be, but all remarkably similar members of it, too."

"Not hybrids, you mean?"

"Certainly not hybrids."

"I see. Yet their mothers must be our usual English mixture of stocks. Would it then be permissible to say that their apparent mothers are not, in fact, their mothers at all?"

"I don't see that any other conclusion is possible."

Bernard meditated for some moments, then he said:

"You must forgive a layman's ignorance, but is this simply a logical conclusion, or is it a known possibility?"

"It is a known possibility. Whether it has actually taken place or not I can't tell you; I've not had the time to go into it thoroughly. However, there is a veterinary technique which has proved satisfactory. It also has a name—xenogenesis."

"H'm," said Bernard. "Is the village in general aware of this?"

"Not in general. The Zellabys are, of course. One or two others also thought of it, but only half-seriously—not, I fancy, as a real, practical possibility. There is a humiliating aspect to it which tends to promote evasion."

Mr. Crimm put in: "My people are of much the same opinion as Dr. Willers, but have felt it better not to mention it in the village. I've not liked to interfere."

"And your views, Doctor?"

"Let 'em come to it gradually for themselves and make their own terms with it. If you go round saying bluntly: 'This baby that you think is your own isn't anything of the kind; you are only its foster-mother,' you'll set up deep emotional conflicts and neuroses in a lot of 'em, with hell to pay. The differences are there. They're gradually discovering that, anyway."

"What differences?"

"Well, non-medically, the babies, while perfectly healthy, do not show the degree of 'chubbiness' to be expected at their age; the size of the head in relation to the body is that normally found in a slightly older child; a curious, somewhat silvery sheen on the skin is appearing—very slight now, but perceptible, and it may increase. A number of the mothers will be the happier for ignoring these things—very well, then, let them do so for as long as circumstances permit."

Bernard nodded, reflected a moment, and then took up another point.

"Richard, here, has told me something of a recent development that seems to need some explanation, the—er—gathering of the clan. Can you throw any light on that, Doctor?"

Willers frowned.

"Right from the beginning this affair has bristled with opportunities for hysteria," he said. "The marvel to me is that so little has actually been displayed."

"That *is* remarkable," Bernard agreed. "And I can understand that the companionship of misadventure could have a unifying influence, but this, I understand, is another hundred-per-cent occurrence . . . ?" He looked at Janet and me for confirmation.

"It is," agreed Janet. "Everyone of them is here now."

"Including the five of mine who were away," supported Mr. Crimm. "Two were on leave, but the other three had officially resigned, shaken the dust off. But back they came, babies and all, and simply dumped themselves. *Nous y sommes, nous y restons,* now find us somewhere to live.

"The establishments branch is just about throwing in the towel, and I can't say that I greatly wonder. There's bound to be an almighty rumpus before long, and once the reasons come out, goodness knows where it will end. And now we're in a position where if we were to send the girls away forcibly there'd be a row of another kind. Besides, it wouldn't work —they'd be back again next day. I'm hanged if I can see how we'll square this all up with the Treasury when their sleuths get onto it."

"You don't need to worry about that, Mr. Crimm," Bernard assured him. "We've not been idle, though it has been sticky. You'll be getting a notification to attend a conference any day now; I can't say more at present."

"I'm extremely glad to hear it," acknowledged Mr. Crimm. "I still don't see why the War Office should want to go into the crêche business. We all find that hard to understand. . . ." He cocked an inquiring eye. "No? Not yet? Ah, well . . . the great unraveler is Time."

"You said," Bernard reminded him, "that they'd be back again next day."

"A manner of speaking," Mr. Crimm admitted. "I should have said that if we were to send the mothers away without the babies—which would really be no solution at all— natural instinct would probably bring them back the next day; but if we were to try to send them *with* the babies, they'd be back the *same* day. And this, I'm afraid is where some of us start to hold different views." He glanced at the doctor, who made no comment, went on: "You see, when it is suggested that they remove their babies, their prompt and unanimous reply is that they *can't,* because the babies themselves *won't let them.* . . .

"Now I believe, without at all understanding what's involved, that they mean exactly what they say, whereas Dr. Willers—"

"Before we start any misunderstandings," the doctor broke in, "I should like the Colonel to know that I, too, believe they mean what they say. In my opinion, however, the phenomena is obviously *subjective*—which is to say that *for them* it appears real, though actually and objectively it has no existence. What we now have in Midwich is a widespread condition of hysteria, after the long period of strain. This has resulted in a manifestation of collective hallucination, which should not greatly surprise anyone in the circumstances. Certainly it doesn't me, I am only thankful it has taken a mild, rather than a distressing, or even dangerous, form."

"My dear Willers," Mr. Crimm put in. "In all, there were a dozen of these golden-eyed babies distributed in different parts of the country *Now* every one of them is back in Midwich. You will admit that it is a requirement of collective hallucination that it should spread infectiously or contagiously from a source; *but* every one of these mothers said, before she had any opportunity of consulting the rest, that she was 'compelled' to bring the baby back here."

"What, exactly, did they mean by 'compelled'?" asked Bernard.

At this point Janet felt that the matter had entered her province.

"I have visited these women and talked to all of them," she said. "What they say—what they *all* say—is that they suddenly become aware of a kind of distress and a feeling of need which they somehow knew would only be assuaged by coming back here. They vary in their attempts to describe the feeling: some say it was similar to hunger or thirst; one remembers feeling a similar need to flee from the noise in an engineering shop; another says she had a sense of being stifled; Zellaby's daughter speaks of intolerable jitters. But whichever way it took them they all felt there was only one way to ease it. To come back here."

"Except, apparently, Miss Lamb," Bernard pointed out.

"Including Miss Lamb," Janet insisted, "only hers was brought by proxy, by Miss Latterly. They were in Eastbourne for a change of air, and then Miss Lamb was rushed off to a nursing home with appendicitis. After the operation Miss Latterly visited her, taking the baby with her. Soon after the visit began Miss Lamb became distressed. She wanted to leave at once and bring the baby back here. That was, of course, impossible, but she continued to grow more distressed until Miss Latterly thought it better to leave, taking the baby with her.

"But when she got away Miss Latterly herself was struck with a violent, nagging compulsion to bring the baby back. She rang up and told Miss Lamb, who seemed to understand and agreed at once. So back she came and parked the baby with Mrs. Brant while she returned to Eastbourne and Miss Lamb—after which, I gather, neither of them felt any more compulsion or anxiety."

"I see," said Bernard. He raised an eyebrow at the doctor.

"If," said Doctor Willers heavily, "*if* we take all old wives' —or young wives'—tales at face value; *if* we remember that the majority of feminine tasks are deadly dull and leave the mind so empty that the most trifling seed that falls there can grow into a riotous tangle, we shall not be surprised by an outlook on life which has the disproportion and the il-logical inconsequence of a nightmare, where values are sym-bolic rather than literal.

"Now, what do we have here? A number of women who are the victims of an improbable, and as yet unexplained, phenomenon, and a number of resultant babies which are not quite like other babies. By a dichotomy familiar to us all a woman requires her own baby to be perfectly normal and at the same time superior to all other babies. Well, when any of these women concerned is isolated from the rest with her own baby, it is bound to become more strongly borne in upon her that her golden-eyed baby is not, in relation to the other babies she sees, quite normal. Her subconscious be-comes defensive, and keeps it up until a point is reached where the facts must either be admitted, or somehow subli-mated. The easiest way to sublimate the situation is to trans-fer the irregularity into an environment where it no longer appears irregular—if there is such a place. And in this case there *is* one, and one only—Midwich. So they pick up their babies and back they go, and everything is comfortably ration-alized—for the time being."

"Comfortably?" said Mr. Crimm. "What about Mrs. Welt?"

"Good heavens! If ever there was a straightforward exam-ple of hysteria . . ." Dr. Willers shrugged.

"And who," inquired Bernard, "is Mrs. Welt?"

"She's a widow who keeps the village shop. Mrs. Brant went in there one day and discovered her jabbing a pin into herself and weeping as she did it. That didn't seem good, so she dragged her off to see Willers. She was still jabbing when she arrived and went on doing so until Willers gave her some kind of anesthetic. When she came round she explained that in changing the baby's napkin she had pricked him with the pin. According to her, the baby just looked at her steadily with its golden eyes and *made* her jab the pin into herself, and go on doing it."

"As plain a case of hysterical remorse as you could find—hair-shirts, and all that," said the doctor.

"And there was Harriman, too," Mr. Crimm continued. "His face was in a shocking mess. Nose broken, couple of teeth knocked out, both eyes blacked. He *said* he was set on by three unknown men, but there's been no trace of them. On the other hand, two of the village boys say they saw him through the window bashing himself with his fists as hard as he could go. And the next day there was a bruise on the side of the Harrimans' baby's face. Janet can support that, I know."

Janet nodded. Willers observed, "If Harriman were to complain of assault by a pink elephant it would not greatly surprise me."

"H'm," said Bernard, noncommittally. "And the general opinion in the village?" he asked. Janet replied to that.

"Mixed, I'd say. Most of the mothers are resisting alarm, so far. That's not quite so difficult as you might think. The notion of some mystic rapport between mother and child is, for no very clear reason, thought to be flattering to the mother; that helps. There is also a touchily defensive attitude of mind, very understandable in the circumstances, and kept alert by whisperings in what Zellaby calls the beldame underground. The men are taking it surprisingly well, on the whole, I think. They look more askance at the children than the women do, but make good efforts to cover up, for their wives' sakes. Would you say that's a fair opinion, Doctor?"

Willers gave a grunt, and nodded.

Bernard said:

"You mentioned Zellaby just now. Surely, on past form, he should have some views about all this?"

"He must have," agreed Mr. Crimm, "but the odd thing—and very odd indeed in Zellaby—is that at any recent discussion Zellaby has been listening, and not talking." He shook his head as if lamenting an infirmity in an old friend.

"I really think I'd better try to see him before I go," Bernard said.

"I wish you would. It has been getting a little awkward for us at times," I told him. "And he's half-aware of you, anyway. He was saying to me a little time ago that he'd like to meet the stage-manager of our little drama."

Before the meeting broke up, Dr. Willers, who had become silent during the latter part, emerged from his reflections with a touch of doggedness, to say:

"I am going to register an official, and professional, protest over all this, Colonel Westcott. I propose to write a letter for submission to the proper quarters, but I don't see why all of you should not hear the gist of it now. It's this: In the first place I do not see why M.I. is concerned in this at all: in the second, that it should be, apparently, an exclusive concern of theirs is outrageous.

"We've grown accustomed to the idea of military interference with science in a number of fields—a lot of it totally unnecessary—but this is really preposterous. Somebody should be making a thorough study of these children; I'm keeping notes, of course, but they're only an ordinary G.P.'s observations. There ought to be a team of experts on the job. The effects of environment, conditioning, association, diet— why, there's the stuff for volumes of precious knowledge here. Something *must* be done about it. . . ."

He went on at some length, with a great deal of earnest feeling.

Bernard listened patiently and sympathetically. At the end he said:

"I understand, and personally I agree. But it doesn't lie with me. All I can say is write your letter. Pitch it as strong as you like and I'll undertake to see that it reaches the highest levels I have contact with."

"I've a good mind to get it raised in the House unless something *is* done—and very soon," Dr. Willers said.

Bernard shook his head and looked at him seriously.

"I'd not advise that, Dr. Willers. I really wouldn't. Just let me have your letter and I'll see there's no delay in its getting into the right hands, I'll promise you that."

When we broke up, and Mr. Crimm and the doctor had left, the latter looking only slightly mollified, Bernard said, frowning a little:

"He's a good chap. It must have been the devil of a strain on him. I do hope he doesn't do anything silly."

"But he *is* right, Bernard, you know," Janet said.

"Of course he is. And the thing will be *put* right. But

this side is the Ministry of Health's job, not ours. I'll get on to them again, and find out where the holdup is. . . ."

In the evening, after dinner, I took him up to Kyle Manor, introduced him to Zellaby and left them to talk. He came back to the cottage about a couple of hours later, looking thoughtful.

"Well," Janet asked him. "What did you make of the sage of Midwich?"

Bernard shook his head and looked at me.

"He's got me wondering, Richard," he said. "Most of your reports have been excellent, Richard, but I doubt that you got him quite right. Oh, there *is* a lot of chatter which sounds like hot air, I know, but what you gave me was too much of the manner and too little of the matter."

"I'm sorry if I misled you," I admitted. "The trouble about Zellaby is that his matter is frequently elusive and often allusive. Not much that he says is reportable fact; he is given to mentioning things *en passant* and by the time you've thought it over you don't know whether he followed them up with serious deductions or was simply playing with hypotheses —nor, for that matter, are you at all sure how much he implied and how much you inferred. It makes things difficult."

Bernard nodded understandingly.

"I appreciate that now. I've just had some of it. He spent quite ten minutes toward the end telling me that it is only recently that he has come to wonder whether civilization is not biologically speaking, a form of decadence. From that he went on to wonder whether the gap between homo sapiens and the rest was not too wide; with the suggestion that it might have been better for our development had we had to contend with the conditions of some other sapient, or at least semi-sapient, species. I'm sure he wasn't being altogether irrelevant, but I'm hanged if I can really pin down the relevance. One thing seems pretty clear though; erratic as he seems, he doesn't miss a lot. He is strong on the same line as the doctor concerning expert observation, particularly on this 'compulsion,' but in that case for the opposite reason: he doesn't consider it hysterical and is anxious to know what it is.

"By the way, you seem to have missed one trick—did you know his daughter tried to take her baby for a drive in her car the other day?"

"No," I said, "what do you mean, 'tried'?"

"Just that after about six miles she had to give up and come back again. He doesn't like it. As he put it, for a child to be tied to its mother's apron strings is bad, but for a mother to be tied to a baby's apron strings is serious. He feels it is time he took some steps about it."

15 · Matters Arising

FOR VARIOUS REASONS almost three weeks went by before Alan Hughes was free to come for a weekend visit, so that Zellaby's expressed intention of taking steps had to be postponed until then.

By this time the disinclination of the Children (now beginning to acquire an implied capital C, to distinguish them from other children) to be removed from the immediate neighborhood was generally accepted as just another inconvenience added to the inconveniences inevitable with babies, anyway.

Zellaby took a less casual view of it, but waited until the Sunday afternoon before putting the matter to his son-in-law. Reasonably certain, then, of a spell without interruption he led Alan to deck chairs under the cedar tree on the lawn where they would not be overheard. Once they were seated he came to the point with quite unusual directness.

"What I want to say, my boy, is this: I'd feel happier if you can get Ferrelyn away from here. And the sooner, I think, the better."

Alan looked at him with an expression of surprise which became changed into a slight frown.

"I should have thought it fairly clear that there is nothing I want more than to have her with me."

"Of course it is, my dear fellow. One could not fail to realize that. But at the moment I am concerned with something more important than interfering in your private affairs; I am not thinking of what either of you wants or would like, so much as of what needs to be done—for Ferrelyn's sake, not for yours."

"She wants to come away. She set out to come once," Alan reminded him.

"I know. But she tried to take the baby with her: it brought her back, just as it brought her here before, and will again if she tries to take it away. Therefore you must take her away without the baby. If you can persuade her to that we can arrange to have it excellently looked after here. The indications are that if it is not actually with her it will not—probably cannot—exert any influence stronger than that of natural affection."

"But according to Willers—"

"Willers is making a loud blustering noise to prevent himself from being frightened. I don't blame the man. He's had enough for the time being; he's tired out and he deserves a rest. But that doesn't mean we must let him obscure the facts. For instance, even if he has observed it, he has not admitted that none of this 'hysteria' has ever been known to manifest itself without one of the babies being present."

"Is that so?" Alan asked, surprised.

"Without exception. Separate the baby from the mother—or perhaps one should say remove the mother from the neighborhood of any of the babies—and the compulsion at once begins to lessen and gradually to die away. It takes longer to fade in some than in others, but that is what happens."

"But I don't see—I mean, how is it done?"

"I've no idea. But my point is this: Ferrelyn cannot take the baby; but if she makes up her mind to go and leave it here, there's nothing to stop her. Your job is to help her make up her mind."

Alan considered.

"Sort of put out an ultimatum—make her choose between baby and me? That's a bit tough, isn't it?"

"My dear fellow, the baby's put the ultimatum already. The only possible alternative would be for you to surrender to the baby's challenge and come to live here, too."

"Which I couldn't, anyway."

"Very well, then. Ferrelyn has been dodging the issue for some weeks now, but sooner or later she must face it. Your job is first to make her recognize the hurdle, and then help her over it."

Alan said slowly, "It's quite a thing to ask, though, isn't it?"

"Isn't the other quite a thing to ask of a man—when it isn't his baby?" Zellaby went on: "And it isn't really her baby, either, or I'd not be talking quite like this. Ferrelyn and the rest are the victims of an imposition. This baby has absolutely nothing to do with either of you, except that, by some process not yet explained, she was placed in a situation which forced her to nourish it. So far is it from belonging to either of you that it doesn't correspond to any known racial classification. Even Willers has to admit that."

"Well . . ." Alan qualified. "I understood him to say that as yet he is unable to classify it definitely."

"That only means he's boggling again. He's tried his damnedest to assign the type, and he can't. But if the type is unknown the phenomenon is not—our ancestors, who did not have Willers' blind faith in the articles of science, had a word for it: they called such things changelings. None of his business would have seemed as strange to them as it does to us because they had only to suffer religious dogmatism which was not so dogmatic as scientific dogmatism.

"The idea of the changeling, therefore, far from being novel is both old and so widely distributed that it is unlikely to have arisen, or to have persisted, without cause, and occasional support. True, one has not encountered the idea of it taking place on such a scale as this, but quantity does not, in this case, affect the quality of the event; it simply confirms it. All these sixty golden-eyed children we have here are intruders, changelings: they are cuckoo-children."

Alan frowned. He said, "I'll grant you quite a lot of that—a certain alien quality, apart from the compulsive factor; their quite astonishing similarity; the fact that Willers can't classify them. But where does it get us? As far as I am concerned it only makes the how and why more baffling."

"We can afford to omit that for the moment," Zellaby went on. "The important thing about the cuckoo is not how the egg got into the nest, nor why that nest was chosen; the real matter for concern comes after it has been hatched; what, in fact, it will attempt to do next. And that, whatever it may be, will be motivated by its instinct for survival, an instinct characterized chiefly by utter ruthlessness."

Alan pondered a little.

"You really think you've got a sound analogy there?" he asked, uneasily.

"I'm perfectly certain of it. Look, my dear fellow. Altogether eleven women, some of them strongly against their wills, have been forced to reassemble in Midwich: and any attempt to remove their babies again more than a few miles from Midwich has been frustrated. And these babies are still not many weeks old. No doubt you have heard about Mrs.

Welt, and about that fellow Harriman, too. Don't their experiences seem to you significant? They do to me."

The two of them fell silent for some little time, Zellaby lying back in his chair with his hands behind his head, Alan staring unseeingly across the lawn.

"All right," he said. "I suppose most of us have been hoping that once the babies arrived it would straighten out. I admit that it doesn't look like it now. But what are you expecting to happen?"

"I'm just being expectant, not specific—except that I don't think it will be anything pleasant," Zellaby replied. "The cuckoo survives because it is tough and single-purposed. That is why I hope you will take Ferrelyn away—and keep her away.

"Nothing satisfactory can come of this, at best. Do your utmost to make her forget this changeling in order that she may have a normal life. It will be difficult at first, no doubt, but not so hard if she has a child that is really her own."

Alan rubbed the furrows on his forehead.

"It *is* difficult," he said. "In spite of the way it happened she does have a maternal feeling for it—a sort of physical affection, and a sense of obligation, you know."

"But of course. That's how it works. That's why the poor hen works herself to death feeding the greedy cuckoo-chick. It's a form of confidence-trick, the callous exploitation of a natural proclivity. The existence of such a proclivity is important to the continuation of a species, but in this case Ferrelyn must simply refuse to be blackmailed through her better instincts."

"If," said Alan slowly, "if Anthea's child had turned out to be one of them what would you have done?"

"I should have done what I am advising you to do for Ferrelyn. Taken her away. I should also have cut off our connection with Midwich by selling this house, fond as we both are of it. I may have to do that yet, even though she is not directly involved. It depends how the situation develops. One waits to see. The potentialities are unknown, but I don't care for the logical implications. Therefore the sooner Ferrelyn is out of it the happier I shall be. I don't propose to say anything about it to her myself. For one thing it is a matter for you to settle between you; for another, there is the risk that by crystallizing a not very clear misgiving I might do the wrong thing—make it appear as a challenge to be met, for instance. You have a positive alternative to offer. However, if it is difficult and you need something to tip the balance, Anthea and I will back you up quite fully."

Alan nodded slowly.

"I hope that won't be necessary; I don't think it will be. We both know really that we can't just go on like this. Now you've given me a push we'll get it settled."

They continued to sit, in silent contemplation. Alan was aware of some relief that his fragmentary feelings and suspicions had been collected for him into a form which warranted action. He was also considerably impressed, for he could recall no previous conversation with his father-in-law in which Zellaby, spurning one tempting divagation after another, had held so stoutly to his course. Moreover the speculations which could arise were interesting and numerous. He was on the point of raising one or two of them himself when he was checked by the sight of Anthea crossing the lawn toward them.

She sat down in the chair on the other side of her husband and demanded a cigarette. Zellaby gave her one and held out the match. He watched her take the first few puffs.

"Trouble?" he inquired.

"I'm not quite sure. I've just had Margaret Haxby on the telephone. She's left."

Zellaby lifted his eyebrows.

"You mean cleared out?"

"Yes. She was speaking from London."

"Oh," said Zellaby, and lapsed into thought. Alan asked Anthea who Margaret Haxby was.

"Oh, I'm sorry. You probably don't know her. She's one of Mr. Crimm's young ladies—or was. One of the brightest of them, I understand. Academically Dr. Margaret Haxby—Ph.D. London."

"One of the—er—afflicted?" Alan inquired.

"Yes. And one of the most resentful," Anthea said. "Now she's made up her mind and gone, leaving Midwich holding the baby. Literally."

"But where do you come in, my dear?" Zellaby inquired.

"Oh, she just decided I was a reliable subject for official notification. She said she'd have rung Mr. Crimm but he's away today. She wanted to arrange about the baby."

"Where is it now?"

"Where she was staying. In the older Mrs. Dorry's cottage."

"And she's just walked out on it?"

"That's it. Mrs. Dorry doesn't know yet. I'll have to go and tell her."

"This could be awkward," Zellaby said. "I can see a pretty panic starting up among the other women who've taken these girls in. They'll all be throwing them out overnight before they get left in the lurch, too. Can we stall? Give Crimm time to get back and do something? After all, his girls aren't a village responsibility—not primarily, anyway. Besides, she might change her mind."

Anthea shook her head.

"Not this one, I think. She's not done it on the spur of the moment. She's been over it pretty carefully, in fact. Her line is: She never asked to come to Midwich she was simply posted here. If they'd posted her to a yellow-fever area they'd be responsible for the consequences; well, they posted her here and through no fault of her own she caught this instead; now it's up to them to deal with it."

"With the upshot that it is now thrown on the parish, unless she intends to pay for it, of course."

"Naturally, I asked about that. She said that the village and the Grange could fight out the responsibility between them; it certainly was not hers. She will refuse to pay anything, since payment might be legally construed as admission of liability. Nevertheless, Mrs. Dorry, or any other person of good character who cares to take the baby on, will receive a rate of two pounds a week, sent anonymously and irregularly."

"You're right, my dear. She has been thinking it out; this is going to need looking into. What is the effect if this repudiation is allowed to go unchallenged? I imagine legal responsibility for the child has to be established somewhere. How is that done? Get the Relieving-Officer in and slap a court order on her, do you suppose?"

"I don't know, but she's thought of something of the kind happening. If it does, she intends to fight it in court. She claims that medical evidence will establish that the child cannot possibly be hers; from this it will be argued that as she was placed *in loco parentis* without her knowledge and consent, she cannot be held responsible. Failing this, it is still open to her to bring an action against the Ministry for negligence resulting in her being placed in a position of jeopardy; or it might be for conniving at assault; or, possibly, procuring. She isn't sure."

"I should think not," said Zellaby. "It ought to be an interesting indictment to frame."

"Well, she didn't seem to think it was likely to come to that," Anthea admitted.

"I imagine she's perfectly right there," agreed Zellaby. "We

have made our own efforts, but the unperceived official mach-
inations to keep all this quiet must have been quite considerable. Even the evidence brought to dispute a court order
would be manna to journalists of all nations. In fact, the
issue of such an order would probably bring Dr. Haxby a
considerable fortune, one way and another. Poor Mr. Crimm
—and poor Colonel Westcott. They are going to be worried,
I'm afraid. I wonder just what their powers in the matter
are . . . ?" He lapsed into thought for some moments before he went on:

"My dear, I've just been talking to Alan about getting Ferrelyn away. This seems to make it a little more urgent. Once
it becomes generally known, others may decide to follow
Margaret Haxby's example, don't you think?"

"It may make up their minds for some of them," Anthea
agreed.

"In which case, and supposing an inconvenient number
should take the same course, don't you think there is a
possibility of some counter-move to stop more desertions?"

"But if, as you say, they don't want publicity—"

"Not by the authorities, my dear. No, I was wondering
what would happen if it were to turn out that the children
are as opposed to being deserted as they are to being removed."

"But you don't really think—?"

"I don't know. I'm simply doing my best to place myself
in the situation of a young cuckoo. As such I fancy I should
resent anything that appeared likely to lessen attention to my
comfort and well-being. Indeed, one does not even have to
be a cuckoo to feel so. I just air the suggestion, you understand, but I do feel that it is worth making sure that
Ferrelyn is not trapped here if something of the sort should
happen."

"Whether it does or not she'll be better away," Anthea
agreed. "You could start by suggesting two or three weeks
away while we see what happens," she told Alan.

"Very well," Alan said. "It does give me a handle to start
with. Where is she?"

"I left her on the verandah."

The Zellabys watched him cross the lawn and disappear
round a corner of the house. Gordon Zellaby lifted an eyebrow at his wife.

"Not very difficult, I think," Anthea said. "Naturally she's
longing to be with him. The obstacle is her sense of obligation. The conflict is doing her harm, wearing her out."

"How much affection does she really have for the baby?"

"It's hard to say. There is so much social and traditional pressure on a woman in these matters. One's self-defensive instinct is to conform to the approved pattern. Personal honesty takes time to assert itself, if it is ever allowed to."

"Not with Ferrelyn, surely?" Zellaby looked hurt.

"Oh, it will with her, I'm sure. But she hasn't got there yet. It's a bit much to face, you know. She's had all the inconvenience and discomfort of bearing the baby, as much as if it were her own, and now, after that, she has to readjust to the biological fact that it is not, that she is only what you call a 'host-mother' to it. That must take a lot of doing."

She paused, looking thoughtfully across the lawn. "I now say a little prayer of thanksgiving every night," she added. "I don't know where it goes to, but I just want it to be known somewhere how grateful I am."

Zellably reached out and took her hand. After some minutes he observed:

"I wonder if a sillier and more ignorant catachresis than 'Mother Nature' was ever perpetrated? It is because Nature is ruthless, hideous and cruel beyond belief that it was necessary to invent civilization. One thinks of wild animals as savage, but the fiercest of them begins to look almost domesticated when one considers the viciousness required of a survivor in the sea; as for the insects, their lives are sustained only by intricate processes of fantastic horror. There is no conception more fallacious than the sense of cosiness implied by 'Mother Nature.' Each species must strive to survive, and that it will do by every means in its power, however foul, unless the instinct to survive is weakened by conflict with another instinct."

Anthea seized the pause to put in, with a touch of impatience:

"I've no doubt you are gradually working round to something, Gordon."

"Yes," Zellaby owned. "I am working round again to cuckoos. Cuckoos are very determined survivors. So determined that there is really only one thing to be done with them once one's nest is infested. I am, as you know, a humane man; I think I may even say a kindly man by disposition."

"You may, Gordon." She nodded.

"As a further disadvantage, I am a civilized man. For these reasons I shall not be able to bring myself to approve of what ought to be done. Nor, even when we perceive its advisability, will the rest of us. So, like the poor hen-thrush we shall feed and nurture the monster and betray our own species. Odd, don't you think? We could drown a litter of kittens that is no sort of threat to us, but these creatures we shall carefully rear."

Anthea sat motionless for some moments. Then she turned her head and looked at him, long and steadily.

"You *mean* that—about what *ought* to be done, don't you, Gordon?"

"I do, my dear."

"It isn't like you."

"As I pointed out. But then it is a situation I have never been in before. It has occurred to me that 'live and let live' is a piece of patronage which can only be afforded by the consciously secure. I now find, when I feel—as I never expected to feel—my situation at the summit of creation to be threatened, that I don't like it a bit."

"But, Gordon, dear, surely this is all a little exaggerated. After all, a few unusual babies . . ."

"Who can at will produce a neurotic condition in mature women—and don't forget Harriman, too—in order to enforce their wishes."

"It may wear off as they get older. One has heard sometimes of odd understanding, a kind of psychic sympathy . . ."

"In isolated cases, perhaps. But in sixty interconnected cases! No, there's no tender sympathy with these, and they trail no clouds of glory, either. They are the most practical, sensible, self-contained babies anyone ever saw. They are also quite the smuggest, and no wonder—they can get anything they want. Just at present they are still at a stage where they do not want very much, but later on—well, we shall see . . ."

"Doctor Willers says—" his wife began, but Zellaby cut her short impatiently.

"Willers rose to the occasion magnificently, so well that it's not surprising that he's addled himself into behaving like a damned ostrich now. His faith in hysteria has become practically pathological. I hope his holiday will do him good."

"But, Gordon, he does at least *try* to explain it."

"My dear, I am a patient man, but don't try me too far. Willers has never tried to *explain* any of it. He has accepted certain facts when they became inescapable; the rest he has attempted to explain away—which is quite different."

"But there must *be* an explanation."

"Of course."

"Then what do you think it is?"

"We shall have to wait until the children are old enough to give us some evidence."

"But you do have some ideas?"

"Nothing very cheering, I'm afraid."

"But what?"

Zellaby shook his head. "I'm not ready," he said again. "But as you are a discreet woman I will put the question to you. It is this: If you were wishful to challenge the supremacy of a society that was fairly stable and quite well weaponed, what would you do? Would you meet it on its own terms by launching a probably costly, and certainly destructive, assault? Or, if time were of no great importance, would you prefer to employ a version of a more subtle tactic. Would you, in fact, try somehow to introduce a fifth column to attack it from within?"

16 · Matters to Arise

THE NEXT FEW MONTHS saw a number of changes in Midwich.

Ferrelyn departed with Alan, leaving her baby to be looked after, for the present at least, in the Zellaby household. Doctor Willers had handed his practice into the care of the locum who had helped him during the crisis, and gone off, accompanied by Mrs. Willers, for a lengthy and well-earned holiday which was said to be taking him round the world.

More sensational, however, was the evacuation of the Grange which took place at only a few days' notice. The researchers themselves heard about it for the first time on a Monday and began to pack up. On the Wednesday large vans began to arrive and by the weekend the house, and the expensive new laboratories, too, stood blank-windowed, empty and echoing, leaving the villagers with a feeling that they had witnessed a demonstration of pantomime magic. Mr. Crimm vanished with his staff, including two of the girls who had resigned in the early summer and been reinstated later, and when the exodus was finished the only mementos of their presence other than the building itself were one young woman who elected to remain with her baby, and four other golden-eyed babies for whom foster-parents had somehow to be found.

A week later a desiccated-looking couple called Freeman, accompanied by a seventeen-year-old daughter who gave promise of being scarcely less parched, moved into the cottage vacated by Mr. Crimm. Freeman introduced himself as a medical man specializing in social psychology, and his wife, too, it appeared, was a doctor of medicine. We were led to understand, in a cautious way, that their purpose was to study the development of the children on behalf of an unspecified official body. This, after their own fashion, they presumably did, for they were continually lurking and peering about the village, often insinuating themselves into the cottages, and not infrequently to be found on one of the seats on the Green pondering weightily and watchfully. They had an aggressive discretion which verged upon the conspiratorial, and tactics which within a week of their arrival caused them to be generally resented and referred to as the Noseys. Doggedness, however, was another of their characteristics, and they persisted in the face of discouragement until they gained the kind of acceptance accorded to the inevitable.

I checked on them with Bernard. He said they were nothing to do with his department, but their appointment was authentic. We felt that if they were to be the only outcome of Willers' anxiety for study of the Children it was as well that he was away.

Zellaby offered, as indeed did all of us, a few cooperative overtures to them, but made no headway. Whatever department was employing them had picked winners for discretion, but we felt that, importantly as discretion might be regarded in the larger sphere, a little more sociability within the community could have brought them fuller information with less effort. Still, they *might*, for all we knew, be turning in useful reports somewhere. All we could do was let them prowl in their chosen fashion.

However interesting scientifically the Children may have been during the first year of their lives there was little about them during that time to cause further misgiving. Apart from their continued resistance to any attempt to remove any of them from Midwich, the reminders of their compulsive powers were mostly mild and infrequent. They were, as Zellaby had said, remarkably sensible and self-sufficient babies—as long as nobody neglected them, or crossed their wishes. With two exceptions their health was so good as to be almost monotonous. The two exceptions were somewhat sickly girls who finally took some virus infection shortly before Christmas and succumbed to it in a few hours.

There was very little about them at this stage to support the ominous ruminations of the beldame group or, for that matter, the differently cast but scarcely less gloomy prognostications of Zellaby himself; and as the time passed with unexpected placidity Janet and I were not the only ones who began to wonder whether we had not all been misled, and if the unusual qualities in the Children were not fading, perhaps to dwindle into insignificance as they should grow older.

And then, in the following summer, Zellaby made a discovery which, as far as anyone in Midwich knew, appeared to have escaped the Freemans, for all their conscientious watching.

Gordon Zellaby turned up at our cottage one sunny afternoon and ruthlessly routed us out. I protested at having my work interrupted, but he was not to be put off.

"I know, my dear fellow, I know. I have a picture of my own publisher with tears in his eyes. But this is important. I need reliable witnesses."

"Of what?" inquired Janet, with little enthusiasm. But Zellaby shook his head.

"I am making no leading statements, incubating no germs. I am simply asking you to watch an experiment and draw your own conclusions. Now here," he fumbled in his pockets, "is our apparatus."

He laid on the table a small ornamental wooden box about half as big again as a matchbox, and one of those puzzles consisting of two large nails so bent that they are linked together, but will, when held in the right positions, slide easily apart. He picked up the wooden box and shook it. Something rattled inside.

"Barley-sugar," he explained. "This is one of the products of feckless Nipponese ingenuity. It has no visible means of opening, but slide aside this bit of the marquetry here and it opens without difficulty, and here's your barley-sugar. Why anybody should trouble himself to construct such a thing is known only to the Japanese, but for us it will, I think, turn out to have a useful purpose after all. Now, which of the Children, male, shall we try it on first?"

"None of these babies is quite one year old yet," Janet pointed out, a little chillingly.

"In every respect except that of actual duration they are, as you very well know, quite well-developed two-year-olds," Zellaby countered. "And in any case, what I am proposing is not exactly an intelligence test. Or, is it?" He broke off uncertainly. "I must admit that I'm not sure about that. However, it doesn't greatly matter. Just name the child."

"All right. Mrs. Brant's," said Janet. So to Mrs. Brant's we went.

Mrs. Brant showed us through into her small back garden where the child was in a play-pen on the lawn. He looked, as Zellaby had pointed out, every bit of two years old and brightly intelligent at that. Zellaby gave him the little box. The boy took it, looked at it, found that it rattled and shook it delightedly. We watched him decide that it must be a box and try unsuccessfully to open it. Zellaby let him go on playing with it for a bit, and then produced a piece of barley-sugar and traded it for the return of his box, still unopened.

"I don't see what that's supposed to show," Janet said, as we left.

"Patience, my dear," Zellaby said, reprovingly. "Which shall we try next, male again?"

Janet suggested the vicarage as convenient. Zellaby shook his head.

"No that won't do. Polly Rushton's baby girl would very likely be on hand, too."

"Does that matter? It all seems very mysterious," said Janet.

"I want my witnesses satisfied," said Zellaby. "Try another."

We settled for the elder Mrs. Dorry's. There he went through the same performance, but after playing with the box a little the child offered it back to him, looking up expectantly. Zellaby, however, did not take it from him. Instead, he showed the child how to open the box, and then let him do it for himself and take out the sweet. Zellaby thereupon put another piece of barley-sugar in the box, closed it and presently handed it to him again.

"Try once more," he suggested, and we watched the little boy open it easily and achieve a second sweet.

"Now," said Zellaby as we left, "we go back to Exhibit One, the Brant child."

In Mrs. Brant's garden again he presented the child in the play-pen with the box, just as he had before. The child took it eagerly. Without the least hesitation he found and slid back the movable bit of marquetry and extracted the sweet, as if he had done it a dozen times before. Zellaby looked at our dumbfounded expressions with an amused twinkle. Once more he retrieved and reloaded the box.

"Well," he said, "name another boy."

We visited three, up and down the village. None of them showed the least puzzlement over the box. They opened it as if it were perfectly familiar to them, and made sure of the contents without delay.

"Interesting, isn't it?" remarked Zellaby. "Now let's start on the girls."

We went through the same procedure again except that this time it was to the third, instead of to the second, child that he showed the secret of opening the box. After that, matters went just as before.

"Fascinating, don't you think?" beamed Zellaby. "Like to try them with the nail-puzzle?"

"Later, perhaps," Janet told him. "Just at present I should like some tea." So we took him back with us to the cottage.

"That box idea was a good one," Zellaby congratulated himself modestly, while wolfing a cucumber sandwich. "Simple, incontestable, and went off without a hitch, too."

"Does that mean you've been trying other ideas on them?" Janet inquired.

"Oh, quite a number. Some of them were a bit too complicated, though, and others not fully conclusive. Besides I hadn't got hold of the right end of the stick to begin with."

"Are you quite sure you have now? Because I'm not at all sure that I have," Janet told him. He looked at her.

"I rather think you do understand," he said, "and that Richard does, too. You don't need to be shy of admitting it."

He helped himself to another sandwich, and looked inquiringly at me.

"I suppose," I told him, "that you are wanting me to say that your experiment has shown that what one of the boys knows, all the boys know, though the girls do not, and vice versa. All right then, that *is* what it appears to show—unless there is a catch somewhere."

"My dear fellow—!"

"Well, you must admit that what it *appears* to show is a little more than anyone is likely to be able to swallow at one gulp."

"I see. Yes. Of course, I myself arrived at it by stages," he nodded.

"But," I said, "it *is* what we were intended to infer?"

"Of course, my dear fellow. Could it be clearer?" He took

the linked nails from his pocket and dropped them on the table. "Take these, and try for yourselves. Or, better still, devise your own little test, and apply it. You'll find the inference—at least the preliminary inference—inescapable."

"To appreciate takes longer than to grasp," I said, "but let's regard it as a hypothesis which I accept for the moment—"

"Wait a minute," put in Janet. "Mr. Zellaby, are you claiming that if I were to tell anything to any one of the boys, all the rest would know it?"

"Certainly—provided, of course, that it was something simple enough for them to understand at this stage."

Janet looked highly skeptical.

Zellaby sighed.

"The old trouble," he said. "Lynch Darwin and you show the impossibility of evolution. But, as I said, you've only to apply your own tests." He turned back to me. "You were allowing the hypothesis . . ?" he suggested.

"Yes," I agreed, "and you said that was the *preliminary* inference. What is the next one?"

"I should have thought that just that one contained implications enough to capsize our social system."

"Couldn't this be just a more developed form of the sort of sympathetic understanding that's sometimes found between twins?" Janet asked.

Zellaby shook his head.

"I think not—or else it has developed far enough to have acquired new features. Besides, we don't have here one single group *en rapport;* we have two separate groups of rapport, apparently without cross-connections. Now if that is so, and we have seen that it is, the question immediately presents itself: to what extent is any of these Children an individual? Each is physically an individual, as we can see. But is he so in other ways? If he is sharing consciousness with the rest of the group, instead of having to communicate with others with difficulty as we do, can he be said to have a mind of his own, a separate personality as we understand it? I don't see that he can. It seems perfectly clear that if A, B and C share a common consciousness, then what A expresses is also what B and C are thinking, and that any action taken by B in particular circumstances is exactly that which would be taken by A and C in those circumstances—subject only to modifications arising from physical differences between them, which may, in fact, be considerable insofar as conduct is very susceptible to conditions of the glands and other factors in the physical individual.

"In other words if I ask a question of any of these boys I shall get exactly the same answer whichever I choose to ask. If I ask him to perform an action, I shall get more or less the same result, but it is likely to be more successful with some who happen to have better physical co-ordination than others; though in point of fact with such close similarity as there is among the Children the variation will be small.

"But my point is this: it will not be an individual who answers me or performs what I ask, it will be an item of the group. And in that alone lie plenty of further questions and implications."

Janet was frowning. "I still don't quite—"

"Let me put it differently," said Zellaby. "What we *seem* to have here is fifty-eight little individual entities. But appearances are deceptive, and we now find that what we actually have are two individuals only—*a* boy and *a* girl—though the boy has thirty component parts with the physical structure and appearance of individual boys; and the girl has twenty-eight component parts."

There was a pause.

"I find that rather hard to take," said Janet, with careful understatement.

"Yes, of course," agreed Zellaby. "So did I."

"Look here," I said. "You are putting this forward as a serious proposition? I mean, it isn't just a dramatic manner of speaking?"

"I am stating a fact—having shown you the evidence first."

I shook my head. "All you showed us was that they are able to communicate in some way that I don't understand. To proceed from that to your theory of non-individualism is too much of a jump."

"On that piece of evidence, perhaps so. But you must remember that though this is the first you have seen, I have already conducted a number of tests, and not one of them has contradicted the idea of what I prefer to call multiple-individualism. Moreover, it is not as strange as it appears at first sight. It is quite a well established evolutionary dodge for getting round a shortcoming. A number of forms that appear at first sight to be individuals turn out to be colonies, and many forms cannot survive at all unless they create colonies which operate as individuals. Admittedly the best examples are among the lower forms, but there's no reason why it should be confined to them. Many of the insects come pretty near it. The laws of physics prevent them increasing in size, so they contrive greater efficiency by acting as a group.

We ourselves combine in groups consciously instead of by instinct for the same purpose. Very well, why shouldn't nature produce a more efficient version of the method by which we clumsily contrive to overcome our own weakness? Another case of nature copying art, perhaps?

"After all, we are up against the barriers to further development, and have been for some time. Unless we are to stagnate we must find some way of getting round them. If we don't evolve we shall die out, like the big reptiles. G.B.S. proposed, you will remember, that the first step should be to extend the term of human life to three hundred years. That might be one way—and no doubt the extension of individual life would have a strong appeal to so determined an individualist—but there are others, and though this is not perhaps a line of evolution one would expect to find among the higher animals, it is obviously not impracticable. Of course, that is by no means to say that it is bound to be successful."

A quick glance at Janet's expression showed me that she had dropped out. When she has decided that someone is talking nonsense she makes a quick decision to waste no more effort upon it and pulls down an impervious mental curtain. I went on pondering, looking out of the window.

"I feel, I think," I said presently, "rather like a chameleon placed on a color it can't quite manage. If I have followed you, you are saying that in each of these two groups the minds are in some way pooled. Would that imply that the boys have, collectively, a normal brain-power multiplied by thirty, and the girls have it multiplied by twenty-eight?"

"I think not," said Zellaby, quite seriously, "and it certainly does not mean normal abilities to the power of thirty, thank heaven; that would be beyond any comprehension. It does appear to mean multiplication of intelligence in some degree, but at their present stage I don't see how that can be estimated, if it ever could be. That may portend tremendous things. But what seems to me of more immediate importance is the degree of will power that has been produced; the potentialities of that strike me as very serious indeed. One has no idea how these compulsions are exerted, but I fancy that if it can be explored we might find that when a certain degree of will is, so to speak, concentrated in one vessel a Hegelian change takes place—that is, that over a critical quantity it begins to display a new quality. In this case, a power of direct imposition. That, however, I frankly admit is speculative; and I can now foresee a devil of a lot to speculate about and investigate."

"The whole thing sounds incredibly complicated to me, if you are right."

"In detail, in the mechanics, yes," Zellaby admitted, "but in principle, I think not nearly so much so as would appear at first sight. After all, you would agree that the essential quality of man is the embodiment of a spirit?"

"Certainly."

"Well, a spirit is a living force; therefore it is not static, it must either evolve or atrophy. Evolution of a spirit assumes the eventual development of a greater spirit. Suppose, then, that this greater spirit, this super spirit, is attempting to make its appearance on the scene. Where is it to dwell? The ordinary man is not constructed to contain it; the superman does not exist to house it. Might it not, then, for lack of a suitable single vehicle, form a group—rather like an encyclopedia grown too large for one volume? I don't know. But if it is so, then two super-spirits, residing in two groups, is no less probable."

He paused, looking out of the open windows, watching a bumble-bee fly from one lavender-head to another, then he added reflectively:

"I have wondered about these two groups quite a lot. I have even felt that there ought to be names for these two super-spirits. One would imagine there were plenty of names to choose from, and yet I find just two out of them all persistently invading my mind. Somehow I keep on thinking of —Adam and Eve."

Two or three days later I had a letter telling me that the job I had been angling for in Canada could be mine if I sailed without delay. I did, leaving Janet to clear things up and follow me.

When she arrived she had little more news of Midwich except for a rather one-sided feud which had broken out between the Freemans and Zellaby.

Zellaby, it appeared, had told Bernard Westcott of his findings. An inquiry for further particulars had reached the Freemans, to whom the whole idea came as a novelty and one which they instinctively opposed. They at once instituted tests of their own, and were seen to be growing gloomier as they proceeded.

"But at least I imagine they'll stop short of Adam and Eve," she added. "Really, old Zellaby! The thing I shall never cease to be thankful for was that we happened to go to London when we did. Just fancy if I'd become the mother of a thirty-first part of an Adam, or a twenty-ninth part of an Eve. It's been bad enough as it is, and thank goodness we're out of it. I've had enough of Midwich and I don't care if I never hear of the place again."

PART TWO

17 · Now We Are Nine

DURING THE NEXT FEW YEARS such visits as we managed were brief and hurried, spent entirely in dashing from one lot of relatives to another, with interludes to improve business contacts. I never went anywhere near Midwich, nor indeed thought much about it. But in the eighth summer after we had left I managed a six-week spell, and at the end of the first week I ran into Bernard Westcott one day in Piccadilly, by chance.

We went to the In and Out for a drink. In the course of chat I asked him about Midwich. I think I expected to hear that the whole thing had fizzled out, for on the few occasions I had recalled the place lately, it and its inhabitants had the improbability of a tale once realistic, but now unconvincing. I was more than half-ready to hear that the Children no longer trailed clouds of anything unconventional, that, as so often with suspected genius, expectations had never flowered and that, for all their beginnings and indicatives, they had become an ordinary gang of village children, with only their looks to distinguish them.

Bernard considered for a moment, then he said:

"As it happens, I have to go down there tomorrow. Would you care to come for the run, renew old acquaintance and so on?"

Janet had gone north to stay with an old school friend for a week, leaving me on my own, with nothing particular to do.

"So you do still keep an eye on the place? Yes, I'd like to come and have a few words with them. Zellaby's still alive and well?"

"Oh, yes. He's that rather desiccated type that seems set to go on forever unchanged."

"The last time I saw him—apart from our farewell—he was

121

off on a weird tack about composite personality," I recalled. "An old spellbinder. He manages to make the most exotic conceptions sound perfectly feasible while he's talking. Something about Adam and Eve, I remember."

"You won't find much difference there," Bernard told me, but did not pursue that line. Instead he went on: "My own business there is a bit morbid I'm afraid—an inquest—but that needn't interfere with you."

"One of the Children?" I asked.

"No," he shook his head. "A motor accident to a local boy called Pawle."

"Pawle," I repeated. "Oh, yes, I remember. They've a farm a bit outside, nearer to Oppley."

"That's it. Dacre farm. Tragic business."

It seemed intrusive to ask what interest he could have in the inquest, so I did not pursue it, and let him switch the conversation to my Canadian experiences.

The next morning, with a fine summer's day already well begun, we set off soon after breakfast. In the car he apparently felt at liberty to talk more freely than he had at the club.

"You'll find a few changes in Midwich," he warned me. "Your old cottage is now occupied by a couple called Welton; he etches, and his wife throws pots. It seems a precarious way of living to me, but at least they are their own masters, and seem to scrape along somehow. I can't remember who is in Crimm's place at the moment; there's been quite a succession of people since the Freemans. But what's going to surprise you most is the Grange. The board outside has been re-painted; it now reads: 'Midwich Grange—Special School— Ministry of Education.' "

"Oh? The Children?" I asked.

"Exactly." He nodded. "Zellaby's 'exotic conception' was a lot less exotic than it seemed. In fact, it was a bull's-eye —to the great discomfiture of the Freemans. It showed them up so thoroughly that they had to clear out to hide their faces."

"You mean his Adam and Eve stuff?" I said incredulously.

"Not that exactly. I mean the two mental groups. It was soon proved that there was this rapport; everything supported that, and it continued. At just over two years old one of the boys learned to read simple words—"

"At two!" I exclaimed.

"Quite the equivalent of any other child's four," he re- minded me. "And the next day it was found that any of the boys could read them. From then on the progress was amazing. It was some weeks later before one of the girls learned to read, but when she did, all the rest of them could, too. Later on, one boy learned to ride a bicycle; right away any of them could do it competently, first shot. Mrs. Brinkman taught her girl to swim; all the rest of the girls were immediately able to swim; but the boys could not until one of them got the trick of it, then the rest could. Oh, from the moment Zellaby pointed it out there was no doubt about it. The thing there has been—and still is—a whole series of rows about, on all levels, is his deduction that each group represents an individual. Not many people will wear that one. A high degree of mutual sensitivity, yes; a number of units with a form of communication not yet clearly understood, perhaps; but a single unit informing physically independent parts, no. There's precious little support for that."

I was not greatly surprised to hear it, but he was going on:

"Anyway, the arguments are chiefly academic. The point is that, however it happens, they *do* have this rapport within the groups. Well, sending them to any ordinary school was obviously out of the question; there'd be tales about them all over the place in a few days if they'd just turned up at Oppley or Stouch schools. So that brought in the Ministry of Education, with the result that the Grange was opened up as a kind of school-cum-welfare-center-cum-social-observatory for them.

"That has worked better than we expected. Even when you were here it was pretty obvious they were going to be a problem later on. They have a different sense of community; their ties to one another are far more important to them than any feeling for the ordinary homes. Some of the homes resented them pretty much, too—they can't really become one of the family, they're too different; they were little good as company for the true children of the family, and the difficulties looked like growing. Somebody at the Grange had the idea of starting dormitories there for them. There was no pressure, no persuasion—they could just move in if they wanted to, and a dozen or more did, quite soon. Then others gradually joined them. It was rather as if they were beginning to learn that they could not have a great deal in common with the rest of the village, and so gravitated naturally toward a group of their own kind."

"It sounds an odd arrangement. What did the village people think of it?" I asked.

"There was disapproval from some, of course, more from convention than conviction, really. A lot of them were relieved to lose a responsibility that had rather scared them, though they didn't feel it proper to admit it. Where the mothers feel affectionately for them the Children keep on good terms and are in and out of the houses as they like. Some others of the Children have made a complete break."

"It sounds the queerest set-up I ever heard of," I said. "What do they do at the Grange?"

"Primarily it is a school, as it says. They have teaching and welfare staff as well as social psychologists, and so on. They also have quite eminent teachers visiting and giving short courses in various subjects. At first they used to hold classes like an ordinary school, until it occurred to somebody that that wasn't necessary. So now any lesson is attended by one boy and one girl, and all the rest know what those two have been taught. And it doesn't have to be one lesson at a time, either. Teach six couples different subjects simultaneously, and they somehow sort it out so that it works the same way."

"But, good heavens, they must be mopping up knowledge like blotting-paper, at that rate."

"They are indeed. It seems to give some of the teachers a touch of jitters."

"And yet you still manage to keep their existence quiet?"

"On the popular level, yes. There is still an understanding with the Press; and, anyway, the story hasn't nearly the possibilities now that it would have had in the early stages, from their point of view. As for the surrounding district, that has involved a certain amount of undercover work. The local reputation of Midwich was never very high—an ingenuous neighborhood is perhaps the kindest way of putting it. Well, with a little helping on we've got it still lower. It is now regarded by the neighboring villages, so Zellaby assures me, as a kind of mental home without bars. Everybody there, it is known, was affected by the Dayout; particularly the Children who are spoken of as 'daytouched'—an almost exact synonym of 'moonstruck'—and are retarded to such an extent that a humane government has found it necessary to provide a special school for them. Oh, yes, we've got it pretty well established as a local deficiency area. There is occasional gossip; but it is accepted as an unfortunate affliction and not a matter that we advertise to the outside world."

"It must," I said, "have involved quite a deal of engineering and maintenance. What I never understood, and still don't understand, is why you were, and apparently are, so concerned to keep the matter quiet. Security at the time of the Dayout is understandable—something made an unauthorized landing; that was a Service concern. But now . . . ? All this trouble to keep the Children hidden away still. This queer arrangement at the Grange. A special school like that couldn't be run for a few pounds a year."

"You don't think that the Welfare State should show so much concern for its responsibilities?" he suggested.

"Come off it, Bernard," I told him.

But he did not. Though he went on talking of the Children and the state of affairs in Midwich he continued to avoid any answer to the question I had raised.

We lunched early at Trayne, and ran into Midwich a little after two. I found the place looking utterly unchanged. It might have been a week that had passed instead of eight years since I last saw it. Already there was quite a crowd waiting at the Green outside the hall where the inquest was to be held.

"It looks," Bernard said as he parked the car, "it looks as if you had better postpone your calls until later. Practically the whole place seems to be here."

"Will it take long, do you think?" I inquired.

"Should be purely routine. Probably all over in half an hour."

"Are you giving evidence?" I asked, wondering why if it was to be so routine he should bother to come all the way from London for it.

"No. Just keeping an eye on things," he said.

I decided that he had been right about postponing my calls, and followed him into the hall. As the place filled up, and I watched the familiar figures trooping in and finding seats, there could be no doubt that almost every mobile person in the place had chosen to attend. I did not quite understand why. Young Jim Pawle, the casualty, was known to them all, of course, but that did not seem quite to account for it, and certainly did not account for the feeling of tension which inescapably pervaded the hall. I could not, after a few minutes, believe that the proceedings were going to be as cut and dried as Bernard had predicted. I had a sense of waiting for an outburst of some kind from someone in the crowd.

But none came. The proceedings were routine, and brief, too. It was all over inside half an hour.

I saw Zellaby slip out quickly as the meeting closed. We found him standing by the steps outside watching us emerge. He greeted me as if we had last met a couple of days ago, and then said:

"How do you come into this? I thought you were in India."

"Canada," I said. "It's accidental." And explained that Bernard had brought me down.

Zellaby turned to look at Bernard.

"Satisfied?" he asked.

Bernard shrugged slightly. "What else?" he asked enigmatically.

At that moment a boy and girl passed us, and walked up the road among the dispersing crowd. I had only time for a glimpse of their faces, and stared after them in astonishment.

"Surely, they can't be . . . ?" I began.

"They are," Zellaby said. "Didn't you see their eyes?"

"But it's preposterous! Why, they're only nine years old!"

"By the calendar," Zellaby agreed.

I gazed after them as they strode along.

"But it's—it's unbelievable!"

"The unbelievable is, as you will recall, rather more prone to realization in Midwich than in other places," Zellaby observed. "The improbable we can now assimilate at once; the incredible takes a little longer, but we have learned to achieve it. Didn't the Colonel warn you?"

"In a way," I admitted. "But those two! They look fully sixteen or seventeen."

"Physically, I am assured, they are."

I kept my eyes on them, still unwilling to accept it.

"If you are in no hurry come up to the house and have tea," Zellaby suggested.

Bernard, after a glance at me, offered the use of his car.

"All right," said Zellaby, "but take it carefully after what you've just heard."

"I'm not a dangerous driver," said Bernard.

"Nor was young Pawle; he was a *good* driver, too," replied Zellaby.

A little way up the drive we came in sight of Kyle Manor at rest in the afternoon sun. I said:

"The first time I saw it it was looking just like this. I remember thinking that when I got a little closer I should hear it purring, and that's been the way I've seen it ever since."

Zellaby nodded. "When I saw it first it seemed to me a good place to end one's days in tranquility, but now the tranquility is, I think, questionable."

I let that go. We ran past the front of the house and parked round the side by the stables. Zellaby led the way to the verandah. We refused drinks in favor of waiting for tea. He waved us to cushioned cane chairs.

"Anthea's out at the moment, but she promised to be back for tea," he said.

I leaned back, absorbing the scene with satisfaction. Zellaby said to Bernard:

"So you're satisfied. You think it will end there?"

"I hope so. Nothing could be undone. The wise course was to accept the verdict, and they did," Bernard told him.

"H'm," said Zellaby. He turned to me. "What, as a detached observer, did you think of our little charade this afternoon?"

"I don't—oh, the inquest, you mean. There seemed to be a bit of an atmosphere, but the proceedings appeared to me to be in good enough order. The boy was driving carelessly. He hit a pedestrian. Then, very foolishly, he got the wind up and tried to make a getaway. He was accelerating too fast to take the corner by the church and as a result he piled up against the wall. Are you suggesting that 'accidental death' doesn't cover it? One might call it misadventure, but it comes to the same thing."

"There was misadventure all right," Zellaby said, "but it scarcely comes to the same thing. Let me tell you what happened—I've only been able to give a brief account to the Colonel yet. . . ."

Gordon Zellaby had been taking his afternoon stroll. "At my time of life," he explained, "the sight of an easy chair after luncheon has to be avoided." The walk, therefore, was a well-established habit. Usually he enjoyed it; at other times, when pressure of the current Work lay on his thoughts, he could not say for certain whether he had been out or not, but assumed that custom had guided him. This particular afternoon, however, had found him almost fully extravert, greeting such of his neighbors as he chanced to meet with amiable benevolence, and even recalling their names.

The nine years since the Midwich Dayout had treated him kindly. The fine silver hair was still as thick, and still as lucent in the August sunshine. The wrinkles about his eyes and the lines on his face were only infinitesimally deeper, and if his lanky figure had become a little sparser it was not by a matter of more than four or five pounds.

Coming out of the village he turned unhurriedly up Hickham Lane, passed the entrance to the Grange drive, climbed the stile on the left and made his way across a couple of fields to St. Accius' Abbey. There, sitting on a sun-dried slab of fallen masonry, he paused to smoke a cigarette. Then he went on across the footbridge over the little stream that had once supplied the brothers' fishpond, took the path back to the Oppley road, and so began to re-approach Midwich.

As he was completing his loop by nearing the turn to Hickham Lane again, four of the Children emerged from it, and made toward the village, walking strung out in a line, ahead of him.

Zellaby studied them with the interest that had never lessened. There were three of the boys, and a girl. The boys were so closely alike that he could not have identified them had he tried, but he had long given up what he regarded as the pointless effort of trying. The girl, too, might as far as he was concerned, have been any of the twenty-eight girls. His inability to distinguish one from another was a shortcoming shared with most of the village—though some of the women seemed genuinely to be seldom in doubt—but unlike the majority he never could feel that it greatly mattered. The Children themselves did not seem to mind in the least, and he was on good terms with both groups.

As always he marveled that they could have crammed so much development into so short a time. That alone set them apart as a different species. It was not simply a matter of maturing early; it was development at almost twice normal speed. Perhaps they were a little light in structure compared with normal children of the same apparent age and height, but it was a lightness of type; there was not the least suggestion of weediness or overgrowth.

As always, too, he found himself wishing he could know them better and learn more of them. It was not for lack of trying that he had made so little headway. He had tried patiently and persistently ever since they were small. They accepted him as much as they accepted anyone and he, for his part, probably understood them quite as well as, if not better than, any of their mentors at the Grange. Superficially they were friendly with him, which they were not with many; they were willing to talk with him and to listen, to be amused, and to learn. But it never went further than the superficial and he had a feeling that it never would. Always, quite close under the surface there was a barrier. Such understanding as passed between himself and them was curiously partial and impersonal; it lacked the dimension of feeling and sympathy. Their real lives seemed to be lived in a world of their own. They were interested, they learned, but one had the feeling that they were simply collecting knowledge—somewhat, perhaps, as a juggler acquires a useful skill which, however he may excel with it, has no influence whatever upon him as a person. Zellaby wondered if anyone would get closer to them. The people up at the Grange were an unforthcoming lot, but from what he had been able to discover even the most assiduous were held back by the same barrier.

Watching the Children walking ahead, talking among themselves, he suddenly found himself wondering whether one of them was Ferrelyn's boy. It really did seem a little reprehensible to be unable to distinguish the boy to whom, according to the register, he was grandfather. It rather bracketed one with Miss Ogle, who got round the difficulty by taking it for granted that any of the boys she happened to meet was her son—and the odd thing about that was that they never disillusioned her.

Presently the quartet in front rounded a corner and passed out of his sight. He had just reached the corner himself when a car overtook him, and he had, therefore, a clear view of all that followed.

The car, a small, open two-seater, was not traveling fast, but it happened that just round the corner and shielded from sight by it the Children had stopped. They appeared, still strung out across the road, to be debating which way they should go.

The driver did his best. He pulled hard over to the right in an attempt to avoid them, and all but succeeded. Another six inches and he would have missed them entirely. But he could not make the extra inches. His front wheel caught the outermost boy and flung him across the road against the fence of a cottage garden.

There was a moment of tableau which remained quite static in Zellaby's mind. The boy against the fence, the three other Children frozen where they stood, the young man in the car in the act of straightening his wheels again, still braking.

Whether the car actually came to a stop Zellaby could never be sure; if it did it was for the barest instant, then the engine roared.

The car sprang forward. The driver changed gears and put his foot down again, keeping straight ahead. He made no attempt whatever to take the corner to the left. The car was still accelerating when it hit the churchyard wall. It smashed to smithereens and hurled its driver headlong against the wall itself.

People shouted, and the few who were near started running toward the wreckage. Zellaby did not move. He stood

half-stunned as he watched the yellow flames leap out and
the black smoke start to pour upward. Then, with stiff movements, he turned to look at the Children. They, too, were
staring at the wreck, a similar tense expression on each face.
He had only a glimpse of it before the three of them turned
to the boy who lay by the fence groaning.

Zellaby became aware that he was trembling. He walked
on a few yards, unsteadily, until he reached a seat by the
edge of the Green. There he sat down and leaned back, pale
in the face, feeling ill, and waiting for the trembling to sub-
side.

Presently, when he was feeling a little steadier, he made
his way to the back door of the Scythe and Stone. Mrs. Williams' air was defensive as she opened it, but at the sight of
his face she asked him in and shut the door behind him.

"Sit there, sir. I'll get you some brandy," she told him.

"Thank you," said Zellaby. "It could be quite a strong one,
please, Mrs. Williams."

She handed him the glass with only a little soda added. He
drank half the contents off and rested his forehead on his left
hand. When he was somewhat recovered he finished the drink
and held the glass out to her.

"Just a small one this time," he said.

When she returned he was lighting a cigarette with a hand
that still shook, but some color was coming into his face.

"You saw it, then, sir?" she asked.

He nodded. "Yes, I saw it, Mrs. Williams, but I didn't see
who it was in the car."

"Young Jim Pawle, it was, from Dacre Farm, just this side
of Oppley."

Gordon Zellaby shook his head.

"I know him, a nice lad."

She nodded.

"Yes, sir. A good boy, Jim. Not one of the wild ones. I
can't think what he was doing driving mad in the village.
Not like him at all. He always drove sensible, did Jim."

"You didn't see it all, then?" Zellaby asked.

"I heard the car come roaring past and I thought, that's
mad, that is. And then I looked out of the window just in
time to see it hit the wall. People started running, and somebody called out that it was Jim Pawle."

Zellaby sipped his drink and drew at his cigarette.

"Before that he hit one of the Children," he said flatly.
Then, remembering that Mrs. Williams' Dayout child had been

a girl, he added: "One of the boys—not very badly, I imagine, but he knocked him across the road."

"One of the Children—" she repeated. She broke off. Her expression changed. "Oh, my God, sir! You don't mean . . . ? Oh, no, they couldn't've . . ." She stared at him, letting the sentence trail away.

Zellaby was recovering, though he still looked several years older than he had an hour before. He swirled the remaining brandy round and watched it spin in the glass.

"Other people saw it, too," he said. "Ask them how it was." He finished off the brandy. "It's never too late to learn, though the process becomes more painful. Perhaps I should have found it less upsetting if at some previous stage of my quite long life I had had the opportunity of witnessing deliberate murder. . . ."

When he finished I looked from him to Bernard. There was no lead whatever in Bernard's expression.

"You're suggesting that the Children did it, that they *made* him drive into that wall?"

"I'm not suggesting," said Zellaby with a regretful shake of his head, "I'm stating. They *did* it, just as surely as they *made* their mothers bring them back here."

"But the witnesses, the ones who gave evidence . . . ?"

"They're perfectly well aware of what happened. They only had to say what they actually *saw*."

"But if they know it's as you claim?"

"Well, what then? What would you have said if you had known, and happened to be called as a witness? In an affair such as this there has to be a verdict acceptable to authority —acceptable, that means, to our well-known figment, the reasonable man. Suppose that they had somehow managed to get a verdict that the boy was willed to kill himself; do you imagine that would stand? Of course it wouldn't. There'd have to be a second inquest called to bring in a 'reasonable' verdict, which would be the verdict we now have, so why should the witnesses run the risk of being thought unreliable, or superstitious, for nothing?

"If you want evidence that they would be, take a look at your own attitude now. You know that I have some little reputation through my books, and you know me personally, but how much is that worth against the thought-habits of the 'reasonable man'? So little that when I tell you what actually occurred your immediate reaction is to try to find ways in which what appeared to me to have occurred could

not in actual fact have done so. You really ought to have
more sense, my dear fellow. After all you were here when
those Children forced their mothers to come back."

"That wasn't quite on a level with what you are telling me
now," I objected.

"No? Would you care to explain the essential difference between being forced into the distasteful, and being forced into
the fatal? Come, come, my dear fellow, since you've been
away you have lost touch with improbability. You've been
blunted by rationality. Here, the unorthodox is to be found
on one's doorstep almost every morning."

I took an opportunity to lead away from the topic of the
inquest.

"To an extent which has caused Willers to abandon his
championship of hysteria?" I asked.

"He abandoned that some little time before he died," Zella-
aby replied.

I was taken aback. I had meant to ask Bernard about the
doctor, but the intention had been mislaid in our talk.

"I'd no idea he was dead. He wasn't much over fifty, was
he? How did it happen?"

"He took an overdose of some barbiturate drug."

"He—you don't mean . . . ? But Willers wasn't that sort!"

"I agree," said Zellaby. "The official verdict was that 'the
balance of his mind was disturbed.' A kindly meant phrase,
no doubt, but not explanatory. Indeed, one can think of
minds so steady that disturbance would be a positive benefit.
The truth is, of course, that nobody had the least idea
why he did it. Certainly not poor Mrs. Willers. But it had
to suffice." He paused, and then added: "It was not until I
realized what the verdict on young Pawle would have to be
that I began to wonder about Willers."

"Surely you don't think it was the Children?" I said.

"I don't know. You yourself said Willers was not that sort.
Now it has suddenly been revealed that we live much more
precariously here than we had thought. That is a shock.

"One has to realize that though it was the Pawle boy who
came round the corner at that fatal moment it might as easily
have been Anthea, or anyone else. It suddenly becomes clear
that she, or I, or any of us may accidentally do something
to harm or anger the Children at any moment. There's no
blame attached to that poor boy. He tried his very best to
avoid hitting any of them, but he couldn't. And in a flare of
anger and revenge they killed him for it.

"So one is faced with a decision. For myself—well, I

NOW WE ARE NINE • 133

don't suppose I have a great deal longer to live in any case, and this is by far the most interesting thing that has ever come my way. I want very much to see how it goes. But Anthea is still quite a young woman, and Michael is still dependent on her, too. . . ."

"Are you seriously thinking of leaving here?" Bernard put in.

Zellaby frowned. "We have already sent Michael away, but I can't quite decide whether the moment has arrived for Anthea to go, too.

"These last few years have been like living on the slopes of an active volcano. Reason tells one that a force is building up inside and that sooner or later there must be an eruption. But time passes with no more than an occasional tremor, so that one begins to tell oneself that the eruption which appeared inevitable may, perhaps, not come after all. One becomes uncertain. I ask myself: is this business of the Pawle boy just a bigger tremor, or is it the first sign of the eruption? I do not know."

Anthea Zellaby, looking very little changed since I had last seen her, emerged from the house onto the verandah a few minutes later. She was so clearly preoccupied that her attention was only brought to bear on us with a visible effort, and after a brief lobbing back and forth of civilities it showed signs of wavering again. A touch of awkwardness was relieved by the arrival of the tea tray. Zellaby bestirred himself to prevent the situation congealing.

"Richard and the Colonel were at the inquest, too," he said. "It was the expected verdict, of course. I suppose you've heard?"

Anthea nodded. "Yes. I was at Dacre Farm, with Mrs. Pawle. Mr. Pawle brought the news. The poor woman's quite beside herself. She adored Jim. It was difficult to keep her from going to the inquest herself. She wanted to go there and denounce the Children—make a public accusation. Mr. Leebody and I managed between us to persuade her not to, and that she'd only get herself and her family into a lot of trouble and do no good to anybody. So we stayed to keep her company while it was on."

"The other Pawle boy, David, was there," Zellaby told her. "He looked as if he were on the point of coming out with it more than once, but his father stopped him."

"Now I'm wondering whether it wouldn't have been better if someone had, after all," Anthea said. "It *ought* to come out. It will have to some time. It isn't just a matter of a dog, or a bull, any more."

"A dog and a bull. I've not heard of them," I put in.

"The dog bit one of them on the hand; a minute or two later it dashed in front of a tractor and was killed. The bull chased a party of them; then it suddenly turned aside, charged through two fences and got itself drowned in the mill pond," Zellaby explained, with unusual economy.

"But this," said Anthea, "is murder. Oh, I don't say they *meant* it that way. Very likely they were frightened and angry and it was their way of hitting out blindly when one of them was hurt. But it was murder, all the same. The whole village knows it, and now everybody can see that they are going to get away with it. We simply can't afford to let it rest there. They don't even show any sign of compunction. None at all. That's what frightens me most. They just did it, and that's that. And now, after this afternoon, they know that as far as they are concerned murder carries no penalty. What is going to happen to anyone who seriously opposes them later on?"

Zellaby sipped his tea thoughtfully.

"You know, my dear, while it's proper for us to be concerned, the responsibility for a remedy isn't ours. If it ever was, and that is highly questionable, the authorities took it away from us a long time ago. Here's the Colonel representing some of them—for heaven knows what reason. And the Grange staff cannot be ignorant of what all the village knows. They will have made their report, so in spite of the verdict the authorities are aware of the true state of affairs. We must wait and see how they move.

"Above all, my dear, I do implore you most seriously not to do anything that will bring you into conflict with the Children."

"I shan't, dear," Anthea shook her head. "I've a cowardly respect for them."

"The dove is not a coward to fear the hawk," said Zellaby, and proceeded to steer the conversation on to more general lines.

My intention had been to look in on the Leebodys and one or two others, but by the time we got up to leave it was clear that unless we were going to be back in London much later than we had intended any further calls would have to be postponed until another visit.

I did not know how Bernard felt when we had made our

farewells and were running down the drive—he had, in fact, talked very little since we had reached the village, and revealed scarcely anything of his own views—but, for my part, I had a pleasantly relaxing sensation of being on my way back to the normal world. Midwich values gave one an odd feeling of having only a finger-tip touch with reality. One had a sense of being several stages behind. While I was back at the difficulties of reconciling myself to the Children's existence, and boggling at what I was told of them, the Zellabys had long ago left all that behind. For them the improbable element had become submerged in familiarity. They accepted the Children and that, for good or ill, they were on their hands; their anxieties now were of a social nature, on whether such a *modus vivendi* as had been contrived was going to collapse. The sense of uneasiness which I had caught from the tension in the village hall had been with me ever since.

Nor, I think, was Bernard unaffected by it. I had the impression that he drove with more than usual caution through the village and past the scene of the Pawle boy's accident. He began to increase his speed a little as we rounded the corner on to the Oppley Road, and then we caught sight of four figures approaching. Even at a distance they were unmistakably a quartet of the Children. On an impulse I said:

"Will you pull up, Bernard? I'd like the chance of a better look at them."

He slowed again and we came to a stop almost at the foot of Hickham Lane.

The Children came on toward us. There was a touch of institutionalism in their dress, the boys in blue cotton shirts and gray flannel trousers, the girls in short, pleated gray skirts and pale yellow shirts. So far I had only set eyes on the pair outside the Hall, and seen little of them but a glimpse of their faces and then their backs.

As they approached I found the likeness among them even greater than I had expected. All four had the same browned complexions. The curious lucency of the skin that had been noticeable in them as babies had been greatly subdued by the sunburn, yet enough trace of it remained to attract one's notice. They shared the same dark-golden hair, straight, narrow noses and rather small mouths. The way the eyes were set was perhaps more responsible than anything for a suggestion of 'foreignness,' but it was an abstract foreignness, not calling to mind any particular race or region. I could not see anything to distinguish one boy from the other; and, indeed, I doubted whether, had it not been for the cut of the hair, I could have told the boys' faces from the girls', with certainty.

Soon I was able to see the eyes themselves. I had forgotten how striking they were in the babies, and remembered them as yellow. But they were more than that: they had a quality like glowing gold. Strange indeed, and disturbing; but if one could disregard the strangeness they had a singular beauty. They looked like living, semi-precious stones.

I watched, fascinated, as they drew level with us. They took no more notice of us than to give the car a brief, unembarrassed glance, and then turned into Hickham Lane.

At close quarters I found them disturbing in a way I could not quite account for, but it became less surprising that a number of the v.   .mes had been unprotestingly willing for them to go and liv. at the Grange.

We watched them a few yards up to the lane, then Bernard reached for the starter.

A sudden explosion close by made us both jump. I jerked my head round just in time to see one of the boys collapse and fall face down on the road. The other three Children stood petrified.

Bernard opened the door and started to get out. The still-standing boy turned and looked at us. The golden eyes were hard and bright. I felt as if a sudden gust of confusion and weakness were sweeping through me. Then the boy's eyes left ours and his head turned further.

From behind the hedge opposite came the sound of a second explosion, more muffled than the first, then, further away, a scream.

Bernard got out of the car and I shifted across to follow him. One of the girls knelt down beside the fallen boy. As she made to touch him he groaned, and writhed where he lay. The standing boy's face was anguished. He groaned, too, as if in agony himself. The two girls began to cry.

Then eerily down the lane, out of the trees that hid the Grange, swept a moan like a magnified echo and, mingled with it, a threnody of young voices, weeping.

Bernard stopped. I could feel my scalp prickling, and my hair beginning to rise.

The sound came again; a ululation of many voices blended in pain, with the higher note of crying piercing through. Then the sound of feet running down the lane.

Neither of us tried to go on. For myself, I was held for a

moment by sheer fright, and then by a sense that I was not wanted, an intruder upon something I did not understand.

We stood there watching while half a dozen boys, all disconcertingly alike, came running to the fallen one and lifted him between them. Not until they had started to carry him away did I become aware of a quite different sound of sobbing coming from behind the hedge to the left of the lane.

I clambered up the bank and looked through the hedge there. A few yards away a girl in a summer frock was kneeling on the grass. Her hands were clenched to her face and her whole body was shaking with her sobs.

Bernard scrambled up beside me, and together we pushed our way through the hedge. Standing up in the field now I could see a man lying prone at the girl's knees, with the butt of a gun protruding from beneath his body.

As we stepped closer she heard us. Her sobs stopped momentarily as she looked up with an expression of terror. Then when she saw us it faded and she went on weeping, helplessly.

Bernard walked closer to her and lifted her up. I looked down at the body. It was a very nasty sight indeed. I bent over it and pulled the jacket up, trying to make it hide what was left of the head. Bernard led the girl away, half supporting her.

There was a sound of voices on the road. As we neared the hedge a couple of men there looked up and saw us.

"Was that you shootin'?" one of them asked.

We shook our heads.

"There's a dead man up here," Bernard said.

The girl beside him shivered and whimpered.

" 'Oo is it?" asked the same man.

The girl said hysterically, "It's David. They've killed him. They killed Jim; now they've killed David, too," and choked in a fresh burst of grief.

One of the men scrambled up the bank.

"Oh, it's you, Elsa, lass," he exclaimed.

"I tried to stop him, Joe. I tried to stop him, but he wouldn't listen," she said through her sobs. "I knew they'd kill him, but he wouldn't listen. . . ." She became incoherent and clung to Bernard, shaking violently.

"We must get her away. Bad shock," I said. "Do you know where she lives?"

"Aye," said the man, and decisively picked the girl up as though she were a child. He scrambled down the bank and carried her, crying and shivering, to the car. Bernard turned to the other man.

"Will you stand by and keep anyone off till the police come?"

"Aye. It'll be young David Pawle?" the man said, climbing the bank.

"She said David. A young man," Bernard told him.

"That'll be him—the bastards." The man pushed through the hedge. "Better call the coppers at Trayne, guv'nor. They got a car there." He glanced toward the body. "Murderin' young bastards!" he said.

They dropped me off at Kyle Manor and I used Zellaby's phone to call the police. When I put the receiver down I found him at my elbow with a glass in his hand.

"You look as if you could do with it," he said.

"I could," I agreed. "Very unexpected. Very messy."

"Just how did it occur?" he inquired.

I gave him an account of our rather narrow angle on the affair. Twenty minutes later Bernard returned, also in need of a drink, and able to tell more of it.

"The Pawle brothers were apparently very much attached," he began. Zellaby nodded agreement. "Well, it seems that the younger one, David, found the inquest the last straw, and decided that if nobody else was going to see justice done over his brother, he'd do it himself.

"This girl Elsa—his girl—called at Dacre Farm just as he was leaving. When she saw him carrying the gun she guessed what was happening and tried to stop him. He wouldn't listen, and to get rid of her he locked her in a shed, and then went off.

"It took her a bit of time to break out, but she guessed he would be making for the Grange, and followed across the fields. When she got to *the* field she thought she'd made a mistake because she didn't see him at first. Possibly he was lying down to take cover. Anyway she doesn't seem to have spotted him until after the first shot. When she did he was standing up, with the gun still pointed into the lane. Then while she was running toward him he reversed the gun and put his thumb on the trigger. . . ."

Zellaby remained silently thoughtful for some moments.

"It'll be a clear enough case from the police view. David considers the Children to be responsible for his brother's death, kills one of them in revenge and then, to escape the penalty, commits suicide. Obviously unbalanced. What else could a 'reasonable man' think?"

"I may have been a bit skeptical before," I admitted, "but I'm not now. The way that boy looked at us! I believe that for a moment he thought one of us had done it—fired that shot, I mean—just for an instant, until he saw it was impossible. The sensation was indescribable, but it was frightening for the moment it lasted. Did you feel that, too?" I turned to Bernard.

He nodded. "A queer, weak and watery feeling," he agreed. "Very bleak."

"It was just—" I broke off, suddenly remembering. "My God, I was so taken up with other business I forgot to tell the police anything about the wounded boy. Ought we to call an ambulance for the Grange?"

Zellaby shook his head.

"They've got a doctor of their own on the staff there," he told us.

He reflected in silence for fully a minute, then he sighed and shook his head. "I think I'll join you two in a drink. I don't much like this development, Colonel. I don't like it at all. Am I mistaken, do you think, in seeing here the very pattern of the way a blood feud starts?"

18 · Midwich Protests

DINNER AT KYLE was postponed to allow Bernard and me to make our statements to the police, and by the time that was over I was feeling the need of it. I was grateful, too, for the Zellabys' offer to put both of us up for the night. The shooting had caused Bernard to change his mind about returning to London; he had decided to be on hand, if not in Midwich itself, then no further away than Trayne, leaving me with the alternatives of keeping him company or making a slow journey by railway. Moreover, I had a feeling that my skeptical attitude toward Zellaby in the afternoon had verged upon the discourteous and I was not sorry for the chance to make amends.

I sipped my sherry, feeling a little ashamed of myself and pondering with some wryness the wonderful self-protective mechanism of the mind: the way, for instance, that mine had during the intervening years belittled the events in Midwich and rationalized nearly all the disquiet out of them until, on my return, they had once more become a novelty I could scarcely accept. Now, after the afternoon's shock, I promised I would manage myself better, I would not let my automatic defense system deprive me of honest evaluation.

At dinner, however, the Zellabys took pains to keep the conversation on subjects unrelated to Midwich and its troubles. Bernard remained somewhat abstracted, but I appreciated the effort and ended the meal, listening to Zellaby discoursing on the desirability of intermittent periods of social rigidity for the purpose of curbing the subversive energies of a new generation, in a far more equable frame of mind than I had started it.

Not until after we had withdrawn to the sitting-room did the peculiar problems of Midwich come back to us, re-entering with a visit by Mr. Leebody. The Reverend Hubert was a badly troubled man and looked, I thought, a lot older than the passage of eight years fully warranted.

Anthea Zellaby sent for another cup and poured him some coffee. His attempts at small talk were valiant if erratic, but when he finally set down his empty cup, it was with an air of holding back no longer.

"Something," he announced to us all, "something will have to be done."

Zellaby looked at him thoughtfully for a moment.

"My dear Vicar," he reminded him gently, "each of us has been saying that for years."

"I mean done soon, and done decisively. We've done our best to find a place for the Children, to preserve some kind of balance—and, considering everything, I don't think we have done too badly—but all along it has been makeshift, impromptu, empiric, and it can't go on like that any longer. We must have a code which includes the Children, some means by which the law can be brought to bear on them as it does on the rest of us. If one section of a community is exempted from the dealings of common justice you have the beginnings of a state of anarchy. Confidence in authority is destroyed, the law falls into contempt and men feel that there is no resort and no protection but private revenge. That is what happened this afternoon."

"We foresaw possible difficulty of the kind, you will remember," Zellaby reminded him again. "We even sent a memorandum on the subject to the Colonel here. And what happened? You, Colonel, passed it on to higher authorities, there the matter ended. Though, I must confess, I sympathize with the Department, for I am still quite unable to see how the Children can be compelled to obey rules of any kind, if they do not choose to."

Mr. Leebody entwined his fingers, looking miserably helpless.

"But something *must* be done," he reiterated. "It only needed an occurrence of this kind to bring it all to a head; now I'm afraid of it boiling over any minute. Almost every man in the village is at the Scythe and Stone tonight. Nobody called a meeting; they've just gravitated there. It's the kind of excuse they've always wanted—or it might be."

"Excuse?" I put in. "I don't quite see . . . ?"

"Cuckoos," explained Zellaby. "You don't think the men have ever honestly *liked* these Children, do you? The fair face they've put on it has been mostly for their wives' sakes. Considering the sense of outrage that must be abiding in their subconsciouses, it does them great credit."

"It has been very difficult," agreed Mr. Leebody, "It cuts right across a proper family relationship. There's scarcely a man who doesn't resent their existence."

"And you think this Pawle business will supply a fatal impetus?" Bernard asked.

"It could. If not, something else will," Mr. Leebody said forlornly. "If only there were something one could *do*."

"There isn't, my dear fellow," Zellaby said decisively. "There's nothing that you or any of us can *do* because the initiative is not ours; it lies with the Children themselves. We can't even anticipate them because we don't understand, on any but the broadest lines, what they want, or how they think. What's happened to that boy who was shot, by the way?"

"Dr. Anderby's up there looking after him. There are quite a number of pellets to be removed, but he thinks he'll recover," said the Vicar.

"I hope he's right. If not I can see us having a real feud on our hands," said Zellaby.

"It is my impression that we already have," Mr. Leebody remarked unhappily.

"Not yet," Zellaby maintained. "It takes two parties to make a feud. So far the agression has been by the village."

"You're not going to deny that the Children murdered the two Pawle boys?"

"No, but it wasn't aggressive. I do have some experience of the Children. In both cases the response was defensive. Overdrastic, I'll grant that, but in intent it was manslaughter rather than murder. Both times they were the provoked, not the provokers. In fact, the one deliberate attempt at murder was by David Pawle."

"If someone hits you with a car, and you kill him for it," said the vicar, "it seems to me to be murder, and *that* seems to me to be provocation. And to David Pawle it *was* provocation. He waited for the law to administer justice and the law failed him, so he took the matter into his own hands. Now was that intended murder—or was it intended justice?"

"The one thing it certainly was not, was justice," Zellaby said firmly. "It was feuding. He attempted to kill one of the Children, chosen at random, for an act they had committed collectively. What these incidents really make clear, my dear fellow, is that the laws evolved by one species are, by their nature inapplicable against a species with different capacities."

The vicar shook his head despondently.

"I don't know, Zellaby . . . I don't know . . . I don't even know for certain whether these Children are imputable for murder."

Zellaby raised his eyebrows.

" 'And God said,' " quoted Mr. Leebody, " 'Let us make man in our image, after our likeness.' Very well, then, *what* are these Children? What *are* they? The image does not mean the outer image, or every statue would be man. It means the inner image, the spirit and the soul. But you have told me, and on the evidence I came to believe it, that the Children do not have individual spirits—that they have one man-spirit, and one woman-spirit, each far more powerful than we understand, that they share between them. What, then, are they? They have the *look* of the genus homo, but not the nature. Murder is, by definition, the killing of one of one's *own* kind. But if we kill one of them, or they kill one of us is it in fact, murder? It would appear not.

"And from that one must go further. If they are another species, are we not fully entitled—indeed, have we not perhaps a duty?—to fight them in order to protect our own species? Or are they rightly to be treated as we treat ourselves because their forms are similar? I don't know. . . . I am, as I said, in a morass. . . ."

"You are, my dear fellow, you are," agreed Zellaby. "Only

a few minutes ago you were telling me with some heat that the Children had murdered both the Pawle boys. Now you argue that if we were to kill them it would be something else. One cannot help feeling that a jurist, lay or ecclesiastical, would find such a proposition ethically unsatisfactory.

"Nor do I altogether follow your argument concerning the 'likeness.' If your God is a purely terrestial God, you are no doubt right, for in spite of one's opposition to the idea it can no longer be denied that the Children have in some way been introduced among us from 'outside.' But, as I understand it, your God is a universal God; He is God on all suns and planets. Would it not be a staggering vanity to imagine that He can manifest Himself only in the form that is appropriate to this particular, not very important planet?

"Our two approaches to such a problem are bound to differ greatly, but—"

He broke off at the sound of raised voices in the hall outside and looked questioningly at his wife. Before either could move, however, the door was abruptly thrust open and Mrs. Brant appeared on the threshold. With a perfunctory 'Scuse me' to the Zellabys, she made for Mr. Leebody and grasped his sleeve.

"Oh, sir. You must come quick," she told him breathlessly.

"My dear Mrs. Brant—" he began.

"You must come, sir," she repeated. "They're all going up to the Grange. They're going to burn it down. You must come and stop them."

Mr. Leebody stared at her while she continued to pull at his sleeve.

"They're starting now," she said desperately. "You can stop them, Vicar. You must. They want to burn the Children. Oh, hurry. Please. Please hurry!"

Mr. Leebody got up. He turned to Anthea Zellaby.

"I'm sorry. I think I'd better—" he began, but his apology was cut short by Mrs. Brant's tugging.

"Has anyone told the police?" Zellaby inquired.

"Yes—no. I don't know. They couldn't get here in time. Oh, Vicar, please *hurry!*" said Mrs. Brant dragging him forcibly through the doorway.

The four of us were left looking at one another. Anthea crossed the room swiftly and closed the door.

"I'd better go and back him up, I think," said Bernard.

"We might be able to help," agreed Zellaby, turning, and I moved to join them.

Anthea was standing resolutely with her back to the door.

"No!" she said, decisively. "If you want to do something useful, call the police."

"You could do that, my dear, while we go and—"

"Gordon," she said in a severe voice, as if reprimanding a child, "stop and think. Colonel Westcott, you would do more harm than good. You are identified with the Children's interests."

We all stood in front of her feeling surprised and a little sheepish.

"But it will be important," protested Zellaby. "We know what the Children can do with individuals; I want to see how they handle a crowd. If they run true to form they'll only have to will the whole crowd to turn round and go away. It will be most interesting to see whether—"

"Nonsense," said Anthea flatly, and with a firmness which made Zellaby blink. "That is *not* their 'form,' and you know it. If it were they'd simply have made Jim Pawle *stop* his car; and they'd have made David Pawle fire his second barrel into the air. But they didn't. They're never content with repulsing —they always counterattack."

Zellaby blinked again.

"You're right, Anthea," he said, in surprise. "I never thought of that. The reprisal *is* always rather too drastic for the occasion."

"It is. And however they handle a crowd, I don't want you handled with it. Nor you, Colonel," she added, to Bernard.

"I might observe—from a distance, perhaps," I suggested meekly.

"If you've any sense you'll stay here out of harm's way," Anthea replied bluntly and turned again to her husband. "Gordon, we're wasting time. Will you ring up Trayne and see whether anyone has told the police there, and ask for ambulances as well."

"Ambulances! Isn't that a bit premature?" Zellaby protested.

"You introduced this 'true to form' consideration, but you don't seem to have considered," Anthea replied. "I have. I say ambulances, and if you don't I will."

Zellaby, with rather the air of a small boy subdued, picked up the telephone. To me he remarked:

"We don't even know—I mean, we've only Mrs. Brant's word for any of it . . ."

"As I recall Mrs. Brant, she was one of the reliable pillars," I said.

"That's true," he admitted. "Well, I'd better risk it."

When he had finished he returned the telephone thoughtfully to the cradle and regarded it for a moment. He decided to make one more attempt.

"Anthea, my dear, don't you think that if one were to keep at a discreet distance . . . ? After all, I am one of the people the Children trust, they're my friends, and—"

But Athea cut him short, with unweakened decision.

"Gordon, it's no good trying to get round me with that nonsense. You're just inquisitive. You know perfectly well that the Children have no friends."

19 · Interview with a Child

THE CHIEF CONSTABLE of Winshire looked in at Kyle Manor the next morning just at the right time for a glass of Madeira and a biscuit, which he accepted with appreciation.

"Sorry to trouble you over this affair, Zellaby. Ghastly business—perfectly horrible. Can't make any sense of it. Nobody in your village quite on target, seems to me. Thought you might be able to put up a picture a fellow can understand."

Anthea leaned forward.

"What are the real figures, Sir John? We've heard nothing officially yet."

"Bad, I'm afraid." He shook his head. "One woman and three men dead. Eight men and five women in the hospital. Several others who look as if they ought to be. Regular riot by all accounts—everybody fighting everybody else. But why? That's what I can't get at. No sense out of anybody." He turned back to Zellaby. "Seeing that you called the police and told them there was going to be trouble, it'd help us to know what put you on to it."

"Well—" Zellaby began cautiously.

His wife cut him short.

"It was Mrs. Brant, the blacksmith's wife," she said, and went on to describe the vicar's departure. "I'm sure Mr. Leebody will be able to tell you more than we can. He was there, you see; we weren't."

"He was there all right and got home somehow, but now he's in Trayne hospital," said the Chief Constable.

"Oh, poor Mr. Leebody. Is he badly hurt?"

"I'm afraid I don't know. The doctor there tells me he's not to be disturbed for a bit. Now." He turned back to Zellaby once more, "you told my people that a crowd was marching on the Grange with the intention of setting fire to it. What was your source of information?"

Zellaby looked surprised.

"Why, Mrs. Brant. My wife just told you."

"Is that all? You didn't go out to see for yourself what was going on?"

"Why, no," Zellaby admitted.

"You mean that on the unsupported word of a woman in a semi-hysterical condition you called out the police, in force, and told them that ambulances would be needed?"

"I insisted on it," Anthea put in, with a touch of chill. "And I was perfectly right. They *were* needed."

"But simply on this woman's word—"

"I've known Mrs. Brant for years. She's a sensible woman."

Bernard put in, "If Mrs. Zellaby had not advised us against going to see for ourselves I'm quite sure we should now be either in the hospital, or worse."

The Chief Constable looked at us.

"I've had an exhausting night," he said, at last. "Perhaps I haven't got this straight. What you seem to be saying is that this Mrs. Brant came here and told you that the villagers here—perfectly ordinary English men and women, and good Winshire stock, were intending to march on a school full of children, their own children, too, and—"

"Not quite, Sir John. The men were going to march, and perhaps some of the women, but I think most of the women would be against it," Anthea objected.

"Very well. These men, then—ordinary, decent, country chaps—were going to set fire to a school full of children. You didn't question it. You accepted an incredible thing like that at once. You did not try to check up, or see for yourselves what was happening. You just called in the police—because Mrs. Brant is a sensible woman?"

"Yes," Anthea told him icily.

"Sir John," Zellaby said, with equal coolness. "I realize you have been busy all night and I appreciate your official position, but I think that if this interview is to continue it must be upon different lines."

The Chief Constable went a little pink. His gaze dropped. Presently he massaged his forehead vigorously with a large fist. He apologized, first to Anthea and then to Zellaby. Almost pathetically he said:

"But there's nothing to get hold of. I've been asking questions for hours and I can't make head or tail of anything. There's no sign that these. people were trying to burn the Grange: they never touched it. They were simply fighting one another, men and a few women, too—but they were doing it in the Grange grounds. Why? It wasn't just the women trying to stop the men, or some of the men trying to stop the rest. No, it appears they all went up from the pub to the Grange together, with nobody trying to stop anybody, except the parson, whom they wouldn't listen to, and a few women who backed him up. And what was it all about? Something, apparently, to do with the children at the school, but what sort of a reason is that for a riot like this? It just doesn't make any sense." He shook his head and ruminated a moment. "I remember my predecessor, old Bodger, saying there was something deuced funny about Midwich. And, by God, he was right. But what is it?"

"It seems to me that the best we can do is to refer you to Colonel Westcott," suggested Zellaby, indicating Bernard. With a slightly malicious touch, he added: "His department, for reasons which have continued to elude me for nine years, preserves a continuing interest in Midwich, so that he probably knows more about us than we do ourselves."

Sir John turned his attention to Bernard.

"And what is your department, sir?" he inquired.

At Bernard's reply his eyes bulged slightly. He looked like a man wishing to be given strength.

"Did you say Military Intelligence?" he inquired, flatly.

"Yes, sir," said Bernard.

The Chief Constable shook his head. "I give up." He looked back at Zellaby, with the expression of a man only two or three straws from the end. "And now Military Intelligence," he muttered.

About the same time that the Chief Constable had arrived at Kyle Manor, one of the Children—a boy—came walking unhurriedly down the drive of the Grange. The two policemen who were chatting at the gate broke off their conversation. One of them turned and strolled to meet the boy.

"And where'll you be off to, son?" he inquired amiably enough.

The boy looked at the policeman without expression, though the curious golden eyes were alert and perceptive.

"Into the village," he said.

"Better if you didn't," advised the policeman. "They're not

feeling too friendly there about your lot, not after last night, they're not."

But the boy neither answered nor checked his walk. He simply kept on. The policeman turned and walked back toward the gate. His colleague looked at him curiously.

"Lumme," he said. "Didn't make much of a job of that, did you? Thought the idea was to persuade 'em to keep out of harm's way."

The first policeman looked after the boy, going on down the lane, with a puzzled expression. He shook his head.

"Funny, that," he said uneasily. "I don't get it. If there's another you have a try, Bert."

A minute or two later one of the girls appeared. She, too, was walking in a casually confident way.

"Right," said the second policeman. "Just a bit of advice—fatherly-like, see?"

He began to stroll toward the girl.

After perhaps four steps he turned round and came back again. The two policemen standing side by side watched her walk past them and into the lane. She never even glanced at them.

"What the hell . . . ?" asked the second policeman, in a baffled voice.

"Bit off, isn't it?" said the other. "You go to do something and then you do something else instead. I don't reckon I like it much. Hey!" he called after the girl. "Hey! you, missie!"

The girl did not look back. He started in pursuit, covered half a dozen yards, and then stopped dead. The girl passed out of sight round the corner of the lane. The policeman relaxed, turned round and came back. He was breathing rather fast and had an uneasy look on his face.

"I definitely *don't* like it," he said unhappily. "There's something kind of funny about this place. . . ."

The bus from Oppley on its way to Trayne via Stouch stopped in Midwich, opposite Mrs. Welt's shop. The ten or a dozen women waiting for it allowed the two offloading passengers to descend, and then moved forward in a ragged line. Miss Latterly, at its head, took hold of the rail and made to step aboard. Nothing further happened. Both her feet appeared to be glued to the ground.

"Hurry along there, please," said the conductor.

Miss Latterly tried again, with no better success. She looked up helplessly at the conductor.

"Just you stand aside and let 'em get on, mum. I'll give you a hand in a minute," he advised her.

Miss Latterly, looking bewildered, took his advice. Mrs. Dorry moved up to take her place and grasped the rail. She, too, failed to get any further. The conductor reached down to take her arm and pull her up, but her foot would not lift to the step. She moved beside Miss Latterly and they both watched the next in turn make an equally fruitless attempt to get aboard.

"What's this? Some kind of joke?" inquired the conductor. Then he saw the expression on the faces of the three. "Sorry, ladies. No offense. But what's the trouble?"

It was Miss Latterly who, turning her attention from the fourth woman's ineffective approach to the bus, noticed one of the Children. He was sitting casually on the mounting-block opposite the Scythe and Stone, with his face turned toward them and one leg idly swinging. She detached herself from the group by the bus and walked toward him. She studied him carefully as she approached. Even so, it was with a touch of uncertainty she said:

"You're not Joseph, are you?"

The boy shook his head. She went on, "I want to go to Trayne to see Miss Foresham, Joseph's mother. She was hurt last night. She's in the hospital there."

The boy kept on looking at her. He shook his head very slightly. Tears of anger came into Miss Latterly's eyes.

"Haven't you done enough harm? You're monsters. All we want to do is to go and see our friends who've been hurt—hurt because of what you did."

The boy said nothing. Miss Latterly took an impulsive half-step toward him and then checked herself.

"Don't you understand? Haven't you any human feelings?" she said, in a shaking voice.

Behind her, the conductor, half-puzzled, half-jocular, was saying, "Come along now, ladies. Make up your minds. The old bus don't bite, you know. Can't wait 'ere all day."

The group of women stood irresolute, some of them looking frightened. Mrs. Dorry made one more attempt to board the bus. It was no use. Two of the women turned to glare angrily at the boy who looked back at them unmoved.

Miss Latterly turned helplessly and began to walk away. The conductor's temper shortened.

"Well, if you're not coming, we're off. Got our times to keep, you know."

None of the group made any move. He hit the bell decisively and the bus moved on. The conductor gazed at them as they dwindled forlornly behind, and shook his head. As he ambled forward to exchange comments with the driver he muttered to himself the local adage:

"In Oppley they're smart, and in Stouch they're smarmy, but Midwich folk are just plain barmy."

Polly Rushton, her uncle's invaluable right hand in the parish ever since she had fled across the unmended breach between the two families, was driving Mrs. Leebody into Trayne to see the vicar. His injuries in the fracas at the Grange, the hospital had telephoned reassuringly, were painful, but not serious: a fracture of the left radius, and a number of contusions. He was in need of rest and quiet, but would be glad of a visit in order to make some arrangements to cover his absence.

Two hundreds yards out of Midwich, however, Polly braked abruptly and started to turn the car about.

"What have we forgotten?" inquired Mrs. Leebody, in surprise.

"Nothing," Polly told her. "I just can't go on, that's all."

"Can't?" repeated Mrs. Leebody.

"Can't," said Polly.

"Well, really," said Mrs. Leebody. "I should have thought that at a time like this . . ."

"Aunt Dora, I said 'can't' not 'won't.' "

"I don't understand what you're talking about," said Mrs. Leebody.

"All right," said Polly. She drove on a few yards, and turned the car again so that it faced away from the village once more. "Now change places, and *you* try."

Unwillingly Mrs. Leebody took the driving seat. She didn't care for driving, but accepted the challenge. They moved forward again, and at precisely the spot where Polly had braked, Mrs. Leebody braked. There came the sound of a horn behind them and a tradesman's van with a Trayne address on it squeezed by. They watched it vanish round the corner ahead. Mrs. Leebody attempted to reach the accelerator-pedal, but her foot stopped short of it. She tried again. Her foot could not get to it.

Polly looked round and saw one of the Children sitting half-hidden in the hedge, watching them. She looked harder at the girl, making sure which one it was.

"Judy," Polly said, with sudden misgiving. "Is it you doing this?"

The girl's nod was barely perceptible.

"But you mustn't," Polly protested. "We want to go to Trayne to see Uncle Hubert. He's in the hospital."

"You can't go," the girl told her, with a faintly apologetic inflection.

"But, Judy, he has to arrange lots of things with me for the time he'll have to be away."

The girl simply shook her head, slowly. Polly felt her temper rising. She drew breath to speak again, but Mrs. Leebody cut in nervously:

"Don't annoy her, Polly. Wasn't last night enough of a lesson for all of us?"

Her advice went home. Polly said no more. She sat glaring at the Child in the hedge with a muddle of frustrated emotion that brought tears of resentment to her eyes.

Mrs. Leebody succeeded in finding reverse, and moved the lever. Then, tentatively, she put her right foot forward and found it now reached the accelerator without any difficulty. They backed a few yards and changed seats again. Polly drove them back to the vicarage in silence.

At Kyle Manor we were still having difficulty with the Chief Constable.

"But," he protested from under corrugated brows, "our information supports your original statement that the villagers were marching on the Grange to burn the place."

"So they were," agreed Zellaby.

"But you also say, and Colonel Westcott agrees, that the children at the Grange were the real culprits; they provoked it."

"That's true," Bernard agreed. "But I'm afraid there's nothing we can do about that."

"No evidence, you mean? Well, finding evidence is our job."

"I don't mean no evidence. I mean no imputability under the law."

"Look," said the Chief Constable, with conscientious patience. "Four people have been killed—I repeat *killed;* thirteen are in the hospital; a number more have been badly knocked about. It is not the sort of thing we can just say 'what a pity' about and leave it at that. We have to bring the whole thing into the open, decide where responsibility lies and draw up charges. You must see that."

"These are very unusual children—" Bernard began.

"I know. I know. Lot of wrong side of the blanket stuff in

these parts. Old Bodger told me about that when I took over. Not quite firing on all cylinders, either—special school for them, and so on."

Bernard repressed a sigh.

"Sir John, it's not that they are backward. The special school was opened because they are *different*. They *are* morally responsible for last night's trouble, but that isn't the same as being legally responsible. There's nothing you can charge them with—and my department doesn't want them publicized."

"Ridiculous," retorted the Chief Constable. "I've heard of those fancy schools. Children mustn't be what-do-you-call-it? —frustrated. Self-expression, co-education, wholemeal bread and all the rest of it. Damned nonsense. Minors can be charged—or somebody responsible for them can."

Zellaby and Bernard exchanged hopeless glances. Bernard decided to try once more.

"These children, Sir John, have strong will power—strong enough when they exert it to be considered a form of duress. But as far as the law is concerned you can prove nothing at all. And, what is more, if you could find a formula to charge them under you'd not get anywhere. They would bring this duress to bear on your officers. You can neither arrest them, nor hold them, if you try to."

"We can leave those finer points to the lawyer fellows— that's their job. All we need is enough evidence to justify a warrant," the Chief Constable assured him. "This schoolmaster fellow at the Grange—what's his name, Torrance? Director of the place. He must hold the official responsibility for these children if anyone does. Saw the chap last night. Struck me as evasive. Everybody round here's evasive, of course."

Zellaby gazed with innocent thoughtfulness at a corner of the ceiling. Bernard had the withdrawn air of a man who might be counting ten, not too quickly. I found myself troubled by a slight cough.

"Dr. Torrance is an eminent psychiatrist, rather than a schoolmaster," Bernard explained. "I think he may be in considerable doubt as to his right course in the matter until he can take advice."

"Don't see what he has to be doubtful about. All he's got to do is tell the truth. Nothing doubtful about the truth, is there?"

"It's not quite as simple as that," Bernard said patiently. "He may not have felt himself at liberty to disclose some aspects of his work. I think that if you will let me come along with you, and see him again he might be more willing to talk, and much better able to explain the situation than I am."

He got to his feet as he finished. The rest of us rose, too. The Chief Constable's leavetaking was gruff. There was a barely perceptible flicker to Bernard's right eye as he said au revoir to the rest of us and escorted him out of the room.

Zellaby collapsed into an easy chair, and sighed deeply. He searched absentmindedly for his cigarette case.

"I've not met Dr. Torrance," I said, "but I already feel quite sorry for him."

"Unnecessary," said Zellaby. "Colonel Westcott's discretion has been irritating, but passive. Torrance's has always had an aggressive quality. If he has now got to make the situation lucid enough for Sir John, it's simply poetic justice.

"But what interests me more at the moment is your Colonel Westcott's attitude. The barrier there is down quite a bit. If he could have got as far as a mutually understandable vocabulary with Sir John, I do believe he might have told us all something. I wonder why? This seems to me just the kind of situation that he has been trying so hard to avoid all along. The Midwich bag is now very nearly too small for the cat. Why, then, doesn't he appear more concerned, more anxious to hold it up?" He lapsed into a reverie, tapping gently on the chair arm.

Presently Anthea, who had left us at the point when Sir John was strengthening himself with his second glass of Madeira, reappeared. Zellaby became aware of her from the far-off. It took him a moment or two to reestablish himself in the here and now, and observe her expression.

"What's the matter, my dear?" he inquired, and added in recollection: "I thought you were bound for Trayne hospital with a cornucopia."

"I started," she said. "Now I've come back. It seems that we're not allowed to leave the village."

Zellaby sat up.

"That's absurd. The old fool can't put the whole place under arrest. As a J.P.—" he began indignantly.

"It's not Sir John. It's the Children. They're picketing all the roads and won't let us out."

"Are they indeed!" exclaimed Zellaby. "That's extremely interesting. I wonder if—"

"Interesting be damned," said his wife. "It's very unpleasant, and quite outrageous. It's also rather alarming," she added, "because one can't see just what's behind it."

Zellaby inquired how it was being done. She explained, concluding:

"And it's only us, you see—people who live in the village, I mean. They're letting other people come and go as they like."

"They must have some reason for it," said Zellaby.

Anthea eyed him resentfully.

"I dare say, and possibly it will be of great sociological interest, but that isn't the point at the moment. What I want to know is what is to be done about it?"

"My dear," said Zellaby soothingly. "One appreciates your feelings, but we've known for some time now that if it should suit the Children to interfere with us we have no way of stopping them. Well, now, for some reason that I confess I do not perceive, it evidently does suit them."

"But, Gordon, there are these people seriously hurt, in Trayne hospital. Their relatives want to visit them."

"My dear, I don't see that there is anything you can do but find one of them and put it to him on humane grounds. They *might* consider that, but it really depends on what their reason for doing it is, don't you think?"

Anthea regarded her husband with a frown of dissatisfaction. She started to reply, thought better of it, and took herself off with an air of reproof. Zellaby shook his head as the door closed.

"Man's arrogance is boastful," he observed, "woman's is something in the fiber. We do occasionally contemplate the once lordly dinosaurs and wonder when and how our little day will reach its end. But not she. Her eternity is an article of her faith. Great wars and disasters can ebb and flow, races rise and fall, empires wither with suffering and death, but these are superficialities: she, woman, is perpetual, essential; she will go on forever. She doesn't believe in the dinosaurs: she doesn't really believe the world ever existed until she was upon it. Men may build and destroy and play with all their toys; they are uncomfortable nuisances, ephemeral conveniences, mere scamperers-about, while woman, in mystical umbilical connection with the great tree of life itself, *knows* that she is indispensable. One wonders whether the female dinosaur in her day was blessed with the same comfortable certainty."

He paused, in such obvious need of prompting that I said: "And the relevance to the present?"

"Is that while man finds the thought of his supersession abominable, she simply finds it unthinkable. And since she cannot think it she must regard the hypothesis as frivolous."

It seemed to be my service again.

"If you are implying that we see something which Mrs. Zellaby fails to see, I'm afraid I—"

"But, my dear fellow, if one is not blinded by a sense of indispensability, one must take it that we, like the other lords of creation before us, will one day be replaced. There are two ways in which it can happen: either through ourselves, by our self-destruction, or by the incursion of some species which we lack the equipment to subdue. Well, here we are now, face to face with a superior will and mind. And what are we able to bring against it?"

"That," I told him, "sounds defeatist. If, as I assume, you do mean it quite seriously, isn't it rather a large conclusion from rather a small instance?"

"Very much what my wife said to me when the instance was considerably smaller, and younger," Zellaby admitted. "She also went on to scout the proposition that such a remarkable thing could happen here, in a prosaic English village. In vain did I try to convince her that it would be no less remarkable wherever it should happen. She felt that it was decidedly a thing that *would* be less remarkable in more exotic places—a Balinese village, perhaps, or a Mexican pueblo; that it was essentially one of those sorts of things that happens to other people. Unfortunately, however, the instance has developed here—and with melancholy logic."

"It isn't the locality that troubles me," I said. "It's your assumptions. More particularly, your taking it for granted that the Children can do what they like, and there's no way of stopping them."

"It would be foolish to be quite so didactic as that. It *may* be possible, but it will not be easy. Physically we are poor weak creatures compared with many animals, but we overcome them because we have better brains. The only thing that can beat us is something with a still better brain. That has scarcely seemed a threat; for one thing, its occurrence seemed improbable and, for another, it seemed even more improbable that we should allow it to survive to become a menace.

"Yet here it is—another little gimmick out of Pandora's infinite evolutionary box: the contesserate mind—two mosaics, one of thirty, the other of twenty-eight, tiles. What can we, with our separate brains only in clumsily fumbling touch with one another, expect to do against thirty brains working almost as one?"

I protested that, even so, the Children could scarcely have accumulated enough knowledge in a mere nine years to oppose successfully the whole mass of human knowledge, but Zellaby shook his head.

"The government has for reasons of its own provided them with some excellent teachers, so that the sum of their knowledge should be considerable—indeed, I know it is, for I lecture to them myself sometimes, you know—that has importance, but it is not the source of the threat. One is not unaware that Francis Bacon wrote: *nam et ipsa scientia postas est*—knowledge itself is power—and one must regret that so eminent a scholar should, at times, talk through his hat. We all know of people who have amazing memories for facts, with no ability to use them; a computing-engine can roll out knowledge by the ream in multiplicate; but none of this knowledge is of the least use until it is informed by understanding. Knowledge is simply a kind of fuel; it needs the motor of understanding to convert it into power.

"Now, what frightens me is the thought of the power producible by an understanding working on even a small quantity of knowledge-fuel when it has an extraction-efficiency thirty times that of our own—if, indeed, the aggregation of the minds is no more than the sum of simple addition—which I doubt. That is the proposition that overwhelms my comprehension even now. What it may produce when the Children are mature I cannot begin to imagine."

I frowned. As always, I was a little unsure of Zellaby.

"You are quite seriously maintaining that we have no means of preventing this group of fifty-eight Children from taking what course they choose?" I insisted.

"I am." He nodded. "What do you suggest we could do? You know what happened to that crowd last night; they intended to attack the Children—instead, they were induced to fight one another. Send police, and they would do the same. Send soldiers against them, and they would be induced to shoot one another."

"Possibly," I conceded. "But there must be other ways of tackling them. Surely, it is a question of learning more about them. What, for instance, is the range at which they are able to exert their duress, as Bernard calls it? There must be some limit. Is its limit visual, is it aural, is it arbitrary? Does it decrease in power as a ratio of distance? Are some classes of persons less susceptible to it than others? And so on. The first essential is more data, so that we really do know what we are up against, and its limitations.

"From what you've told me, nobody knows nearly enough about them. They appear to have detached themselves emotionally from their host-mothers quite early—if, indeed, they ever had the emotions we normally expect. Most of them chose to adopt progressive segregation as soon as it was offered. As a result the village knows extremely little of them. In quite a short time most people seem scarcely to have thought of them as individuals. They found them difficult to tell apart, got into the habit of regarding them collectively so that they have tended to become two-dimensional figures with only a limited kind of reality."

Zellaby looked appreciative of the point.

"You're perfectly right, my dear fellow. There is a lack of normal contacts and sympathies. But that is not entirely our shortcoming. I have myself kept as close to them as I can, but I am still at a distance. In spite of all my efforts I still find them, as you excellently put it, two-dimensional. And it is strongly my impression that the people at the Grange have done no better."

"Then the question remains," I said. "How do we get more data?"

We contemplated that for a while until Zellaby emerged from his reverie to say:

"Has it occurred to you to wonder what your own status here is, my dear fellow? If you were thinking of leaving to-day it might be as well to find out whether the Children regard you as one of us, or not?"

That was an aspect that had not occurred to me, and I found it a little startling. I decided to find out.

Bernard had, it appeared, gone off in the Chief Constable's car, so I borrowed his for the test.

I found the answer a little way along the Oppley road. A very odd sensation. My hand and foot were guided to bring the car to a halt by no volition of my own. One of the girl Children was sitting by the roadside, nibbling at a stalk of grass, and looking at me without expression. I tried to put the gear in again. My hand wouldn't do it. Nor could I bring my foot on the clutch pedal. I looked at the girl and told her that I did not live in Midwich and wanted to get home. She simply shook her head. I tried the gear lever again and found that the only way I could move it was into reverse.

"H'm," said Zellaby, on my return. "So you are an honorary villager, are you? I rather thought you might be. Just remind me to tell Anthea to let the cook know, there's a good fellow."

At the same time that Zellaby and I were talking at Kyle Manor, more talk, similar in matter but different in manner, was going on at the Grange. Dr. Torrance, feeling some sanction in the presence of Colonel Westcott, had endeavored to answer the Chief Constable's questions more explicitly than before. A stage had been reached, however, when lack of co-ordination between the parties could no longer be disguised, and a noticeably off-beat query caused the doctor to say, a little forlornly:

"I am afraid I cannot have made the situation quite clear to you, Sir John."

The Chief Constable grunted impatiently.

"Everybody keeps on telling me that, and I'm not denying it; nobody round here seems to be capable of making anything clear. Everybody keeps on telling me, too—and without producing a scrap of evidence that I can understand—that these infernal children are in some way responsible for last night's affair. Even you who I am given to understand are in charge of them. I agree that I do not understand a situation in which young children are allowed to get so thoroughly out of hand that they can cause a breach of the peace amounting to a riot. I don't see why I should be expected to understand it. It is as a constable that I wish to see one of the ringleaders and find out what he has to say about it."

"But, Sir John, I have already explained to you that there are no ringleaders."

"I know, I know. I heard you. Everyone is equal here, and all that. All very well perhaps in theory, but you know as well as I do that in every group there are one or two that stand out, stronger personalities. Those are the chaps you've got to get hold of. Manage them, and you can manage the rest." He paused expectantly.

Dr. Torrance exchanged a helpless look with Colonel Westcott. Bernard gave a slight shrug and the faintest of nods. Dr. Torrance's look of unhappiness increased. He said uneasily:

"Very well, Sir John, since you make it virtually a police order I have no alternative, but I must ask you to watch your words carefully. The Children are very sensitive."

His choice of the final word was unfortunate. In his own vocabulary it had a somewhat technical meaning; in the Chief Constable's it was a word used by doting mothers about spoiled sons, and did nothing to make him feel more sympa-

thetically disposed toward the Children. He made a vowel-
less sound of disapproval as Dr. Torrance got up and left
the room. Bernard half opened his mouth to reinforce the
doctor's warning, and then decided that it would only increase the Chief Constable's irritation, thus doing more
harm than good. The difficulty with Sir John's type was that,
given the full picture, he would reject it all out of hand as a
kind of lunacy; but given only such parts of it as seemed
likely to fall within his grasp it became less coherent, and
therefore less comprehensible as a whole. So the two waited
in silence until the doctor presently returned, bringing one
of the boy-Children with him.

"This is Eric," he said, by way of introduction. To the boy
he added, "Sir John Tenby wishes to ask you some questions.
It is his duty as Chief Constable, you see, to make a report
on the trouble last night."

The boy nodded and turned to look at Sir John. Dr. Torrance resumed his seat at his desk and watched the two of
them uneasily.

The boy's regard was steady, careful, but quite neutral; it
gave no trace of feeling. Sir John met it with equal stead-
iness. A healthy-looking boy, he thought. A bit thin—well, not
exactly thin in the sense of being scraggy, slight would be a
better word. It was difficult to make much of a judgment
from the features; the face was good-looking, though without
the weakness which often accompanies male good looks. On
the other hand, it did not show strength; the mouth, indeed,
was a little small, though not petulant. There was little to be
learned from the face as a whole. The eyes, however, were
even more remarkable than he had been led to expect. He
had been told of the curious golden color of the irises,
but no one had succeeded in conveying to him their striking
lambency, their strange effect of being softly lit from
within. For a moment it disquieted him, then he took himself
in hand, reminded himself that he had some kind of freak
to deal with; a boy only nine years old, yet looking every
bit of sixteen, brought up, moreover, on some of these fid-
dle-faddling theories of self-expression, non-inhibition and
so on. He decided to treat the boy as if he were the age he
looked, and constrained himself into that man-to-boy attitude
that is represented by its practitioners as man-to-man.

"Serious business last night," he observed. "Our job to clear
it up and find out what really happened, who was responsible
for the trouble, and so forth. People keep on telling me that

you and the others here were. Now, what do you say to that?"

"No," said the boy promptly.

The Chief Constable nodded. One would scarcely expect an immediate admission, in any case.

"What happened, exactly?" he asked.

"The village people came here to burn the Grange down," said the boy.

"You're sure of that?"

"It was what they said, and there was no other reason to bring them here at that time," said the boy.

"All right, we'll not go into the whys and wherefores just now. Let's take it from there. You say some of them came intending to burn the place. Then I suppose others came to stop them doing it, and the fighting started?"

"Yes," agreed the boy, but less definitely.

"Then, in point of fact, you and your friends had nothing to do with it. You were just spectators?"

"No," said the boy. "We had to defend ourselves. It was necessary, or they would have burned the house."

"You mean you called out to some of them to stop the rest, something like that?"

"No," the boy told him patiently. "We made them fight one another. We could simply have sent them away, but if we had they would very likely have come back some other time. Now they will not; they understand it is better for them to leave us alone."

The Chief Constable paused, a little nonplused.

"You say you 'made' them fight one another. How did you do that?"

"It is too difficult to explain. I don't think you could understand," said the boy, judicially.

Sir John pinked a little.

"Nevertheless, I'd like to hear," he said, with an air of generous restraint that was wasted.

"It wouldn't be any use," the boy told him. He spoke simply, and without innuendo, as one stating a fact.

The Chief Constable's face became a deeper pink. Dr. Torrance put in hurriedly:

"This is an extremely abstruse matter, Sir John, and one which all of us here have been trying to understand, with very little headway, for some years now. One can really get little nearer to it than to say that the Children 'willed' the people in the crowd to attack one another."

Sir John looked at him and then at the boy. Presently,

after two or three deep breaths, he spoke to the boy again, but now with his tone a little ruffled.

"However it was done—and we'll have to go into that later—you are admitting that you were responsible for what happened?"

"We are responsible for defending ourselves," the boy said.

"To the extent of four lives and thirteen serious injuries—when you *could* you say, have simply sent them away."

"They wanted to kill us," the boy told him, indifferently.

The Chief Constable looked lengthily at him.

"I don't understand *how* you can have done it, but I take your word for it that you did, for the present; also your word that it was unnecessary."

"They would have come again. It would have been necessary then," replied the boy.

"You can't be sure of that. Your whole attitude is monstrous. Don't you feel the least compunction for these unfortunate people?"

"No," the boy told him. "Why should we? Yesterday afternoon one of them shot one of us. Now we must protect ourselves."

"But not by private vengeance. The law is for your protection, and for everyone's."

"The law did not protect Wilfred from being shot: it would not have protected us last night. The law punishes the criminal *after* he has been successful: it is no use to us, we intend to stay alive."

"But you don't mind being responsible—so you tell me—for the deaths of other people."

"Do we have to go round in circles?" asked the boy in a bored tone. "I have answered your questions because we thought it better that you should understand the situation. As you apparently have not grasped it I will put it more plainly. It is that if there is any attempt to interfere with us or molest us by anybody we shall defend ourselves. We have demonstrated our ability to defend ourselves, and we hope that that will be warning enough to prevent further trouble."

Sir John stared at the boy speechlessly while his knuckles whitened and his face empurpled. He half rose from his chair as if he meant to attack the boy, and then sank back, thinking better of it. Some seconds passed before he could trust himself to speak. Presently, in a half-choked voice he addressed the boy, who was watching him with a kind of critically detached interest.

"You damned young blackguard! You insufferable little prig! How dare you speak to me like that? Do you understand that I represent the police force of this county? If you don't, it's time you learned it, and I'll see that you do, b'God. Talking to your elders like that, you swollen-headed little upstart! So you're not to be 'molested,' you'll defend yourselves, will you! Where do you think you are? You've got a lot to learn, m'lad, a whole—"

He broke off suddenly and sat staring at the boy.

Dr. Torrance leaned forward over his desk.

"Eric—" he began in protest, but made no move to interfere.

Bernard Westcott remained carefully still in his chair, watching.

The Chief Constable's mouth went slack, his jaws fell a little, his eyes widened and seemed to go on widening. His hair rose slightly. Sweat burst out on his forehead, at his temples and came trickling down his face. Inarticulate gobblings came from his mouth. Tears ran down the sides of his nose. He began to tremble, but seemed unable to move. Then, after long rigid seconds, he did move. He lifted hands that fluttered and fumbled them to his face. Behind them, he gave queer thin screams. He slid out of the chair to his knees on the floor and fell forward. He lay groveling and trembling, making high whinnying sounds as he clawed at the carpet, trying to dig himself into it. Suddenly he vomited.

The boy looked up. To Dr. Torrance he said, as if answering a question:

"He is not hurt. He wanted to frighten us, so we have shown him what it means to be frightened. He'll understand better now. He will be all right when his glands are in balance again."

Then he turned away and went out of the room, leaving the two men looking at one another.

Bernard pulled out a handkerchief and dabbed at the sweat that stood in drops on his forehead. Dr. Torrance sat motionless, his face a sickly gray. They turned to look at the Chief Constable. Sir John was lying slackly now, seemingly unconscious, drawing long, greedy breaths, shaken occasionally by a violent tremor.

"My God!" exclaimed Bernard. He looked at Torrance again. "And you have been here three years!"

"There's never been anything remotely like *this*," the doctor said. "We've suspected many possibilities. They know we're here to teach and try to understand them. There's never been any enmity—thank God for that!"

"Yes, you could well do worse than that," Bernard told him. He looked at Sir John again.

"This chap ought to be got away before he pulls round. We'd be better out of the way, too; it's the sort of situation where a man can't forgive the witnesses. Send in a couple of his men to collect him. Tell them he's had an attack of some kind."

Five minutes later they stood on the steps and watched the Chief Constable driven off, still only semi-conscious.

" 'All right when his glands are in balance!' " murmured Bernard. "They seem better at physiology than at psychology. They've broken that man, for the rest of his life."

20 · Impasse

AFTER A COUPLE of strong ʋhiskies Bernard began to lose some of the shaken look with which he had returned to Kyle Manor. When he had given us an account of the Chief Constable's disastrous interview at the Grange, he went on:

"You know, one of the few childlike things about the Children, it strikes me, is their inability to judge their own strength. Except, perhaps, for the corralling of the village, everything they have done has been overdone. What might be excusable in intent they contrive to make unforgivable in practice. They wanted to scare Sir John in order to convince him that it would be unwise to interfere with them, but they did not do simply what was necessary for that; they went so much farther that they reduced the poor man to a state of groveling fear near the brink of imbecility. They induced a degree of personal degradation that was sickening and utterly unpardonable."

Zellaby asked in his mild, reasonable tone, "Are we not perhaps looking at this from too narrow an angle? You, Colonel, say 'unpardonable,' which assumes that they expect to be pardoned. But why should they? Do we concern ourselves whether jackals or wolves will pardon us for shooting them? We do not. We are concerned only to make them innocuous.

"In point of fact our ascendancy has been so complete that most of us have quite forgotten what it means to have to fight in a personal way against another species. But, when the need arises we have no compunction; we give no quarter, and certainly expect no pardon.

"The situation vis-á-vis the Children would seem to be that we have not grasped that they represent a danger to our species, while they are in no doubt that we are a danger to theirs. And they intend to survive. We might do well to remind ourselves what that intention implies. We can watch it any day in a garden; it is a fight that goes perpetually, bitterly, lawlessly, without trace of mercy or compassion. . . ."

His manner was quiet, but there was no doubt that his intention was pointed; and yet, somehow, as so often with Zellaby, the gap between theory and practical circumstances seemed too inadequately bridged to carry conviction.

Presently Bernard said, "Surely this is quite a change of front by the Children. They've exerted persuasion and pressure from time to time, but, apart from a few early incidents, almost no violence. Now we have this outbreak. Can you point to the start of it, or has it been working up?"

"Decidedly," said Zellaby. "There was no sign whatever of anything in this category before the matter of Jimmy Pawle and his car."

"And that was—let me see—last Wednesday, the third of July. I wonder . . ." he was beginning, but broke off as the gong called us to luncheon.

"My experience, hitherto, of interplanetary invasion," said Zellaby, as he concocted his own particular taste in salad-dressing, "has been vicarious—indeed, one might even say hypothetically vicarious, or do I mean vicariously hypothetical?" He pondered that a moment, and resumed: "At any rate it has been quite extensive. Yet, oddly enough, I cannot recall a single account of one that is of the least help in our present dilemma. They were, almost without exception, unpleasant; but also they were almost always forthright, rather than insidious.

"Take H. G. Wells's Martians, for instance. As the original exponents of the death-ray they were formidable, but their behavior was quite conventional: they simply conducted a straightforward campaign with a weapon which outclassed anything that could be brought against it. But at least we could try to fight back, whereas in this case—"

"Not cayenne, dear," said his wife.

"Not what?"

"Not cayenne. It gives you hiccups," Anthea reminded him.

"So it does. Where is the sugar?"

"By your left hand, dear."

"Oh, yes . . . where was I?"

"With H.G.'s Martians," I told him.

"Of course. Well, there you have the prototype of innumerable invasions. A super-weapon which man fights valiantly with his own puny armory until he is saved by one of several possible kinds of bell. Naturally, in America it is all rather bigger and better. Something descends and something comes out of it. Within ten minutes, owing no doubt to the excellent communications in that country, there is a coast-to-coast panic and all highways out of all cities are crammed by the fleeing populace—except in Washington. There, by contrast, enormous crowds stretching as far as the eye can reach stand grave and silent, white-faced but trusting, with their eyes upon the White House, while somewhere in the Catskills a hitherto ignored professor and his daughter with their rugged young assistant strive like demented midwives to assist the birth of the *dea ex laboratoria* which will save the world at the last moment, minus one.

"Over here, one feels, the report of such an invasion would be received in at least some quarters with a tinge of preliminary skepticism, but we must allow the Americans to know their own people best.

"Yet, over-all, what do we have? Just another war. The motivations are simplified, the armaments complicated, but the pattern is the same and, as a result, not one of the prognostications, speculations, or extrapolations turns out to be of the least use to us when the thing actually happens. It really does seem a pity when one thinks of all the cerebration the prognosticators have spent on it, doesn't it?"

He busied himself with eating his salad.

"It is still one of my problems to know when you are to be taken literally and when metaphorically," I told him.

"This time you can take him literally, with assurance," Bernard put in.

Zellaby cocked a sideways look at him.

"Just like that? Not even reflex opposition?" he inquired.

"Tell me, Colonel, how long have you accepted this invasion as a fact?"

"For about eight years," Bernard told him. "And you?"

"About the same time, perhaps a little before. I did not like it, I do not like it, I am probably going to like it even less. But I had to accept it. The old Holmes axiom, you know: 'When you have eliminated the impossible, whatever remains, *however improbable,* must be the truth.' I had not known, however, that my views were shared in official circles. What did you decide to do about it?"

"Well, we did our best to preserve their isolation here and to see to their education."

"And a fine helpful thing that turns out to have been, if I may say so. Why?"

"Just a minute," I put in. "I'm in between the literal and the figurative again. You are both of you seriously accepting as a fact that these Children are a kind of invaders? That they do originate somewhere outside the Earth?"

"See?" said Zellaby. "No coast-to-coast panic. Just skepticism. I told you."

"We are," Bernard told me. "It is the only hypothesis that my department has not been forced to abandon—though, of course, there are some who still won't accept it, even though we had the help of a little more evidence than Mr. Zellaby did."

"Ah!" said Zellaby, brought to sudden attention with a forkful of greenstuff in mid-air. "Are we getting closer to the mysterious interest Military Intelligence have shown in us?"

"There's no longer any reason why it should not have a restricted circulation," Bernard admitted. "I know that in the early stages you did quite a little inquiring into our interest on your own account, Zellaby, but I don't believe you ever discovered the clue."

"Which was?" inquired Zellaby.

"Simply that Midwich was not the only, nor even the first place to have a Dayout. Also, that during the three weeks around that time there was a marked rise in the radar detection of unidentified flying objects."

"Well, I'm damned!" said Zellaby. "Oh, vanity, vanity . . .! There are other groups of Children besides ours, then? Where?"

But Bernard was not to be hurried; he continued deliberately, "One Dayout took place at a small township in the Northern Territory of Australia. Something apparently went badly wrong there. There were thirty-one pregnancies, but for some reason the Children all died; most of them a few hours after birth, the eldest at a week old.

"There was another Dayout at an Eskimo settlement on Victoria Island, north of Canada. The inhabitants are cagey about what happened there, but it is believed that they were so outraged, or perhaps alarmed, at the arrival of babies so unlike their own kind that they exposed them almost at once. At any rate, none survived. And that, by the way, taken in conjunction with the time of the Midwich babies' return here, suggests that the power of duress does not develop until they are a week or two old, and that they may be truly individuals until then. Still another Dayout—"

Zellaby held up his hand.

"Let me guess. There was one behind the Iron Curtain."

"There were two *known* ones behind the Curtain," Bernard corrected him. "One of them was in the Irkutsk region, near the borders of Outer Mongolia—a very grim affair. It was assumed that the women had been lying with devils, and they perished as well as the Children. The other was directly to the east, a place called Gizhinsk, in the mountains northeast of Okhotsk. There may have been others that we didn't hear of. It's pretty certain it happened in some places in South America and in Africa, too, but it's difficult to check. The inhabitants tend to be secretive. It's even possible that an isolated village would miss a day and not know it, in which case the babies would be even more of a puzzle. In most of the instances we know of, the babies were regarded as freaks and were killed, but we suspect that in some villages they may have been hidden away."

"But not, I take it, in Gizhinsk?" put in Zellaby.

Bernard looked at him with a small twitch to the corner of his mouth.

"You don't miss much, do you, Zellaby? You're right, not in Gizhinsk. The Dayout there took place a week before the Midwich affair. We had the report of it three or four days later. It worried the Russians quite a lot. That was at least some consolation to us when it happened here; we knew that they couldn't have been responsible. In due course they presumably found out about Midwich, and were also relieved —though there is no evidence of that. Meanwhile, our agent kept an eye on Gizhinsk, and reported the curious fact that every woman there was simultaneously pregnant. We were a little slow in appreciating any significance in that—it sounded like useless tittle-tattle—but presently we discovered the state of affairs in Midwich and began to take more interest. Once the babies were born the situation was easier for the Russians than for us; they practically sealed off Gizhinsk—a place about twice the size of Midwich—and our information from there virtually ceased. We could not exactly seal off Midwich, so we had to work differently and, in the circumstances, I don't think we did too badly."

Zellaby nodded. "I see. The War Office view being that it did not know quite what we had here, or what the Russians had there. But if it should turn out that the Russians had a flock of potential geniuses, it would be useful for us to have a similar flock to put up against them?"

"More or less that. It was quite quickly clear that the Children were something unusual."

"I ought to have seen that," said Zellaby. He shook his head sadly. "It simply never crossed my mind that we in Midwich were not unique. It does, however, now cross my mind that something must have happened to impel your present confidence. I don't quite see why the events here should justify it, so it probably happened somewhere else, say in Gizhinsk? Has there been a new development there that our Children are likely to display shortly?"

Bernard put his knife and fork neatly together on his plate, regarded them for a moment, and then looked up.

"The Far-East Army," he said slowly, "has recently been equipped with a new medium-type atomic cannon, believed to have a range of between fifty and sixty miles. Last week they carried out the first live tests with it. The town of Gizhinsk no longer exists. . . ."

We stared at him. With a horrified expression, Anthea leaned forward.

"You mean—everybody there?" she said incredulously.

Bernard nodded. "Everybody. No one there could have been warned without the Children getting to know of it. Besides, that way it could be officially attributed to an error in calculation or, possibly, to sabotage."

Zellaby looked down, and traced the damask pattern of the tablecloth for some moments. Then he raised his eyes again:

"Last week, you say. Which day?"

"Tuesday, the second of July," Bernard told him.

Zellaby nodded several times, slowly.

"But how, I wonder, did ours know . . .?" he said, pensively.

Soon after luncheon was finished Bernard announced that he was going up to the Grange again.

"I didn't have a chance to talk to Torrance while Sir John was there—and after that, well, we both needed a bit of a break."

"I suppose you can't give us any idea of what you intend to do about the Children?" Anthea asked.

He shook his head. "If I had any ideas I suppose they'd have to be official secrets. As it is, I'm going to see whether Torrance, from his knowledge of them, can make any suggestions. I hope to be back in an hour or so," he added as he left us.

As he emerged from the front door he made automatically toward his car and then, as he reached for the handle, changed his mind. A little exercise, he decided, would freshen him up and he set off briskly down the drive.

Just outside the gate a small lady in a blue tweed suit looked at him, hesitated, and then advanced to meet him. Her face went a little pink, but she pushed resolutely on. Bernard raised his hat.

"You won't know me. I am Miss Lamb, but of course we all know who you are, Colonel Westcott."

Bernard acknowledged the introduction with a small bow, wondering how much 'we all' (which presumably comprehended the whole of Midwich) knew about him and for how long they had known it. He asked what he could do for her.

"It's about the Children, Colonel. What is going to be done?"

He told her, honestly enough, that no decision had yet been made. She listened, her eyes intently on his face, her gloved hands clasped together.

"It won't be anything severe, will it?" she asked. "Oh, I know last night was dreadful, but it wasn't their fault. They don't really understand yet. They're so very young, you see. I know they look twice their age, but even that's not very old, is it? They didn't really *mean* the harm they did. They were frightened. Wouldn't any of us be frightened if a crowd came to our house wanting to burn it down? Of course we should. We should have a right to defend ourselves, and nobody could blame us. Why, if the villagers came to my house like that I should defend it with whatever I could find— perhaps an ax."

Bernard doubted it. The picture of this small lady setting about a crowd with an ax was one that did not easily come into focus.

"It was a very drastic remedy they took," he reminded her gently.

"I know. But when you are young and frightened it is very easy to be more violent than you mean to be. I know when I was a child there were injustices which positively made me burn inside. If I had the strength to do what I wanted to do it would have been dreadful, really dreadful, I assure you."

"Unfortunately," he pointed out, "the Children do have that strength, and you must agree that they can't be allowed to use it."

"No," she said. "But they won't when they're old enough to understand. I'm sure they won't. People are saying they must be sent away. But you won't do that, will you? They're so young. I know they're willful, but they need us. They aren't wicked. If they can stay here we can teach them love and gentleness, show them that people don't really mean them any harm. . . ."

She looked up into his face, her hands pressed anxiously together, her eyes pleading, with tears not far behind them.

Bernard looked back at her unhappily, marveling at the devotion that was able to regard six deaths and a number of serious injuries as a kind of youthful peccadillo. He could almost see in her mind the adored slight figure with golden eyes which filled all her view. She would never blame, never cease to adore, never understand. There had been just one wonderful, miraculous thing in all her life. His heart ached for Miss Lamb.

He could only explain that the decision did not lie in his hands, but assure her, trying not to raise any false hopes, that what she had told him would be included in his report; and then detach himself as gently as possible to go on his way, conscious of her anxious, reproachful eyes at his back.

The village, as he passed through it, was wearing a sparse appearance and a subdued air. There must, he imagined, be strong feelings concerning the corralling measure, but the few people about, except for one or two chatting pairs, had a rather noticeable air of minding their own business. A single policeman on patrol round the Green was clearly bored with his job. Lesson One, from the Children—that there was danger in numbers—appeared to have been understood. An efficient step in dictatorship: no wonder the Russians had not cared for the look of things at Gizhinsk.

Twenty yards up Hickham Lane he came upon two of the Children. They were sitting on the roadside bank, staring up ward and westward with such concentration that they did not notice his approach.

Bernard stopped and turned his head to follow their line of sight, becoming aware at the same time of the sound of jet engines. The aircraft was easy to spot, a silver shape against the blue summer sky, approaching at about five thousand feet. Just as he found it, black dots appeared beneath it. White parachutes opened in quick succession, five of them, and began the long float down. The aircraft flew steadily on.

He glanced back at the Children just in time to see them exchange an unmistakable smile of satisfaction. He looked up again at the aircraft serenely pursuing its way, and at the five gently sinking white spots behind it. His knowledge of aircraft was slight, but he was fairly certain that he was looking at a Carey light long-range bomber that normally carried a complement of five. He looked thoughtfully at the two Children again, and at the same moment they noticed him.

The three of them studied one another while the bomber droned on, passing overhead.

"That," Bernard observed, "was a very expensive machine. Someone is going to be very annoyed about losing it."

"It's a warning. But they'll probably have to lose several more before they believe it," said the boy.

"Probably. It's a very unusual accomplishment," he paused, still studying them. "You don't care for the idea of aircraft flying over you, is that it?"

"Yes," agreed the boy.

Bernard nodded. "I can understand that. But, tell me, why do you always make your warnings so severe—why do you always carry them a stage further than necessary?"

"We *could* have made him crash," said the girl.

"I suppose so. We must be grateful that you didn't, I'm sure. But it would have been no less effective to turn him back, wouldn't it? I don't see why you have to be so drastic."

"It makes more of an impression. We should have to turn a lot of aircraft back before anyone would believe we were doing it. But if they lose an aircraft every time they come this way they'll take notice," the boy told him.

"I see. The same argument applies to last night, I suppose. If you had just sent the crowd away, it would not have been warning enough," Bernard suggested.

"Do you think it would?" asked the boy.

"It seems to me to depend how it was done. Surely there

was no need to make them fight one another, murderously? I mean, it seems to me, to put it on its most practical level, politically unsound always to take that extra step that simply increases anger and hatred?"

"Fear, too," the boy pointed out.

"Oh, you *want* to instill fear, do you? Why?" inquired Bernard.

"It is a means, not an end," said the boy. "It gives us the initiative, and if we have that we set the course." He looked up at Bernard with a steady, earnest look in his golden eyes. "Sooner or later," he explained, "you will try to wipe us out. You will try to kill us, whatever we do, but there is no reason why you should have the initiative."

The boy spoke quite calmly, but his words pierced right through the front that Bernard had adopted.

In one startled flash he was hearing an adult, seeing a six-teen-year-old, knowing that it was a nine-year-old who spoke.

"For a moment," he said, later, "it bowled me right over. I was near panic. The child-adult combination seemed to be full of a terrifying significance . . . an outrage on the proper order . . . I suppose it does seem a small point now; but at the time it hit me like a revelation, and, by God, it frightened me . . . I suddenly saw them double: individually still children; collectively adult; talking to me on my own level . . ."

The effect must have shown.

The boy said:

"You needn't be afraid of us: we want to talk to you."

Bernard pulled himself together. Deliberately, he sat down on the bank beside them, and forced a reasonable tone.

"Wanting to kill you seems a very large assumption. Naturally, if you do the sort of things you have been doing lately, we shall hate you, and take revenge—or, one might say, protect ourselves from you. But if you don't . . ." He shrugged. "Do you have such a great hatred of us? If you don't, then surely some kind of *modus vivendi* might be contrived."

The boy shook his head.

"You're putting this on the wrong level. It isn't a matter of hates, or likes. They make no difference. Nor is it something that can be arranged by discussion. It is an inescapable biological obligation. You cannot afford *not* to kill us, for if you don't you are finished." He paused to give that weight, and then went on: "Already, some of your politicians who know about us must be wondering whether something like the Russian solution could not be managed here."

"Oh, so you *do* know about them?"

"Yes, of course. As long as the Children of Gizhinsk were alive we did not need to look after ourselves, but when they died, two things happened: one was that the balance was destroyed, and the other was that we realized the Russians would not have destroyed the balance unless they were quite sure that a colony of the Children was more of a liability than a possible asset.

"The biological obligation will not be denied. The Russians fulfilled it from political motives, as, no doubt, you will try to do. The Eskimos did it by primitive instinct. But the result is the same.

"For you, however, it will be more difficult. In Russia, the individual exists to serve the State; if he puts self above State, he is a traitor, and it is the duty of the community to protect itself from traitors whether they are individuals or groups. In this case, then, biological duty and political duty coincided. But you have the conception that the State exists to serve the individuals who compose it. Therefore your consciences will be troubled by the thought that we have 'rights.'

"Our first moment of real danger has passed. It occurred when you first heard of the Russian action against the Children there. A decisive man might have arranged a quick 'accident' here. It had suited you to keep us hidden away here, and it suited us to be hidden, so it might have been cunningly managed without too much trouble. Now, however, it cannot. Already, the people in Trayne hospital will have talked about us; in fact, after last night there must be talk and rumors spreading all round. The chance of making any convincing 'accident' has gone. So what are you going to do to liquidate us?"

Bernard shook his head.

"Look," he said, "suppose we consider this thing from a more civilized standpoint—after all, this is a civilized country and famous for its ability to find compromises. I'm not convinced by the sweeping way you assume there can be no agreement."

It was the girl who answered this time:

"This is not a civilized matter," she said, "it is a very primitive matter. If we exist we shall dominate you—that is clear and inevitable. Will you agree to be superseded, and start on the way to extinction without a struggle? I do not think you are decadent enough for that. And then, politically, the question is: Can *any* State, however tolerant, afford to harbor an increasingly powerful minority which it has no power to control? Obviously the answer is again, no.

"So what will you do? We are very likely safe for a time while you talk about it. The more primitive of you, your masses, will let their instincts lead them—we saw the pattern in the village last night—they will want to hunt us down and destroy us. Your more liberal, responsible-minded and religious people will be greatly troubled over the ethical position. Opposed to any form of drastic action at all, you will have your true idealists—and also your sham idealists: the quite large number of people who profess ideals and are content to lay up slavery and destitution for their descendants so long as they are enabled to produce personal copybooks of elevated views at the gate of heaven.

"Then, too, with your Government of the Right reluctantly driven to consider drastic action against us, your politicians of the Left will see a chance of party capital and possible dismissal of the Government. They will defend our rights as a threatened minority, and children at that. Their leaders will glow with righteousness on our behalf. They will claim, without referendum, to be representing justice, compassion and the great heart of the people. Then it will occur to some of them that there really *is* a serious problem and that if they were to force an election there would very likely be a split between the promoters of the party's official Warm-hearted policy, and the rank and file whose misgivings about us will make them a Cold-feet faction; so the display of abstract righteousness and the plugging of well-tested, best-selling virtues will diminish."

"You don't appear to think very highly of our institutions," Bernard put in. The girl shrugged.

"As a securely dominant species you could afford to lose touch with reality and amuse yourselves with abstractions," she replied. Then she went on: "While these people are wrangling, it will come home to more of them that the problem of dealing with a more advanced species than themselves is not going to be easy, and will become less easy with procrastination. There may be practical attempts to deal with us. But we have shown last night what is going to happen to soldiers if they are sent against us. If you send aircraft they will crash. Very well, then, you will think of artillery, as the Russians did, or of guided missiles whose electronics we cannot effect. But if you send them you won't be able to kill only us, you will have to kill all the people in the village as well—it would take you a long time even to contemplate such an action, and if it were carried out, what government in this country could survive such a massacre of innocents on the grounds of expediency? Not only would the party that sanctioned it be finished for good, but if they were successful in removing the danger the leaders could then be safely lynched, by way of atonement and expiation."

She stopped speaking, and the boy took up:

"The details may vary, but something of the sort will become inevitable as the threat of our existence is more widely understood. You might easily have a curious epoch when both parties are fighting to keep out of office rather than be the one that has to take action against us." He paused, looking out thoughtfully across the fields for some moments, then he added:

"Well, there it is. Neither you, nor we, have wishes that count in the matter; or should one say that we both have been given the same wish—to survive. We are all, you see, toys of the life-force. It made you numerically strong, but mentally undeveloped; it made us mentally strong, but physically weak. Now it has set us at one another, to see what will happen. A cruel sport, perhaps, from both our points of view, but cruelty is as old as life itself. We are improving by degrees: humor and compassion are very recent inventions that only came in with man; they are not firmly established yet, but they promise well." He smiled. "Pure Zellaby, that. Our first teacher." Then he went on: "But the life-force is not to be denied. It will have its blood-sport. However, it has seemed to us not impossible that the serious stage of the combat might possibly be postponed. And that is what we want to talk to you about. . . ."

21 · Ultimatum

"THIS," ZELLABY SAID reprovingly to a golden-eyed girl who was sitting on the branch of a tree beside the path, "this is a quite uncalled for circumscription of my movements. You know perfectly well that I *always* take an afternoon stroll. and that I always return for tea. Tyranny easily becomes a very bad habit. Besides, you've got my wife as a hostage."

The Child appeared to think it over, and presently pushed a boiled-sweet into one cheek.

"All right, Mr. Zellaby," she said.

Zellaby advanced. This time his foot passed unobstructedly over an invisible barrier that had stopped it before.

"Thank you, my dear," he said, with a polite inclination of his head. "Come along, Gayford."

We passed on into the woods, leaving the guardian of the path idly swinging her legs and crunching her sweet.

"A very interesting aspect of this affair is the demarcations between the individual and the collective," Zellaby remarked. "I've really made precious little progress in determining it. The Child's appreciation of her sweet is indubitably individual, it could scarcely be other; but her permission for us to go on was collective, as was the influence that stopped us. And since the mind is collective, what about the sensations it receives? Are the rest of the Children vicariously enjoying her bulls-eye, too? It would appear not, yet they must be aware of it, and perhaps of its flavor. A similar problem arises when I show them my films and lecture to them. In theory, if I had two of them only as my audience, all of them would share the experience—that's the way they learn their lessons, as I told you—but in practice I always have a full house when I go up to the Grange. As far as I can understand it, when I show a film they *could* get it from one representative of each sex, but presumably in the transmission of visual sensation something is lost, for they all very much prefer to see it with their own eyes. Apparently individual experience of a picture is more satisfactory to them. And there's a point that sets off a whole train of questions."

"I can believe that," I agreed, "but they are postgraduate questions. As far as I am concerned, the basic problem of their presence here at all gives me quite enough to be going on with."

"Oh," said Zellaby, "I don't think there is much that's novel about that. Our presence here at all raises the same problem."

"I don't see that. We evolved here, but where did the Children come from?"

"Aren't you taking a theory for an established fact, my dear fellow? It is widely *supposed* that we evolved here, and to support that supposition it is *supposed* that there once existed a creature who was the ancestor of ourselves, and of the apes—what our grandfathers used to call 'the missing link.' But there has never been any satisfactory proof that such a creature existed; not a trace of him have we found. And *the* missing link, why, bless my soul, the whole proposition is riddled with missing links, if that is an acceptable metaphor. Can you see the whole diversity of races evolving from this one link? I can't, however hard I try. Nor, at a later stage, can I see a nomadic creature segregating the strains which would give rise to such fixed and distinctive characteristics of race. Think of the number of generations we should have to go back to trace the blacks, the whites, the reds and the yellows to a common ancestor. There should be innumerable traces of this development left by millions of evolving ancestors, yet we find practically nothing but a great blank. Why, we know more about the age of reptiles than we do about the age of supposedly evolving man. We had a complete evolutionary tree for the horse many years ago. If it were possible to do the same for man we should have done it by now. But what do we have? Just a few, remarkably few, isolated specimens. Nobody knows where, or if, they fit into an evolutionary picture because there is no picture—only supposition. The specimens are as unattached to us as we are to the Children . . ."

For half an hour or so I listened to a discourse on the erratic and unsatisfactory phylogeny of mankind, which Zellaby concluded with an apology for his inadequate coverage of a subject which was not susceptible to a condensation into half a dozen sentences, as he had attempted.

"However," he added, "you will have gathered that the conventional assumption has more lacunae than substance."

"But if you invalidate it, what then?" I inquired.

"I don't know," Zellaby admitted, "but I do refuse to accept a bad theory simply on the grounds that there is not a better, and I take the lack of evidence that ought, if it were valid, to be plentiful, as an argument for the opposition—whatever that may be. As a result I find the occurrence of the Children scarcely more startling, objectively, than that of the various other races of mankind that have apparently popped into existence fully formed, or at least with no clear line of ancestral development."

So dissolute a conclusion seemed unlike Zellaby. I suggested that he probably had a theory of his own.

Zellaby shook his head.

"No," he admitted honestly. Then he added: "One has to

speculate, of course. Not very satisfactorily, I'm afraid, and sometimes uncomfortably. It is, for instance, disquieting for a good rationalist such as myself to find himself wondering whether perhaps there is not some Outside Power arranging things here. When I look round the world it does sometimes suggest a rather disorderly testing-ground. The sort of place where someone might let loose a new strain now and then, To see how it will make out in our rough and tumble. Fascinating for an inventor to watch his creations acquitting themselves, don't you think? To discover whether this time he has produced a successful tearer-to-pieces, or just another torn-to-pieces; to observe the progress of the earlier models and see which of them have proved really competent at making life a form of hell for others . . . You don't think so? Ah, well, as I told you, the speculations tend to be uncomfortable."

I told him: "As man to man, Zellaby, not only do you talk a great deal, but you talk a great deal of nonsense, and make *some* of it sound like sense. It is very confusing for a listener."

Zellaby looked hurt.

"My dear fellow, I always talk sense. It is my primary social failing. One must distinguish between the content, and the container. Would you prefer me to talk with that monotonous dogmatic intensity which our simpler minded brethren believe, God help them, to be a guarantee of sincerity? Even if I should, you would still have to evaluate the content."

"What I want to know," I said firmly, "is whether, having disposed of human evolution, you have any serious hypothesis to put in its place?"

"You don't like my Inventor speculation? Nor do I, very much. But at least it has the merit of being no less improbable, and a lot more comprehensible than many religious suggestions. And when I say 'Inventor,' I don't necessarily mean an individual, of course. More probably a team. It seems to me that if a team of our own biologists and geneticists were to take a remote island for their testing-ground they would find great interest and instruction in observing their specimens in ecological conflict. And, after all, what is a planet but an island in space? But a speculation is, as I said, far from being a theory."

Our circuit had taken us round to the Oppley road. As we were approaching the village a figure, deep in thought, emerged from Hickham Lane, and turned to walk ahead of us. Zellaby called to him. Bernard came out of his abstraction. He looked round, and waited for us to catch up.

"You don't look," remarked Zellaby, "as though Torrance has been helpful."

"I didn't get as far as Dr. Torrance," Bernard admitted. "And now there seems to be little point in troubling him. I've been talking to a couple of your Children."

"Not to a couple of them," Zellaby protested gently. "One talks either to the Composite Boy or the Composite Girl, or to both."

"All right. I accept the correction. I have been talking with *all* the Children—at least, I think so, though I seemed to detect what one might call a strong Zellaby flavor in the style of both boy and girl."

Zellaby looked pleased.

"Considering we are lion and lamb, our relations have usually been good. It is gratifying to have had some educational influence," he observed. "How did you get on?"

"I don't think 'get on' quite expresses it," Bernard told him. "I was informed, lectured and instructed. And finally I have been charged with bearing an ultimatum."

"Indeed? And to whom?" asked Zellaby.

"I am really not quite sure. Roughly, I think, to anyone who is in a position to supply them with air transport."

Zellaby raised his brows. "Where to?"

"They didn't say. Somewhere, I imagine, where they will be able to live unmolested."

He gave us a brief version of the Children's arguments.

"So it really amounts to this," he summed up. "In their view, their existence here constitutes a challenge to authority which cannot be evaded for long. They cannot be ignored, but any government that tries to deal with them will bring immense political trouble down on itself if it is not successful, and very little less if it is. The Children themselves have no wish to attack, or to be forced to defend themselves—"

"Naturally," murmured Zellaby. "Their immediate concern is to survive, in order eventually to dominate."

"—therefore it is in the best interests of all parties that they should be provided with the means of removing themselves."

"Which would mean, game to the Children," Zellaby commented, and withdrew into thought.

"It sounds risky, from their point of view, I mean. All conveniently in one aircraft," I suggested.

"Oh, trust them to think of that. They've considered quite a lot of details. There are to be several aircraft. A squad is to be put at their disposal to check the aircraft and search for time-bombs or any such devices. Parachutes are to be provided, some of which, picked out by themselves, are to be tested. There are quite a number of similar provisos. They've been quicker to grasp the full implications of the Gizhinsk business than our own people here, and they aren't leaving much scope for sharp practice."

"H'm," I said. "I can't say I envy you the job of pushing a proposition like that through the red tape. What's their alternative?"

Bernard shook his head.

"There isn't one. Perhaps ultimatum wasn't quite the right word. Demand would be better. I told the Children I could see very little hope of getting anyone to listen to me seriously. They said they would prefer to try it that way first—there'd be less trouble all round if it could be put through quietly. If I can't put it across, and it is pretty obvious I shall not be able to by myself, then they propose that two of them shall accompany me on a second approach.

"After seeing what their 'duress' could do to the Chief Constable, it isn't a pleasant prospect. I can see no reason why they should not apply pressure at one level after another until they reach the very top, if necessary. What's to stop them?"

"One has, for some time, seen this coming, as inevitably as the change of the seasons," Zellaby said, emerging from his reflections. "But I did not expect it so soon, nor do I think it would have come for years yet if the Russians had not precipitated it. I would guess it has come earlier than the Children themselves would wish, too. They know they are not fully ready to face it. That is why they want to get away to some place where they can reach maturity unmolested.

"We are presented with a moral dilemma of some niceness. On the one hand, it is our duty to our race and culture to liquidate the Children, for it is clear that if we do not we shall, at best, be completely dominated by them, and that their culture, whatever it may turn out to be, will extinguish ours.

"On the other hand, it is our culture that gives us scruples about the ruthless liquidation of unarmed minorities, not to mention the practical obstacles to such a solution.

"On the—oh dear, how difficult—on the third hand, to enable the Children to shift the problem they represent to

the territory of a people even more ill equipped to deal with
it is a form of evasive procrastination which lacks any moral
courage at all.

"It makes one long for H.G.'s straightforward Martians,
for this would seem to be one of those unfortunate situations where no solution is morally defensible."

Bernard and I received that in silence. Presently I felt compelled to say:

"That sounds to me the kind of masterly summing-up that
has landed philosophers in sticky situations throughout the
ages."

"Oh, surely not," Zellaby protested. "In a quandary where
every course is immoral there remains the ability to act for
the greatest good of the greatest number. Ergo, the Children
ought to be eliminated at the least possible cost, with the
least possible delay. I am sorry to have to arrive at that conclusion. In nine years I have grown rather fond of them.
And, in spite of what my wife says, I think I have come as
near friendship with them as possible."

He allowed another, and longer, pause, and shook his head.

"It is the right step," he repeated. "But, of course, our authorities will not be able to bring themselves to take it—for
which I am personally thankful because I can see no practical
course open to them which would not involve the destruction
of all of us in the village, as well." He stopped and looked
about him at Midwich resting quietly in the afternoon sun.
"I am getting to be an old man, and I shall not live much
longer in any case, but I have a younger wife, and a young
son, and I should like to think, too, that all this will go on as
long as it may. No, the authorities will argue, no doubt, but
if the Children want to go, they'll go. Humanitarianism will
triumph over biological duty—is that probity, would you
say? Or is it decadence? But so the evil day will be put off—
for how long, I wonder . . .?"

Back at Kyle Manor tea was ready, but after one cup Bernard rose and made his farewells to the Zellabys.

"I shan't learn any more by staying longer," he said. "The
sooner I present the Children's demands to my incredulous
superiors, the sooner we shall get things moving. I have no
doubt your arguments are right, on their plane, Mr. Zellaby,
but I personally shall work to get the Children anywhere out
of this country, and quickly. I have seen a number of unpleasant sights in my life, but none that has ever frightened
me quite so much as the degradation of your Chief Constable. I'll keep you informed how it goes, of course."

He looked at me.

"Coming with me, Richard?"

I hesitated. Janet was still in Scotland, and not due back for a couple of days yet. There was nothing that needed my presence in London, and I was finding the problem of the Midwich Children far more fascinating than anything I was likely to encounter there. Anthea noticed.

"Do stay, if you would like to," she said. "I think we'd both be glad of some company just now."

There was no doubt that she meant it, and I accepted.

"Anyway," I said to Bernard. "We don't know that your new courier status includes a companion. If I were to try to come with you we'd probably find I was still under the ban."

"Oh, that ridiculous ban. I must talk to them seriously about that—a quite absurd panic-measure," said Zellaby.

We accompanied Bernard to the door and watched him set off down the drive with a wave of his hand.

"Yes, game to the Children," Zellaby said again, as the car turned out into the road. "And set . . . ?" He shrugged faintly, and shook his head.

22 · Zellaby of Macedon

"MY DEAR," said Zellaby, looking along the breakfast table at his wife, "if you happen to be going into Trayne this morning, will you get one of those large jars of sweets?"

Anthea switched her attention from the toaster to her husband.

"Darling," she said, though without endearment, "in the first place, if you recall yesterday, you will remember that there is no question of going to Trayne. In the second, I have no inclination to provide the Children with sweets. In the third, if this means that you are proposing to go and show them films at the Grange this evening, I strongly protest."

"The ban," said Zellaby, "is raised. I pointed out to them last night that it was really rather silly and ill-considered. Their hostages cannot make a concerted flight without word reaching them, if only through Miss Lamb or Miss Ogle. Everybody is inconvenienced to no purpose; only half, or a quarter, of the village makes as good a shield for them as the whole of it. And furthermore, that I proposed to cancel my lecture on the Aegean Islands this evening if half of them were going to be out making a nuisance of themselves on the roads and paths."

"And they just agreed?" asked Anthea, wonderingly.

"Of course. They're not stupid, you know. They are very susceptible to reasoned argument."

"Well, really! After all we've been through—!"

"But they are," protested Zellaby. "When they are jittery, or startled, they do foolish things, but don't we all? And because they are young they overreach themselves, but don't all the young? Also, they are anxious and nervous— and shouldn't we be nervous if the threat of what happened at Gizhinsk were hanging over us?"

"Gordon," his wife said coldly, "I don't understand you. The Children are responsible for the loss of six lives. They have *killed* these six people whom we knew well, and hurt a lot more, some of them badly. At any time the same thing may happen to any of us. Are you *defending* that?"

"Of course not, my dear. I am simply explaining that they can make mistakes when they are alarmed, just as we can. One day they will have to fight us for their lives; they know that, and out of nervousness they made the mistake of thinking that the time had come."

"So now all we have to do is to say: 'We're so sorry you killed six people by mistake. Let's forget all about it.' "

"What else do you suggest? Would you prefer to antagonize them?" asked Zellaby.

"Of course not, but if the law can't touch them as you say it can't, that still doesn't mean we've got to take no notice and pretend it never happened. There are social sanctions, as well as legal ones."

"I should be careful, my dear. We have just been shown that the sanction of power can override both," Zellaby told her seriously.

Anthea looked at him with a puzzled expression.

"Gordon, I don't understand you. We think alike about so many things, but now I seem to have lost you. We *can't* just ignore what has happened: it would be as bad as condoning it."

"You and I, my dear, are using different yardsticks. You are judging by social rules, and finding crime. I am considering an elemental struggle, and finding no crime—only grim, primeval danger." The tone in which he said the last words was so different from his usual manner that it startled both of us into staring at him. For the first time in my knowledge I saw another Zellaby; the man whose incisive hints made the Works more than they seemed now showed clearly through, a younger and stronger man than the familiar, dilettante spinner of words. Then he slipped back to his usual style. "The wise lamb does not enrage the lion," he said. "It placates him, plays for time, and hopes for the best. The Children like sweets, and will be expecting them."

His eyes and Anthea's held for some seconds. I watched the puzzlement and hurt fade out of hers, and give place to a look of trust so naked that I was embarrassed.

Zellaby turned to me.

"I'm afraid there is some business that needs my attention this morning, my dear fellow. Perhaps you would care to celebrate the lifting of our siege by escorting Anthea into Trayne?"

When we got back to Kyle Manor, a little before lunchtime, I found Zellaby in a canvas chair in front of the verandah. He did not hear me at first, and as I looked at him I was struck by the contrasts in him. At breakfast there had been a glimpse of purpose and vigor; now he looked old and tired, older than I had ever thought him; showing, too, something of the withdrawal of age as he sat with the light wind stirring his silky white hair and his gaze on things far, far away.

Then, as my foot gritted on the bricks he changed. The air of lassitude left him, the vacancy went out of his eyes and the face he turned to me was the Zellaby countenance I had known for ten years.

I took a chair beside him, and set down the large bottle of bull's-eyes that was my burden, on the bricks. His eyes rested on it a moment.

"Good," he said. "They're very fond of those. After all, they are still children with a small 'c,' too."

"Look," I said, "I may be intrusive, but do you think it's wise of you to go up there this evening? After all, one can't really put the clock back. Things have changed. There is acknowledged enmity now between them and the village, if not between them and all of us. They have tasted their power and are aware of it. They must suspect that there will be moves against them. Their ultimatum to Bernard isn't going to be accepted right away, if it is at all. You said they were nervous, well, they must still be nervous—and, therefore, still dangerous."

Zellaby shook his head.

"Not to me, my dear fellow. I began to teach them before the authorities took any hand in it, and I've gone on teaching them. I wouldn't say I understand them, but I think I know them better than anyone else does. The most important thing is that they trust me. . . ."

He lapsed into silence, leaning back in his chair, watching the poplars sway with the wind.

"Trust—" he was beginning when Anthea came out with the sherry decanter and glasses and he broke off to ask what they were saying about us in Trayne.

At lunch he talked less than usual, and afterward disappeared into the study. A little later I saw him setting off down the drive on his habitual afternoon walk, but as he had not invited me to join him I made myself comfortable in a deck chair in the garden. He was back for tea, at which he warned me to eat well as dinner was replaced by a late supper on the evenings that he lectured to the Children.

Anthea put in, though not very hopefully:

"Darling, don't you think—? I mean, they've seen all your films. I know you've shown them the Aegean one twice before, at least. Couldn't you put it off, and perhaps hire a film that will be new to them?"

"My dear, it's a good film; it will stand seeing more than once or twice," Zellaby explained, a little hurt. "Besides, I don't give the same talk every time; there's always something more to say about the Isles of Greece."

At half past six we started loading his gear into the car. There seemed to be a great deal of it. Numerous cases containing projector, resistance, amplifier, loudspeaker, a case of films, a tape-recorder so that his words should not be lost, all of them very heavy. By the time we had the lot in, and a stand microphone on top, it began to look as if he were starting on a lengthy safari rather than an evening's talk.

Zellaby himself hovered round while we were at work, inspected, counted everything over, including the jar of sweets, and finally approved. He turned to Anthea.

"I've asked Gayford if he'll drive me up there and help to unload the stuff," he said. "There's nothing to worry about." He drew her to him and kissed her.

"Gordon—" she began. "Gordon—"

Still with his left arm round her he caressed her face with his right hand, looking into her eyes. He shook his head in gentle reproof.

"But, Gordon, I'm afraid of the Children now. Suppose they—?"

"You don't need to be anxious, my dear. I know what I'm doing," he told her.

Then he turned and got into the car, and we drove down the drive with Anthea standing on the steps, looking after us unhappily.

It was not entirely without misgiving that I drove up to the front door of the Grange. Nothing in its appearance, how-ever, justified alarm. It was simply a large, rather ugly Victor-ian house, incongruously flanked by the new, industrial-look-ing wings that had been built as laboratories in Mr. Crimm's time. The lawn in front of it showed little sign of the battle of a couple of nights before, and though a number of the sur-rounding bushes had suffered, it was difficult to believe in what had actually taken place.

We had not arrived unobserved. Before I could open the car door to get out, the front door of the house was pulled violently back and a dozen or more of the Children ran excit-edly down the steps with a scattered chorus of "Hullo, Mr. Zellaby." They had the rear doors open in a moment, and two of the boys began to hand things out for the others to carry. Two girls dashed back up the steps with the microphone and the roller screen, another pounced with a cry of triumph on the jar of bull's-eyes, and hurried after them.

"Hi, there," said Zellaby, as they came to the heavier cases, "that's delicate stuff. Go gently with it."

A boy grinned at him and lifted out one of the black cases with exaggerated care to hand to another. There was nothing odd or mysterious about the Children now unless it was the suggestion of musical-comedy chorus work given by their similarity. For the first time since my return I was able to appreciate that the Children had "a small 'c,' too." Nor, was there any doubt at all that Zellaby's visit was a popular event. I watched him as he stood watching them with a kindly, half-wistful smile. It was impossible to associate the Children, as I saw them now, with danger. I had a confused feeling that these could not be *the* Children, at all; that the theories, fears and threats we had discussed must have to do with some other group of Children. It was hard indeed to credit them with the deliquium of the vigorous Chief Constable that had shaken Bernard so badly. All but impossible to believe that they could have issued an ultimatum which was being taken seriously enough to be carried to the highest levels.

"I hope there'll be a good attendance," Zellaby said, in half-question.

"Oh, yes, Mr. Zellaby," one of the boys assured him. "Everybody, except Wilfred, of course. He's in the sickroom."

"Oh, yes. How is he?" Zellaby asked.

"His back hurts still, but they've got all the pellets out and the doctor says he'll be quite all right," said the boy.

My feeling of schism went on increasing. I was finding it harder every moment to believe that we had not all of us been somehow deluded by a sweeping misunderstanding about the Children, and was more incredulous that the Zellaby who stood beside me could be the same Zellaby who had spoken that morning of 'grim, primeval danger.'

The last of the cases was lifted out of the car. I remembered that it had bêen in the car already when we loaded the rest. It was evidently heavy, because two of the boys carried it between them. Zellaby watched them up the steps a little anxiously, and then turned to me.

"Thank you very much for your help," he said, as though dismissing me.

I was disappointed. This new aspect of the Children fascinated me; I had decided I would like to attend his talk and study them when they were relaxed, all together, and being children with a small 'c.' Zellaby caught my expression.

"I would ask you to join us," he explained. "But I must confess that Anthea is considerably in my thoughts this evening. She is anxious, you know. She has always been uneasy about the Children and these last few days have upset her more than she shows. She would, I think, be the better for company this evening. I was rather hoping that you, my dear fellow . . . It would be a great kindness . . ."

"But of course," I told him. "How inconsiderate of me not to have thought of it. Of course." What else could one say?

He smiled and held out his hand.

"Excellent. I am most grateful, my dear fellow. I'm sure I can rely on you."

Then he turned to three or four of the Children who still hovered near, and beamed on them.

"They'll be getting impatient," he remarked. "Lead on, Priscilla."

"I'm Helen, Mr. Zellaby," she told him.

"Ah, well. Never mind. Come along, my dear," said Zellaby, and they went up the steps together.

I got back into the car and drove off unhurriedly. On the way through the village I noticed that the Scythe and Stone seemed to be doing well, and was tempted to pause there to find out how local feeling was running now, but with Zellaby's request in mind I resisted and kept going. In the Kyle Manor drive I turned the car round and left it standing, ready to fetch him back later on, and went in.

In the main sitting-room Anthea was sitting in front of the open windows, with the radio playing a Haydn quartette. She turned her head as I came in, and at the sight of her face I was glad Zellaby had asked me to come back.

"An enthusiastic welcome," I told her, in answer to her unspoken question. "For all I could tell they might—apart from the bewildering feeling that one was seeing multiple—have been a crowd of decent schoolchildren anywhere. I've no doubt he's right when he says they trust him."

"Perhaps," she allowed, "but *I* don't trust *them*. I don't think I have, ever since the time they forced their mothers back here. I managed not to let it worry me much until they killed Jim Pawle, but ever since then I've been afraid of them. Thank goodness I packed Michael off at once. There's no telling what they might do at any time. Even Gordon admits that they are nervous and panicky. It's nonsense for us to go on staying here, with our lives at the mercy of any childish fright or temper that comes over them.

"Can you see anybody taking Colonel Westcott's 'ultimatum' seriously? I can't. That means that the Children will have to do something to show that they *must* be listened to; they've got to convince important, hard-headed, and thick-headed people, and goodness knows how they may decide to do that. After what's happened already I'm frightened—I really am. They just don't care what becomes of any of us."

"It wouldn't do much good their making their demonstration here," I tried to console her. "They'll have to do it where it counts. Go up to London with Bernard, as they threatened. If they treat a few bigwigs there as they treated the Chief Constable—"

I broke off, interrupted by a bright flash like lightning, and a sharp tremor that shook the house.

"What—" I began. But I got no further.

The blast that blew in through the open window almost carried me off my feet. The noise came, too, in a great, turbulent, shattering breaker of sound, while the house seemed to rock about us.

The overwhelming crash was followed by a clatter and tinkle of things falling, and then by an utter silence.

Without any conscious purpose I ran past Anthea, huddled in her chair, through the open french windows, out onto the lawn. The sky was full of leaves torn from the trees and still fluttering down. I turned and looked at the house. Two great swatches of creeper had been pulled from the wall. Every window in the west front looked blankly back at me, without a pane of glass left. I looked the other way again, and through and above the trees there was a white and red glare. I had not a moment's doubt what it meant. . . .

Turning again I ran back to the sitting-room, but Anthea had gone, and the chair was empty. I called to her, but there was no answer.

I found her at last, in Zellaby's study. The room was littered with broken glass. One curtain had been torn from its hangings and was draped half across the sofa. A part of the Zellaby family record had been swept from the mantelshelf and now lay shattered in the hearth. Anthea herself was sitting in Zellaby's working chair, lying forward across his desk, with her head on her bare arms. She did not move nor make any sound as I came in.

The opening of the door brought a draft through the empty window-frames. It caught a piece of paper lying on the desk beside her, slid it to the edge and sent it fluttering to the floor.

I picked it up. A letter in Zellaby's pointed handwriting. I did not need to read it. The whole thing had been clear since I had seen the red and white glow in the direction of the Grange, and recalled on the instant the heavy cases which I had supposed to contain his recording-machine and other gear. Nor was the letter mine to read, but as I put it back on the desk beside the motionless Anthea I caught sight of a line or two in the middle:

". . . no bitterness, my love. We have lived so long in a garden that we have all but forgotten the true face of Nature. It has been said: *Si fueris Romae, Romani vivito more,* which was possibly sensible. It is, however, a more fundamental expression of the same sentiment to say: If you wish to keep alive in the jungle, you must live as the jungle does. . . ."

1972 SELECTIONS FROM THE PUBLISHER OF THE BEST SCIENCE FICTION IN THE WORLD

TIME'S LAST GIFT	$.95	**ALPHA 3**	$1.25
Philip José Farmer		Robert Silverberg, editor	
FIRST PERSON, PECULIAR	$.95	**WHEN HARLIE WAS ONE**	$1.25
T. L. Sherred		David Gerrold	
SEED OF STARS	$.95	**WOLFWINTER**	$1.25
Dan Morgan and John Kippax		Thomas Burnett Swann	
THE TAR-AIYM KRANG		**ALPH**	$1.25
Alan Dean Foster	$.95	Charles Eric Maine	
THE REALITY TRIP AND OTHER IMPLAUSI-BILITIES	$.95	**THE RESURRECTION OF ROGER DIMENT**	$.95
Robert Silverberg		Douglas R. Mason	
STARFLIGHT 3000	$.95	**TIMETRACKS**	$.95
R. M. Mackelworth		Keith Laumer	
THE GOLD AT THE STARBOW'S END	$1.25	**SPACE SKIMMER**	$.95
Frederik Pohl		David Gerrold	
LIFEBOAT	$1.25	**WITH A FINGER IN MY I**	
James White		David Gerrold	$.95
		THE BEST SCIENCE FICTION OF THE YEAR	
		Terry Carr, editor	$1.25